The Tipping Point

Michael Ardern Robinson

Supplement Publications
2007

The Tipping Point

A CIP catalogue record for this book is available from the British Library.

SP2-PR75-10-07

ISBN 978-0-9557585-0-8

Published by

Supplement Publications

4, Waldron Gardens,
Wistaston,
Crewe,
CW2 8UT

For Renee, Sally, and Beth.

One /

This would be the last time and somehow he had to break it to her. He watched as she unpacked some tins from a big box.

"Just the job! Must have been a weight?" she remarked as she fiddled and fussed with each tin.

He shuffled his feet. It had, but he shook his head and smiled and watched her every move, tensed himself. He felt ashamed, and unkind. It had to be said and done with. Her hunched back angled precariously over the box, and he felt sick, chest tightening, breath hard to draw as he watched her awkwardness and age. She had grown ugly to him.

He had hope now, and in his hope his eyes had seen sunshine and possibility. "I put them on my bike. Makes it easier," he said feebly, hoping she wouldn't pick-up the anxiety in his voice. She didn't miss a trick, always on the look-out for signs. Always.

"Oh, yes, of course." Her preoccupation with the latest haul kept her attention away from him. It was important work, counting, working out, seeing how much more time they bought.

"Miss Jones…" It had to be now. It had to be said, to jump in and risk drowning. If he left it any longer he wondered if he would ever find the courage.

"Yes?" she said absently, placing some tins under the floorboards.

"I won't be coming again." His voice was a whisper as he watched for a reaction and guilt hung on him like a tail, like she said it would. 'We carry guilt around like a tail.' How terrible the prospect of letting her down, not wanting to believe anymore.

"You won't what?" she asked. "Sorry, I was counting…"

"I won't be coming again." The words were terrible, stark and real. He felt cold, and his body trembled slightly with an ache of tension arising in him. It was as if he'd hurled a stone at her, aiming to shock her into reality. This was the way it had to be, and short of

doing that there seemed to be no other way in which she would hear him.

She turned quickly, her eyes stabbing into his. He looked down at his feet and cleared his throat, getting ready to defend himself. In his short life he felt emotions that were uncertain, huge and chaotic. It would be better to run, to shove her away and make a dash for freedom so he that could breathe again. He had to tell her, make it clear, and end it.

"I don't care about it anymore, Miss Jones," he stammered, wrestling with the words. It was so hard to disentangle from her passionate presence.

"What are you saying?" Her mouth tightened as her eyes shrivelled into two dark, shrill points, and her tongue darted out and over her thin, dry lips. She became a lizard, stub-nosed, wary and winding-up a reaction.

"I don't want this." His heart pounded against his bones, and his ribs felt as if they'd crack under her scrutiny. How awful it was to end it. How awful, and yet he knew he couldn't do other than this. It was time not to believe anymore. It was time to live and to hope and to feel like the world was okay. His feet pathered the dry dust on the floorboards, made a nervous dance as he anticipated her inevitable anger.

She stood as upright as her crooked back would allow.

"What? You don't want what anymore?" Her face creased in pain. He'd wounded her with the very thought that it might be over. It didn't look like him. He was no longer the sweet-faced kid who'd crept into her head and heart.

"I've got to go now, see..." He pointed to the door, his finger awkward as he expressed a clumsy show of intent, showing them both where he wanted to go, hoping it would be enough for her comprehension, hoping it would be all he had to say.

"Go? Go where?" Miss Jones demanded more.

"I've got to get away." The finger straightened before his

hand clenched and withdrew under her wide-eyed horror at the gesture.

"What? Get away? What, from me? What have I done? How can you say that? All my plans, our plans, will be ruined!" A high-pitched note rose as she felt anxiety and disappointment rise in her. She'd never given way to hysteria; her sense of discipline had been an iron rod driven through to the core, rigid and entirely trustworthy, but at this moment the sense of betrayal shook her so violently she envisioned what people meant when they said they were losing it. How long was it since she'd felt such fear? She struggled to regain control and not fling her arms and fists at him, slap his small face, and cause the big eyes to drop big tears of repentance. In the moment she knew how much she'd come to rely on him. How much! It was against all she'd imagined possible. Such failure! What a fool to have allowed it to come to this!

"Miss Jones, I... I..."

"I trusted you," she said coldly. Hardness crept through her, blood chilling at the prospect of isolation. "I let you into my secret and then made provision for you, for your future. And it's that easy is it? I've had enough Miss Jones, cheerio! Is it that easy? You were my greatest ally. My best friend! You are my boy! My boy!" Her voice broke and she let out a huge cry which made him flinch as it cut through to his bones.

He shook his head vigorously. "It's me. I've changed...I've..." Her words scared him more now than ever. The words rang like metal, clanged like a steel-shuttered window, and he knew now how dark it had all become, how airless and joyless. Her boy? How could he be that? How could he be her boy? Framing the idea hardened his resolution. It was time to go.

She stood upright now, and pushed a hand through her hair, tugged the elastic band holding the bun hard against her scalp, before coughing and shaking her head, letting the thin grey hair fall across her wild and flushing face. Blood boiled and burned. She steeled herself. Her eyes might burst and let out her agony of disappointment, but she would not show it, would not let him know how ferociously this hurt. A beating heart ached inside her and she wondered, feared, if a stroke would stop this, put an end to it all, all this, the planning, the preparation, the cost. What betrayal. It was enough to kill her.

"Anyway, it's your choice! Go! I don't need you. There'll be enough here for me now. Go on! Go! I won't keep you; hold you against your will. Go on, you're free!" She busied herself again with the boards, replacing them over the hole in the sitting room floor, fingers scrabbling in the dust, and ignored the thin boy who stood awkwardly by the door. It was as if, suddenly, he'd become invisible. I will survive, she repeated again and again in her head, feeling the brain boil under the fragile skull, pressuring the blue veins into bulges on her porcelain-white temples. The pressure built as she tried to ignore him.

More than anything in the world Dean wanted to go, but his legs were rigid and his breath caught fast in his chest, a cold stone lodged in the airways. He was letting her down, but look, she was old, a pathetic old woman. God! How much he wanted to make an enemy of her, hate her and make it easier to go – but he had slowly grown towards the light she showed him, and encouraged him to see. The light had diminished over the recent past and now he fought with his misguided sense of loyalty to find himself, to hold on to a new sense of things.

He moved to the door, so near to going, so near to escaping from all this, from her, a withered old lady with a crazy dream, his nightmare. She shrank before his eyes, as the illusion had before her. He could see it now. She was the way of all of them, all grown-ups were like this. Bloody stupid! Stupid bastards! Dean had admitted to his sense of loss, and the death of dependency, but it propelled him towards a different possibility, and one where he wanted to take the risk of letting life back in. There was another way to be and he knew he had to become it.

"You'll be sorry when it comes, and you'll be damned! You'll be damned!" she said suddenly, her eyes wide and wild. "Don't you come running back here, young man, when it starts. You will suffer along with them. You are a traitor. A traitor! When the end comes, don't come back here crawling like a snake on your belly begging and whining. You will deserve it!" But as she said the words her heart heaved in the rickety basket of her bony chest and she wanted to wail like a banshee at his going.

He reached for the door handle, cranked his heavy heart and tired legs into a wild leap as he flew along the path, across the blue-bricks, under the apple tree, under the blue sky a thousand miles high, his lungs filling with a sweetness of air he had long lost the taste for. He could breathe! At last he could breathe again!

Later when he stood at the end of the road, looking back at the old house, he tried to recall when the world shifted and turned in the way it had. When had his life taken on such a drive, manifested such a dread of dying? This weird creation of fear cultivated anxiety, and anxiety had changed the way in which he'd lived. If life had been awful before it was doubly so now, and this sudden grab for freedom, to take the risk of going, breaking away, was the hardest decision he'd ever had to take, and despite his age he felt as if he'd grown old before his time. At the age of twelve he had witnessed the terrible visions, heard the prophecies of doom, and in the end all it served to do was to push him to take a breath and feel what it means to breathe again.

His eyes opened on the world, and it buzzed before him, in innocence and in light. But now, how would it resolve itself? What joy would be there for him? He looked back along Wellington Road towards the big house hunched against the sky, and remembered the beginning, of the end, of the world.

Two /

It was a mossy place behind red-brick walls, high as a castle, where trees whispered and raggy bushes swayed in the early autumn heat. Under the gate a crack of bright green light was as seductive and inviting as the neon clusters in the town's takeaways. This was the place drawing him steadily, hypnotically, despite the white anxiety he felt. Such risky stuff leads a curious boy and the notion of being caught causes more excitement. He took the risk as a way of getting back and levelling things. In some places the grass was as high as he was and he crept through it like a cat, eyes sharp slits against the strong light, peering around the rough brush of tall unkempt plants.

"Hey, you! Get out! What are you doing? Snooping?" she shouted in the small orchard at the back of the big house in Wellington Road, which years before had been one of the better places in Nantwich. It bordered a big expanse of grass on Brookfield Park, where once a year the carnival procession ended and girls danced in troupes beyond the visiting fairground, and where lads scrambled around the backs of the once-posh places to smudge their walls with aerosol tags.

Instinctively they eyed each other with a mixture of fear and anger, quickly gauging size and strength, and whether to fight or run. Shocked to be caught so soon, he ran, and stumbled in the brambles. Nettles gently touched and hooked their barbs into skin and a rash rushed across his thighs and arms. At first he thought she was going to beat him with her walking stick. Her eyes flashed behind her glasses as she loomed over him, teeth clenched in anger; big teeth, straight yellow tiles gleaming through the tight crack of a dark-edged mouth. But when she saw the bulges in his scruffy fleece she changed suddenly.

He looked quite pathetic, a pale ghost of a boy, the pockets laden with a quick steal, a pocket full of promise. His mouth would have been wetting in anticipation of the first crunch beyond the hard green skin into acid-sharp juice, the slight ache in the jaws denied by discovery. If she thought hard enough she would recall this moment of an age away – her time of being a child, but it was far away now. She tore a dock leaf from the tangle of weeds and dropped it at his feet.

"It's a dock, rub it on," she said without emotion, hoping to stay in charge. "It'll take away the sting and stop the red lumps from getting bigger."

"I know," he said impatiently. "Sod it! It hurts!"

As the boy smeared cool green sap over the biting red lumps, she found herself asking him numerous questions.

"Where are you from?"

"Up the road…"

"And what did you say your father did?"

"I didn't. He's a plumber."

"That's useful"

"Yeah."

"And Mother?"

"Nothing."

"At home? I see. What school do you attend? Malbank or Brine Lees?"

"Malbank," he lied. If she complained it would be to the wrong school, and she would look stupid.

"Dreadful place! Mind you the other's no better. And do you raid my orchard often?"

"No."

"Of course, you would say that. Mind you, I don't care. Not much use saving apples. They won't store for as long as I'd like them to. What I don't want is people snooping! Do you hear me? I don't like snoopers; in fact I dislike them just as much as thieves. Anyway, apples are pretty useless!"

"You could make cider," he said, impudently. What the hell was she talking about? He glanced up at her, trying to distract himself from the buzzing rash on his legs. Old people were easy meat. What could they do? They were *old*. They wouldn't be a threat to him, especially this old bird. He could hardly make out her face from this angle, dark against the huge blue sky draped around her shoulders, making her shrink into a shadow.

"Cider? There's no future in cider!" she laughed. "What's your name?" The question surprised her. *His name*! *Why in the world do I need to know that?* Reaching into her chest she tried to rescue a stern note, a voice to provoke him into fear. It would do no good to laugh at him as he might take advantage; stealing apples was one thing, but it might be the thin end of the wedge.

He would lie, give her a false name. Shifting under the light he saw her eyes, piercing and demanding, but her eyes held no fear for him, meant nothing. They were not like the eyes he knew so well, eyes which made him shrink inside, so much so that sometimes he hoped he would shrivel up and become invisible. He could face this old bird out.

"Barry," he lied. He hardly had to think about it.

"Barry, what?"

"Barry Jones." Barry Jones was a dumb kid at school and his name had been given away in situations like these maybe a hundred times.

"Jones? Really? I'm a Jones, too, you know!" she exclaimed, her voice temporarily warming with delight again. "Maybe we're related!" It was an absurd notion, and she tried to throttle her note of warmth. *Be careful, be very careful*, a tiny voice nagged, feeling aggravated by this display of optimism. What was it about this boy? She should shake her stick at him.

It wouldn't have been possible to be related to her even if he was Barry Jones, he thought. Barry's family, like his, came from the Cronkinson Oak estate, a planner's attempt at modernising the terraced families by stacking people upwards rather than sideways. They didn't talk like this in Cronkinson Oak. She was a lady, tall despite the crooked back, and thin and well dressed. She was posh, like someone in an old-fashioned black and white film on the telly, so boring and so dull. He hated black and white films, and sometimes he'd have to sit and endure one when his mother got sentimental and wanted him to be near. She'd wet his shirts as she cried over him, and despite his age he understood her tears were deeper than that, deeper than the stuff on the television. The films only served to pull the trigger.

She smiled and shook her head. It would be best to dismiss him with an air of benevolence and let him go without a grudge on either part, better just to let him go rather than push him into a corner and cultivate a need for him to get one back at her. Go in peace, she thought, a memory stirring somewhere on the very edge of awareness.

"Get along then, Barry Jones. Take the blessed apples, but let this be a lesson to you! I don't like thieves and snoopers!"

"I wasn't snooping, honest. I was only nicking your apples. Anyway, I'm sorry, really sorry. I didn't know anyone lived here," he lied again. Lying was easy for him. He survived on lies. He knew her. He'd seen her often at the front window overlooking the street, stern face pushing through the gap in the curtains. The risk of getting caught hadn't occurred to him then; he didn't see her as a threat of any kind. He could handle her, give her some crappy apology and then hoof it.

"I accept your apology. A rare thing today! Now, if you please, get on your way, young man." She thought it was charming that he'd apologised; mostly the children gave her a 'v' sign.

He didn't move, and for a second she looked into his wide eyes, and then looked away as a breath caught in her bony chest. As he rubbed his legs, hair fell across his eyes. He pushed it away and as he looked up his eyes pierced her. It was wounding. She knew that, felt it instantly, the look got through and hurt her deep inside. Those eyes challenged and defied her, and yet in her heart she moved towards them while her body moved the other way.

Struggling to his feet, scratching another bright rash on the back of his hand, he watched her limp down the uneven blue brick path, slow and awkward, and he disliked her slightly stooped back and the stale smell of perfume, an old woman's smell that caught his nostrils. Her hair was tight in a bun at the back of her head, a small, thin, grey lump bouncing around like something out of a cartoon. The pull of hair made her forehead seem high and white, her eyes stark and starey, like a fish, like the many fish he'd caught and watched, eyes dimming as they gasped on the sandy shoreline of the mere. He paused and stuffed another apple into the lining of his coat and wondered whether to give her some abuse and do a runner, but stopped the words in his throat from erupting, and made ready to go. But Miss Jones hesitated too and turned as if she sensed his eyes on the back of her head. There was something about this child. For a moment she tried to suppress the feeling that welled-up inside her. It was dangerous. At her age, as much as she resented the idea, she had to be cautious. Children were dangerous. Many years of observing them had abnegated any desire she may have had in the past to bear one. Not that she had much opportunity. Coughing into her chest she galvanized herself against sentimentality. She'd been a target for lots of the children from the local schools and neighbourhood, and mostly she ignored the stealing of apples. One time she'd seen someone snooping near the house, and for a time she feared they'd break in and see everything, and the game would be up. But nothing came from it other than she increased her capacity for neurotic vigilance. Mostly she kept well out of sight until they'd gone. It was a difficult house to break in to, she'd made sure of that, but inevitably, she worried. But this lad had done something, and she felt a shift inside. Despite her fear she knew she didn't want him to go, at least, not just now. It had been like turning her face towards the sun on a cold day.

He exuded something warm and attractive, but a thought pierced into consciousness like a shard of bright glass, and she shrugged and shoved it away. It was too painful, and to relocate this was absurd. She wouldn't think of it. Better to dismiss him now, this instant. She opened her mouth to tell him so.

"You want a cup of tea?" She was shocked by this spontaneity. She'd not done this before. Maybe it was his big eyes that appealed to her, or the scruffy mop of hair that fell into them. Certainly, his clothes wrinkled around him in an effort to fit the small, poorly formed body. She felt a slight shift in her chest – *the curse of compassion*, she thought, and again, tried to dismiss this other idea almost as soon as it ruptured into consciousness. There was no place for sentimentality, no point in looking back; it served no purpose whatsoever other than to hurt her deeply. And yet, she felt drawn to leading him along the lumpy garden path, felt the risk was somehow worth taking, as she admitted him into a little bit of her life.

"Tea? I don't like tea," he responded, wondering if he sounded hard enough. Tea was his favourite drink, but for some reason he felt an urge to refuse her offer rather than the drink.

For a moment she couldn't comprehend his reply, but then recovered her wits. "Yes, of course you do. You haven't tasted my tea. It's not the type you get in those baggy things. This is proper tea," she laughed at herself. That was the kind of thing her mother would have said. She glanced at him over her shoulder, and felt another whip of endearment. Perhaps she'd been lonely for too long, she thought, but once again tried to suppress the shift in her, the vague sense of longing, or returning. *No. It wouldn't do*, she thought, reprimanding herself for following that old cul-de-sac of an idea.

Despite her inner tussle she led him towards the high-sided house, a big red-bricked building which once boasted a chest-puffing eloquence among the other houses squatting along the wide road, beyond the railway station. Once upon a time people walked past the place full of admiration, with a longing to emulate such style. In those days Miss Jones was regarded as a beauty too, a wealthy catch in a small town. Then the house and its inhabitant were remarkable, and envied, in sharp contrast now to the dour ageing of both.

He thought she was a bit stupid, all that stuff about proper tea, and felt the urge again to call her an *old cow* and run for it. Something stopped him. She looked stern and yet her eyes were soft and sad and seemed full of the same hurt he'd seen in his poor Auntie Jessie, when Uncle Ralph died.

"Okay," he said, despite himself, feeling a little of the same warmth he had for his aunt. *She* was okay. Maybe this old bird would be okay too, but he flinched when she beckoned him to hurry along behind her. He felt a weird kind of reluctance older people sometimes pulled out of him, an uneasiness rather than disrespect of their wrinkles and half-hunched awkwardness. Maybe it was the way their skin sagged and fingers knotted, but at the drop of a hat he could run like the wind, and the thought reassured him. He could run and leap and be away before she had time to clack her teeth.

"Come on then! Not often one meets a young gentleman."

Me, a gentleman? He wanted to laugh at the stupid remark. How easily she'd fallen for it. If you kept a straight face and gave nothing away people would believe anything. It was becoming a bit of interesting business so he followed quickly, pushing his hands into his pockets and dropping the apples one by one into the long grass as she led the way. He didn't feel any guilt; they knocked against his ribs and thighs as he moved. He could pick them up again when he left. She talked incessantly, her voice sharp and clear, echoing across the walled backyard of the dark Victorian house, speaking the words properly, not like people he knew. Nothing she said was slurred or slang or shortened. He kind of liked it. Even the teachers in school didn't say things the way she did, in a sing-song way. It was nice. Her voice sounded younger than she looked, and for a moment he shut his eyes and listened as she moved down the path. Yes, she had a young voice, a little girl voice which was good and pretty. He really liked that about her – at least it was something, but another part of him felt she was weird too, and although he followed he did so cautiously. The false name he'd given to Miss Jones gave him a sense of security – a way to do this stuff and not get caught. The idea excited him, and yet troubled him too. Sure, he was excited to see how things would go, what would happen next, and maybe she had things in the house which would be worth seeing. Maybe too, there might be things worth nicking. It wasn't something he was quick to do, but he knew it would earn him respect in some places. Although he tried hard to catch the eye of his peers they usually ignored him. He wasn't odd enough to be bullied, but mostly he was avoided. It wasn't who or what he was, but rather the reputation following him. It was usual not to give him a second look, or any disrespect in case his dad waited at the school gates, or stormed into the school itself.

He listened to her again, and the voice softened him, so he decided she was just a lonely old bird like Mrs Santos from the top flat in his block – she wouldn't let you go once she got going. Old Miss Jones was probably harmless too, and not an old witch. He decided she was a mad woman.

As they walked along the blue-brick path he looked across the tangle of her garden. The house stood in a decaying part of town, and he'd felt a strong pull just to get inside the walls and explore this green chaos. Sure, he'd nick some apples, but the risk of getting in became more important than that. It crossed his mind that he could build a den maybe, a place to run to whenever he needed it. The teacher was reading *Robinson Crusoe* to his class, and he thought this was a kind of island, a secret place where no-one would find him. Isolation on an island appealed to him, and he wouldn't wish for rescue. The old lady at the window wouldn't know he was there if he was careful. The dream dissolved away like dirt and dust on the mucky puddles down at the end of his street. Miss Jones was a crazy old bird, but he realised it wouldn't be a good place to hang-out now.

Suddenly she stopped in front of him and pointed her stick, the brass tip inches from the bridge of his nose. His legs tingled and his breath tasted strange. It was like a gun being pointed at his head. It excited him. He wanted to laugh, but the sensation prevented the possibility, and made him feel woozy. It was an unusual buzz that tingled in his balls. Normally if he got threatened in any way he would do a runner, quick as a squirrel running across a road between cars. It was mad that she even tried to scare him.

"One thing!" she said, "You tell no-one about what you see in here, right?" Her voice had gone hard now, as did her eyes, like his dad's did when he was going to get done for some wrongdoing. But Miss Jones' voice was a thin sliver of hardness compared to his.

"What, in the garden?" he asked.

"Yes, in the garden, but more especially in my house!"

"Yes, right, *Mrs* Jones," he said deliberately, trying to bring her down to size. The brandished walking stick thrilled him but the note of bossiness was annoying, and he felt he had to say something to let her know he was tough.

"*Miss* Jones. *Miss*," she said quietly, though insistently, and hobbled down the path, quite unperturbed by his response.

The kitchen was dark after the sunlit garden and it took some moments before his eyes adjusted to the gloom. It smelled of gas and boiled cabbage, and although it was untidy, it was nothing like the kitchen at home. She had lots of cupboards reaching from the red-brick floor up to the flaky ceiling. It was a mad kitchen, chaotic, crazy like the garden, and he wondered why she needed so many drawers. The ceiling and walls took some understanding – they were there somewhere, but too difficult to make out in the gloom. If there was paint or wallpaper it was well hidden. Pipes straddled around doorframes and skirting boards as if they'd grown there like roots in the dark. In places they had bellied and when she filled a kettle they boomed and rattled. The fizz of water sent a shiver down his spine. It was spooky in here, cold and scary. A single light bulb struggled against a duvet of dark, shrugging faint beams against the weight of gloom. It looked like a pathetic tear about to drop and splatter on the red tiled floor.

Miss Jones peered at him before she placed the kettle on the stove. She wanted to trust him. His emaciated face, pale and curious, appealed even more to her. She felt a pang of something maternal, a slight shift from her usual acute defensiveness and wondered if he'd be good boy, a boy she could trust, or would he be like everyone else? Life had been a profound disappointment to her, and people were life, spoiled life, killed life, and ultimately destroyed everything. The risk was acknowledged and yet she was drawn to let him in, to peek into her high stacked world.

Her eyes followed his as they wandered over the scullery. He looked even smaller under the big-fronted cupboards. It was strange to see him here, in her house, her home. He was the first person for a long time to gain entrance, and she was curious as to why it gave her such a strange degree of quite intense pleasure as well as doubt and a measure of pain. He was just a poor, scruffy child who had climbed into her garden to steal apples. Surely this was mischief, not the cynical robbing of everything she'd planned and saved for? Could he be capable of hurting her, spoiling this quite extraordinary moment? He tried to look tough, but how hard was he?

"Master Jones, can you keep a secret?" she blurted, feeling both doubt and excitement on the verge of his answer. How could she stop herself? Every time she tried to divert an idea, an impulse, the opposite expressed itself. Conscious decisions were overwhelmed and usurped by unconscious emotions rupturing through, demanding expression and attention.

He peered intently into her old face and nodded. Yes. Secrets were easy for him – keeping secrets, telling lies, and being ready to duck and dive. You keep your mouth shut and you don't grass. Better to do that than anything. It gave you respect even if it didn't give you friends.

“Go through into the sitting room,” she gently ordered, and pointed her long knotty finger toward a door where the paint peeled.

The door creaked like they do in old films and it was spookily dark inside. The light dazzled him momentarily when she flicked the switch, and he blinked until the sense got back into his eyeballs. He felt uneasy, and wondered if she would do something awful to him. There were things he wouldn’t do even for money. His imagination began to roll, and he thought of bodies in freezers, all cut up and stiff, like the one the police had found in the west end of town. They never caught anyone either. Maybe now would be the time to do a runner, get away, but she was old and he could give her one good shove and knock her flying. It felt horrible to think like that, but it was better than ending up as a stiff piece of meat in an old bird’s fridge. If he had to survive, he would. He could. But despite his feelings of uncertainty, he hesitated because it was too fascinating to run just now. He couldn’t understand what he saw in the room and stood open-mouthed in the doorway. Rooms in houses weren’t like this. How could this be her home? Perhaps it was a shop, he thought, or a storeroom like those in the back of Supersaver. Boxes were stacked on boxes, and the floor dipped under the weight. In one corner a stack reached all the way to the ceiling, and everywhere cardboard boxes leaned and bellied, their sides bursting to reveal tins, and bottles. It was a mad store right in the middle of the old woman’s mad house. If he had any sense he’d get out while the going was good. She was mad, he knew now, and recalled the look he’d seen on her face the days before he climbed over the wall, the way she stared out through the window with eyes full of knives and bullets waiting to blow you away. She stood in his way, framed by the doorway, and yet he was distracted still as his eyes discovered more sagging shelves running over the door behind her, bowed with more dusty brown cardboard boxes, each one numbered in chalk, Why would anyone want all this stuff? he wondered.

She watched him, followed his eyes as they rummaged in the stacks, then patting his head pushed him further inside. Miss Jones wanted to laugh, but understood he might react to that, so she smiled and nodded at her boxes. “My insurance,” she said, chuckling a little, despite herself. “This is my insurance for what is to come.” Her voice was tremulous, and she amazed herself again that she’d gone this far, said this much. Relying on intuition, she knew somewhere inside herself that he was okay. Barry Jones appeared to be a decent little lad.

Her hand felt funny on him. He didn’t like to be touched, but he pretended not to notice and moved out of reach. Head arched upwards and angled first to one side and then another, he tried to comprehend what it all meant. Glancing into other rooms, beyond heavy doors, he saw stack upon stack.

“For the future,” she said, suddenly becoming more serious. “And I’ll be ready.”

“What? Pardon?” He grappled with what she meant. *Ready for what?*

“When the end of the world comes!” she hissed, sounding like a snake about to strike.

“The end of the world?”

“Oh, yes,” she said, emphatically. “The end of the world is coming. The tipping point isn’t far away. And when it comes…”

He’d never heard a grown-up talk like that. A shiver ran down his spine. People’s faces didn’t usually look like this, and they didn’t say things like that either, not unless they were taking the mickey or something. But her face was pulled into a tight and serious look and he knew she meant it, whatever it was she meant. He knew anger, sadness, even rage, the kind of rage which was white-faced and dangerous, but he’d never seen a look like this – all happy and serious at the same time – and like she was looking into the distance even though her eyes rested on his.

“I’m ready, you see,” she laughed. “I’m going to survive it!”

Excitement threaded itself through her words, and she hoped he would feel it too.

What was she talking about? *Mad, crazy old cow!* He should run now while he could, but it was like an accident on the ring-road. The worse the smash the more you wanted to look. He knew she was crazy because of the stuff she was saying, and yet he couldn't go. He wanted to take a good look and see what was mangled-up in her head. Miss Jones turned to go back into the kitchen and he watched her scuttle around making the *proper* tea. It was as if he was watching a film and he couldn't quite get the angle. Here he was watching a weird movie and he didn't know the next line, let alone the plot. Sitting next to his mum through loads of films hadn't prepared him for this one.

She placed a tin of biscuits on a tiled coffee table by a high-backed wooden chair. "Sit down," she commanded, firmly and gently, nodding to the floor. He knelt close beside her, a corner of a wooden crate sticking in his back, the floor hard against his knees. Despite his discomfort he knew he shouldn't move, couldn't fidget. She was going to let him in on something, and even though he felt scared, he wanted to know what it was. *The end of the world?* What was it she knew?

She had a serious look about her now, and she became angular and stiff as she tried to hold onto her vision and make it real for Barry. Her joints cracked as she sat next to him.

"This is my secret," she confided, her voice almost imperceptible. She peered intently into his eyes, checking him out for any sign of a problem. If he so much as grinned he'd be out, she thought. No-one, no-one had ever been party to this, and the risk in telling him, sharing it with another soul, terrified her, but for some reason now she'd started she had to keep going. Deep down she wanted to understand her need to tell him, to make sense of why she wanted him to know. Maybe if it made sense to him, it would be okay and it wasn't just a silly obsession. "This is my secret," she repeated, tapping the side of her nose.

"Yes, right. You mean the end of the world is a secret?" he checked out.

"You must promise to tell no-one. No-one! Not even your parents!"

That wouldn't be difficult, he thought, he hardly ever saw them, and when he did they hardly ever spoke to him, unless they needed something from the off-licence. Often they went for weeks and said very little to him, barely acknowledged that he existed at all, and then suddenly he would be back in the grip of Mum's sentimentality or Dad's wrath. In both places he became uneasy and evasive.

"I promise, Miss Jones." He played along. His face was dead-pan. A teacher at school said he was inscrutable, and couldn't make him out. He asked his dad what 'inscrutable' meant, and he said, 'I haven't got a bloody clue, but whatever it is you'd better make sure to stop being it. Don't bring any shit into my house.' When his dad warned him about anything, the boy did what he said, so from then on he tried not to look like he was inscrutable.

Miss Jones stopped. In an instant she found herself unnerved, anxiety stiffening her muscles and making her feel short of breath. Panic spread through her old body at split second speed and with it her sense of stupidity and vulnerability. What was it? What caused this instantaneous shift?

It felt an age as she peered at him, tried to get into the thoughts behind the eyes, and despite her warmth for the boy she suddenly had terrible pangs of regret she'd invited him into the house. He didn't move. He was like a small well formed statue, not a real boy. He was a piece of art, a deceit. The boy's face was a mask; it registered nothing. An acute fear sharpened in her and she allowed herself to see that which she'd concealed and denied. She was talking to an illusion. He wasn't real. He was stringing her along. She'd fallen for an illusion. He seduced her with his cute perfection, big eyes and floppy hair, and she had responded, projected her deep-seated grief and need onto him. Beyond this was the reality, the truth. He was mere flesh and blood and he would rob her blind if he got the chance, and the silly old fool of a woman that she was had fallen for it.

Barry blinked, shifted his feet, and broke the stillness of the moment.

"You don't like tea," she stated, indifferently. Her body rose and shifted into an awkward angle away from him; closed off – shut him out.

"What?" He sensed a change in her. What happened? One minute she was all over him and now she looked at him like he was a weirdo or something.

"You said you didn't like tea and yet you come into my home and expect me to offer it to you?"

"What? Sorry, I…" She was crazy.

"*Sorry. Sorry. Sorry*. What an absurd little word coming from an absurd little thief. You must go now please," she insisted. Her face had hardened into rock – grey and unyielding. If she moved she would crush him.

"I'm not a thief," he protested. She really was crazy and she was turning on him. It was time to go. He watched her carefully thinking she might strike out. Muscles tensed in him and he made ready to leap away. He was like the hard-coiled springs he saw on the beat-up old cars in the scrap-yard; springs so strong they'd break fingers if their pent-up energy found release. If he had to, as a last resort, he would break her fingers if she tried to grab or push him.

"You must go now please, and don't come into my garden again."

She spoke so quietly now he hardly caught her words, but despite that he understood. The business was over.

"Yeh, okay." He didn't understand why he felt a slight pang of sadness for her. If she was mad he might be in danger, but he pitied her madness and was fascinated by it. Her voice changed from being sing-song into flat and dull words, as cold and indifferent as the words chiselled on headstones where he went to see Uncle Ralph's grave.

He must go, and cautiously rose to his feet. Her words might be a prelude to something more dangerous. Both his mum and dad were like that, fine one minute then going ballistic the next, fighting like crazy over stupid things. Miss Jones would explode soon.

"This way?" he asked, nodding at the way he'd come, suddenly conscious again of teetering stacks of boxes. What was in them? His thoughts began to race and he had visions of skulls and bones crumbling to chalk in those big boxes in the dry and dusty rooms where the pipes rumbled like distant thunder and the doors looked so heavy that if they shut he would be lost forever. It was darker and scarier than any film he'd ever seen. For the first time he understood the drama of black and white in the shadows of this big house. One minute he knew one thing, the next he knew nothing at all. He wondered why life did this to him.

"You must go. Now." Miss Jones demanded, her voice disturbingly quite. "I want you to go, please, this minute."

As he shuffled quickly through the scullery, she watched, forehead tight, eyes shrinking against a sudden shaft of sunlight, watched, as the small and beautiful boy ran down the blue brick path and beyond the tangle of green strangling the thickening bases of the apple trees. It *hurt*, but now it was too late. A memory pierced her breast and despite the effort to close the wound, she bled until the tears quenched and cooled that old and exquisite pain.

Three /

The door scraped over the uneven floor. Dad cursed for weeks and insisted the wood laminate was warped and faulty. It had to be; he was impervious to doubt about his abilities. If he did something it was right. If he said something it had the same strength of singularity – what others would call narrow-minded, even stupid - but never in earshot of Billy Cartwright. Dean steered a more careful path around him these days. It seemed that every time he noticed his son it cranked him into a fury, and Dean learned to ghost in and out of the flat, a pale boy moving in and out of shadows and the clutter of old furniture bought from car boot sales, or the stacks of cast-offs in the local church sale, stuff that just crossed the boundary of the nearly-good-enough. His mother collected clutter like a mangy dog attracted fleas, and no amount of shifting or scratching made any difference to the constant irritants strewn across the room. Unfortunately it fuelled Billy's moods, and added to his deepening malevolence. Tools were strewn over the floor again as the irate man tussled to wrench up another length of faulty wood, and he frowned so hard his eyebrows hurt and he developed one of his thundering headaches.

Keep well away, Dean thought. *One bad move and he'll do me.* The thick arms, rough with coarse black hair, could break him in two. Sometimes when he lashed out and caught Dean with his hammer-fists, the boy would be in a daze for hours afterwards – his ears buzzing, and his eyes unable to bring the world back into focus. But worst of all it made him slow and awkward and unable to keep out of his way. Dean hated the feeling of helplessness.

"Where the friggin' hell have you been?" his father barked.

"Nowhere," Dean replied, voice edgy and strained. His eyes widened and his muscles tensed. He was ready for flight. Under his trainers he felt a floorboard shift and squeak.

"No-one can be no-friggin'-where! You've got to have been somewhere!"

"I've just been coming back from school." Dean tried to make the words easy, smooth, and without the smallest trace of cheek, of confrontation. He'd learned never to speak his mind to his father.

"It's six, Dean!" The man looked up, his eyes narrowing when he saw the boy's slight shift, the feet gently pathering a nervous dance against the floorboards.

"Yes, I'm sorry. I got caught up with my mates." Maybe this would be a good reason; one to get him off the hook. Dad was always telling him he was a loner, making it sound like an accusation.

"Mates? You? Since when?" The accusatory tone rang like a cracked bell.

Dean didn't want to go any further. He wanted a way out. Dad could be merciless when he got going. He had a persecutory look on his face, eyes narrow, mouth drawn tight, like a snake about to spit venom. Dean shifted uneasily from foot to foot, unable to stop the weird little dance of nerves. The man reached for a screwdriver, and snarled as he grabbed the plastic handle. It looked menacing in his huge hand. Keeping quiet, moving slow, Dean tried to ease his way into the kitchen and possible refuge. He crawled among the tools, and the dangerous splinters of a broken board lying around the floor like fractured bones. He dreaded catching anything and disturbing the fragility of his father's mood. One awkward step, a slight teeter, any show of uncertainty and he'd cop it.

"Since when did Deano have mates then? Come on *Billy-no-mates*, since when?" He taunted him now. He played with the shaft of the steel, slapping the handle into his palm, pushing his words, like prodding fingers at Dean's uncertainty, gaining power as the boy gave his away under the pressure of the man's brutality.

Dean tried to deflect his attention. "Is Mum back? Do you

want me to make you a drink? Do you want a can, Dad?" It worked. His father's face unfurled at the mention of beer, but he nodded indifferently not wanting to show any enthusiasm for the boy's suggestion. *Never show your feelings*, he drummed into the kid. *Never let anyone know what's going on in your head. Face them out.* And Dad did. Whoever came along, whatever they said, or threatened to do to him, meant nothing. Police, Probation Officers, Social Workers, were all met with his hard face peering straight at them. No-one withstood the malevolence of his anger.

The boy was an appeaser. At just eleven years he'd learned the art of manipulation, the art of survival. Scared he might be, but equipped he certainly was. It was a tough apprenticeship he was serving. Dad's pressure created another way of coping. Facing them was useless in the hostile schoolyard. Dean learned the art of deceit, telling people what he knew they wanted to hear; let them hang on to their illusion of power. He remembered telling the old woman his dad was a plumber and she didn't question him. He lied without doubting he'd be believed. He didn't even think about it anymore. A lie was just something you said and did and it didn't matter one bit. It got you by and getting by was where it was for him. It got him through the day; no one knew him – teachers, coppers, and other kids, Dad or Mum. He got by. Dean survived by facing no one. He gradually turned his face away from the world.

As he cracked open a can and waited until the fizz settled into froth on the blue steely top, his mind wandered back to the old woman. She kept popping up. All the way home at the corner of every street, lurking in the dark alleys, she whispered about the end of the world. And now as he stood by the dented tub of a fridge he saw her face as clearly as if it had been reflected in the mirror by the doorway. Snapping his eyes shut, he tried to get her out of his mind.

The end of the world. It hurt his head to think about it. What would it be like? How would it end? Would everyone be burned or drowned or crushed by earthquakes or trashed by hordes of devils coming out of the ground and sky. He didn't want to imagine the pain, the terror. Just the other night, on the television, people had been going on about it, saying that the world was moving towards dreadful changes in the climate. If things weren't done soon, they said with concerned faces, it would be too late. Miss Jones' face loomed large again in his mind, her sing-song voice both soothing and frightening him at the same time. It would be really good, he thought, if he could go to Dad and ask him, check out what it meant, and then find reassurance and maybe even a hug. Dad would tell him it was nonsense and not to worry, and push him, josh him along, until Miss Jones and the end of the world faded away. But Dean's dad wasn't like that. Quickly he shut her out of his head and took the can to him.

"Where've you been? Shift your arse, Deano! I could've brewed it the time you took to get it here."

Dean didn't answer. Anything he said would have been wrong so he kept a still tongue. He backed away as the man swigged and gulped the beer. One can made things easy for a time – sometimes Dad even joked with him, and not in a sarcastic, shrivelling way. Dean watched the bulge at the front of his neck and thought about cartoons he'd seen in comic books, drawings of ostriches swallowing spanners, and balls, and buckets, and the shapes stuck through the narrow neck and you could tell exactly what they'd got in there. He knew what the bulge would be like in Dad's neck after a few cans. It would be the shape of anger slipping down to his big belly where it turned to fire and spread upwards onto his face, and he would become sweaty and fierce. He would become dangerous. His eyes would redden, shrivel and burn, his mouth would get fat with insults, and his fists would rip through the battered doors. Dean secretly cursed the floor and the beer understanding that in combination they would rouse his father to madness. It was a small flat and Mum was still out, and there was nowhere to hide.

*

Miss Jones lost count several times and gradually became cross with herself. What a stupid, useless old bat she'd become. If she was to survive she needed to keep her wits about her, and today, foolishly, she'd let sentimentality rule objectivity. And yet the child stayed with her for the whole evening and ruined her attention and concentration. At one point she swore at her lack of focus and tried to banish him from her thoughts by reminding herself of what a lucky escape she'd had and counting back from one hundred in sevens. It was usually a successful technique in regaining control against persistent worries – the werreting loop she occasionally got into – but it failed and her thoughts were invaded again by anxieties.

In newspapers she'd read about the youngest of children doing the most horrible things to old and vulnerable people. Just a few weeks back she'd caught the news on the radio. Some children had kicked a pensioner to death, and not for the sake of robbery. The horror lay in the probability that they did it for status, or even pleasure. She tried to switch off her sense of aroused vulnerability, but the effort to keep both the afternoon's events at bay and her neurotic reactions, wore her down. What if he told other children about what he'd seen? She'd be a prime target and before long she'd be overrun by little thieves, or worse still, their elder and more cynical siblings. She had heard too on the radio how old people were murdered in their beds for a few measly pounds, and here she was sitting on a storehouse of treasure. Some of the children in this town would stop at nothing. She knew. She'd seen their faces as they passed her house. And she, such an old fool, had let one of them in. She despised her age, her folly, almost as much as she despised the world.

Later in another attempt to banish him, she carelessly tipped a too-large tot of whisky into her tea and the alcohol gradually seeped into her heart and unfroze her feelings. Barry Jones' face strayed back into her consciousness. She remembered the lovely big eyes and mop-top of hair. How extraordinary that a boy could look so beautiful. He *was* a lovely child *wasn't* he, and he *had* apologised *hadn't* he? *Not many children did that.* There was such a look on his face when he stepped into the sitting room, his eyes like lamps, flashing and bright, announcing his amazement, and she released a little laugh when she pressed the cup to her lips. It resonated in the white porcelain, and sent tiny ripples in the tea. This was a good moment, she thought. She felt at ease. Had she been too hard on him? Maybe there was nothing to worry about? Was *every* child capable of nasty acts towards the elderly? In this moment she doubted it, but such moments pass.

*

Dean waited behind the kitchen door as his father let rip at the floor, smashing a hammer under the thin ridges of veneer and yanking them away from the polythene sheet beneath. He waited for another command for beer, and at each quick draught his dad lost more control. First the chuntering followed by a string of curses getting louder by the word. '*Friggin' useless crap. Friggin' garbage. What's the friggin' point?*' Several more cans discharged his rage, moving him quickly from vile words to clumsy actions. He fizzed and popped and cursed, spat his wrath, then threw anything within an arm's span across the narrow hallway. At each thud or crash, Dean trembled; his body deeply affected by the wild behaviour unleashed just a few strides away on the other side of the door. He didn't dare to move and hoped the shaking of his limbs wouldn't render him so much out of control it brought attention. Terrifying though it was he had to keep still, keep hidden, until Dad lurched out and vented himself in a pub brawl somewhere, if he was able to find a place he hadn't been barred from. And if he failed to find a landlord stupid enough to give him access, and booze, he'd start something in the street.

This was what the end of the world would be like, Dean thought. Men would become monsters like this and turn on each other and rip heads off, hearts out, break bones and tear and slash until the streets were stained with blood. And maybe afterwards it would be a better world when all the humans had gone. Occasionally the anger ebbed quickly and his dad would fall asleep on the sofa, his mouth agape, snores resounding through the flat. Though not tonight. He'd got the taste now and had the singular intention to, 'get wrecked.'

The door banged so hard Dean felt it as if he'd caught it in the face, and he was so tense he thought the racket would shatter him like glass. Dad had gone, but he hardly dare let go of the breath caught in his chest. Gradually, he craned his stiff neck so he could peep through the crack in the door. The hall was empty. The door had been so forcibly slammed that the hinge had broken at the top, and it leaned awkwardly in its frame. Even though it gave up any idea of security it hardly mattered, as there was nothing worth stealing in the hotchpotch flat, and who would dare to anyway? Billy's reputation was a dark devil hovering over the block.

It was late now, and Dean began to wonder where Mum was. Sometimes she worked late, and occasionally she didn't come home at all. It depended on how many rows had gone on, how angry they'd become, how violent. The darker the bruises the more time she spent away. He couldn't settle, and wanted to run away, but where to? Auntie Jessie had taken him in sometimes, in the past, but when Uncle Ralph died she became very sad and her hair fell out. She didn't go out at all, and she no longer wanted Dean to visit. The house she kept was neat and clean and it was possible to walk in a straight line across the coloured carpets. It had corners too, and a shed where Uncle Ralph kept his fishing rods. She said she didn't want the hassle, not now. Dean heard his mum say she was suffering from depression and he tried to understand how great sadness must be before it became depression, black enough to remove her and take her away from life. Mum said everyone gets 'pissed off' and swore not to see her again. He'd really liked Auntie Jessie, but the last time he saw her he was alarmed by the ugliness of her balding head, and the darkness that weighed down her eyes. The world became so much emptier then. There wasn't any place to run to, and no-one to hold him and try to make it better.

He poked through the cupboards to find something to eat. It was likely Mum wouldn't be back. It was never discussed. No-one talked about it. Sometimes she was there, sometimes she wasn't. This was his family and that was the way it was. He loved them both, he really did, but his sadness was remorseless as he grew to realise it was probably him, Dean, who caused them such misery. They shouted and screamed and she said often enough it was only *the kid* that kept them together, caused this Hell. Dean was the rope binding them in their misery, and guilt was a sack of bricks he carried on his shoulders. He worried that if his sadness grew any bigger it too might become depression and his hair would fall out.

Eventually he found a bag of crisps and a chocolate bar, and carefully counted the cans heaped in the fridge. There were enough and he knew Dad wouldn't miss one – not now after filling up on seven cans and a belly full of anger. Beer and anger made Dad stupid. Dean liked the effect of beer. It made him high for a time. The worst fear would subside and usually, though not always, it would bring sleep. It made him laugh too. He'd drink tonight and think of the stupid old woman and he'd laugh at her, and the end of the world. Dragging himself on top of the bed, still fully clothed, he recalled the chaotic garden and the weird thrill of the walking stick just a short distance from the bridge of his nose. Sensations returned and he smiled under the weight of alcoholic giddiness. The room moved around him and he clutched his duvet, held on tight as his head fell back in the pillow. If the world were to end he would get drunk like this. If the end of everything felt as smooth and as light as this, it would be okay. What a mad old bird she was to be afraid. How could she know anything as serious as this anyway? She wasn't a scientist, or at least she didn't look like one. He trembled slightly. The alcohol dipped and took him sliding backwards into a darker place. But if the end really came he couldn't imagine not being anyone anymore. No body, no arms, no legs, no face, no eyes, no mind, no thoughts, no feelings, no words, nothing. It filled him with horror. And what if there was a Hell like a teacher said in school? What then? How could he not be taken there?

*

Miss Jones pulled the eiderdown around her neck and settled back in bed. She gazed at the cobweb hanging from the centre of the ceiling, and wondered how many spiders would be hiding behind the boxes. She didn't like spiders, but as long as they stayed where she couldn't see them she was happy enough. The boxes were rarely moved nowadays; there were so many and it was an effort to shift them. She did a count every so often so that she could make her calculations, but lately she abandoned the idea in favour of simply collecting until she'd filled every space. She reckoned she was old enough for it to last out her lifetime despite the fact she came from a family blessed with longevity. Great Aunt Sarah Jane had lived to one hundred and three years, but she, like Miss Jones had never married. Mother had lived to ninety-five despite having a husband who expired much earlier. Having reached seventy-three, Miss Jones reckoned fairly good health would sustain her for another twenty, and by her calculations twenty years of supplies would be achieved.

It was strange and awful, she thought, this allotting of life spans – who would die early, who would die late. She'd known such losses and yet they served to galvanize her effort to live her life as fully as possible, to extract every bit, every morsel, as she chewed her existence, hoping to nourish herself against the coming of the end. A world may die but she would continue, not in a vain desire for immortality, but rather as a well planned, deliberate choice. If they couldn't see the signs, acknowledge what blew in the dark and gathering clouds, then so be it. They would die, all would cease, and she would live on. But as she reflected on her triumph she pictured Barry, face down and pressed against the earth, a body broken by Nature's revenge absorbed into the black and cold soil. As his little face dissolved she felt a pang of affection and sadness. Touching her face, feeling to see if there were tears, she chided this stupid sentimentality and tried to reinstate the importance of her vision. Remaining objective had to be the key for her survival. There was no room for anything else and yet now in this moment she felt the cold and unwelcome hug of loneliness as it grabbed and enshrouded her from head to toe. There could be no-one. She was alone.

"Damn, blast and jump to it," she snapped. Tomorrow, when she got up, she'd brush away the cobweb on the ceiling and she'd prepare the pantry. There was a good, usable space and she could dismantle an old meat safe and use the cold marble slab underneath as another shelf. It was dark and there would be spiders but if she did it quickly and flushed the walls and floor with a boiling kettle they'd be killed and shrivel into oblivion. She wouldn't think about the boy again. What happened today had happened, and it was of no use worrying about it. It was unlikely he'd be back anyway. As she admitted the thought she felt a reflux from her stomach. She winced, and wondered whether to get up and go down to the scullery for a glass of milk and a cap of *Gaviscon* to coat and quell the burning acid. Deep down she understood that no amount of milk and antacid could dampen the sharpness of memories shifting in the depths of her gut. Miss Jones knew that a mind may wish to forget but every cell was impregnated with memories. A mind filled each cell and made emotion physical; feelings became sensations. If there was a place to hide she couldn't find it, and every effort to quieten the past only

served to delay the pure physical power of its potential eruption. Better to distract herself, she thought. Better to be so busy, make her plans, beaver away at her dream, collect and save, buy and store, and not face those feelings again. As hard as she tried a face reappeared and acid fizzed inside as her body attempted to devour itself.

Four /

Dean hadn't intended to go, but as the school day dragged on he began to think about her, and the sing-song voice. The day, typically, hadn't gone well for him as in the morning he'd been caught up in an event which exposed him and reinforced his sense of alienation. They'd been messing about in the classroom, John Deacon a red-faced, big boned idiot at the centre of it. Deacon fancied himself as the best fighter in the class, and he was in fact a strong boy, but his strength resolved into a brutal regime of bullying and coercion of the other children and inane displays of his power. Today he'd arm wrestled his way into near omnipotence and looked for another victim. When he noticed Dean in the back corner of the room he immediately dismissed him. Cartwright was weird, always on the edge of things, and perhaps deep down Deacon feared him a little. He decided the strange kid was neither here nor there, and to challenge him didn't matter and wouldn't add to his status, but Ray Pennington's eyes alighted on the boy whose head was in the distance and dragged him into everyone's view.

"You've got arms like a girl," he hissed and pointed at Dean who didn't flinch. "Are you going to take on Johnny or are you a big girl's blouse?"

Deacon smiled uneasily but when Dean caught his eye he flicked back his head in what he thought would look like a gesture of contempt. The class began to enjoy the stand-off and buzzed in anticipation. The loner was pointed out and watched keenly for a reaction. Dean stood up and walked across the room towards John Deacon. This couldn't hurt him. It was nothing compared to what he knew. The room shrank into a tight red-edged space filled with noise, the clamour of thirty or so kids jostling for the best view. Deacon blanched but kept his nerve.

"Have you got girl arms?" he asked, making everyone laugh,

especially Pennington who'd invented the notion. "You want to take me on, Deano?"

Dean would do it. He'd take him on. It wasn't courage or confidence which coursed through him. This was nothing.

They moved to a table and sat facing each other, Deacon shifting position several times before putting his elbow on the table top. He checked Dean's eyes repeatedly while trying to fix a grin on his face. The tension between what he did to retain his status and what he feared at the loss of it, made his heart thump and the sweat bloom on his shirt. By now the place was in uproar as the kids yelled almost exclusive support for John Deacon. Pushing and shoving they circled the table. Those who secretly wished for Dean to win held back and remained silent. They expected it to go Deacon's way and it would implicate them in future trouble if they displayed their preference. Better to stay silent and hope for the best as there was always someone in the wild crowd who noticed support for the loser. That's how they saw Dean, and how they saw themselves, and to disturb the status quo was a risky fantasy. They knew their place.

It was a strange sensation for Dean to be at the centre like this, making his own bit of history, becoming pivotal and important, and yet as he looked around it meant nothing. Then he fixed his eyes on John Deacon's eyes and knew that whatever happened he must not move them. Perhaps this was what Dad meant by, *facing them out.* And now it was as if he looked down a tunnel at Deacon's face and everything, everyone around him faded and disappeared and the noise dimmed too until he sat in stillness and calm. Dean held up his *girl's* arm and spread his fingers. Deacon slapped his hand hard against them and grabbed them so tightly Dean wasn't able to manoeuvre a better grip. High on the fingers Deacon had the advantage but if Dean felt anything he didn't show it. His eyes looked down the tunnel.

And suddenly it began and despite the excitement and garrulous expectations of the crowd it was over in a moment. Seizing his advantage Deacon slammed Dean's hand and arm against the table top. The noise stopped at the moment Mrs Bradshaw, the Assistant Head, walked into the room and yelled at a louder and higher pitch. She couldn't see what the crazy congregation surrounded, and Deacon slipped away into temporary anonymity. Dean quietly resumed his loser's seat in the corner of the room while she demanded answers from the big group of silent conspirators.

Drawn by curiosity and fascination, two powerful magnets, he passed the house again and saw her sitting in the window. It was a weird challenge, to go back, to face her out. At the same time Miss Jones moved nearer to the filmy glass to watch the activity in the street. Her severe face brightened when she watched him hesitate and peep beyond the wall and she waved and beckoned, pointed to the front door. An arthritic finger drew him in.

Last night in a thumping mood brought on by a second can of beer, he was absolutely sure he'd given her the *heave-ho*. Dad was getting tolerant to the drink, and Dean hadn't realised the alcohol content was at a much higher percentage than usual. After mauling his duvet and rummaging for his clothes in the squalor that was his bedroom, he rooted around the kitchen for something to absorb the alcoholic slush heavy in his stomach. Settling for dry bread with the flaky crusts torn off he felt relief after an initial retching, and it soaked up some of the stagnant broth. At that moment the very idea of the world ending was a positive and desirable event and Miss Jones' fantasy, for the morning at least, slowly dissolved as his stomach eventually purged itself of its contents. But now, partly through regaining a clear head, and partly at the relief of being out of school at last, he quickly felt the final conversion of negative energy to this strange positive that her friendly gestures evoked in him, and his curiosity returned. There wasn't a good reason to go home anyway as both his parents were absent that morning and neither had rumbled around the house like distant thunder, or worse, an erupting volcano.

Oblivious to his condition and despite everything that had gone on the previous day, Miss Jones seemed glad to see him. He was pleased too – to see her face and the smile she gave him. She'd bugged him, of that there was no doubt, and there was so much he was left wondering about; she'd intrigued him, despite filling him with fear. It was a very mysterious house with the teetering stacks of boxes and the narrow rows lined with tins and bottles. She said she had insurance. He wasn't sure what it meant, but felt now that if she let him get into the house he'd be able to ask her.

"Drink?" she mouthed, through the glass panel, tipping her hand in a drinking motion. He nodded, and realised the smile was the first he'd given to anyone that day. School had been a serious business, and the hangover added to the deep feelings of gloom and despondency he carried from the moment he shrugged on his clothes and trainers.

He wiped his feet on the rush mat in the porch and smiled again when the door crack widened and he saw her chalky-white face, as white and brittle as a porcelain jug Mum kept behind the cracked glass of a rickety cabinet. Blue veins threaded her temples and reached into the hollow cheeks, and he thought how transparent her skin was, and if she crossed before a strong light she would be like the glass in the door panel – opaque and fragile. Dean felt something approaching pity, but quickly resigned himself to caution. She might flip again.

"I can give you some orange squash if you like," she offered. "You don't like tea." Her manner was straight and good-humoured, and although she felt a great delight in seeing him again, there was still reluctance and she knew she had to be vigilant.

They approached each other like a pair of sniffing dogs, each tense and alert, vigilant for any sign of threat, though locked in fascination. It was a strange choreography and as one moved the other followed, mirroring unconsciously, as they instinctively tested each other.

"Honest, I don't mind. Tea's okay I suppose." It was time to be open now, he felt, especially as she was beginning to look as if she was pleased to see him. He couldn't recall the last time he'd seen a face approaching such openness. It was a long time since Uncle Ralph died; he vaguely remembered how in those days Auntie Jessie had shown him such warmth, and had smiled at him in the way Miss Jones did now.

"Actually, tea's my favourite drink," he blurted, wanting to hold onto her smile and this sharp sense of acceptance. It meant something and he watched her with an even keener eye. He found himself trying to please her now, and held his smile as wide as he could. If she was crazy it was in a nice way, not like the madness he knew and experienced as frequently as the turn of bleak weekdays into miserable weekends.

She didn't hear him but as they walked into the hallway she looked at him intently.

"I hardly recognised you. You look different today. How thin you are, young man. Do you have school dinners?" There was genuine concern in her voice.

"Sometimes. I usually spend my money on sweets on Monday." It was a straight answer. He felt he couldn't disguise it any longer. He shouldn't lie.

"On sweets! What does your Mother say?"

"Nothing. She doesn't know. She doesn't ask."

She thought it better not to pursue the matter. It was their business after all, not up to some old busybody to make an investigation. Not wanting to disturb the boy or give him any sense she was going to turn on him again, she too smiled as brightly as she could, her face eventually melting and the sensation becoming effortless.

"I wanted to see you and apologise about my manner yesterday." Miss Jones tilted her head to one side and widened her cycs. "It was quite rude of me considering you had the decency to apologise to me."

"It's okay, honest." Dean was surprised. A grown-up had never said sorry to him.

"No, really. I am sorry. I suddenly felt very worried that you'd take advantage of me. It's not a very nice world out there." She nodded, and frowned. *Was it necessary to justify this; explain it to the boy?* She couldn't help herself. His face was a picture of innocence. When she looked at him she wanted to laugh and cry at the same time. It was acute like the stir of a dark nostalgia in the pit of the stomach, and she tried to deny herself its subtle push for acknowledgement by turning her eyes from his and leading him towards the scullery.

"What do you mean? I didn't want to worry *you*," Dean said emphatically, "I'm sorry for nicking the apples, and I can keep secrets, honest, I can. *Truly*, I can. "

"It wasn't the apples. It's all this stuff." She nodded towards the shelves along the hallway. Even here the passage way felt like a clogged artery as they made their way through the oppressive gloom. "People might take advantage. They might…"

"You mean I'd rob you?" he cut in, and suddenly felt ashamed that he'd thought about it. By admitting to its possibility he worried she'd react.

"Well, yes. It did cross my mind." She stopped, and turned to look at him, peered down into his face. "Would you? Could you do that to me?"

"No. *No.* I wouldn't." Dean meant it too, now. Taking apples was one thing, but to break into her home and rummage through and steal the stuff in the boxes was something he felt sure he wouldn't do; though he wondered what she hoarded. As he stared up at her he felt a rush of sadness and a fleeting rush of shame at yesterday's more negative notion. The smile she maintained reached him, and held him like a hug. But she looked very old and tired, and even though she was frightened, she'd let him in again. That was courageous in Dean's mind.

"Barry Jones, I believe you," she said in her sing-song way again. And at that point she felt a release, as if the tension held by fear and doubt dissipated or forgot itself.

He felt bad. Really bad. How could she trust him now if he admitted to a lie? He hesitated for a moment, watching the look of expectation on her face. Was it going to be over now, just when it seemed like something good was starting? It wasn't possible to tell her, nor was it possible to hold the lie in place.

Miss Jones knew she'd touched on something and was worried he'd cool off and want to go, and then felt surprised at herself that it mattered at all.

"What's the matter?" she asked, voice quietening to encourage a response.

"I'm not Barry Jones," he blurted, face reddening.

"Oh?" Miss Jones strained to hide the disappointment. She'd liked the idea that they shared the same surname. It gave her some qualification for allowing herself to be easy with him.

"That's not my real name." He felt stupid, awkward. For the first time he felt uncomfortable with a lie and the sensation made him wonder why she had the power to shame him like this. What was going on?

"Who are you?" she asked as gently as she could. She recognised his awkwardness and pitied his discomfort despite her doubt. "What is your real name?"

"Dean."

"That's a good name." She smiled warmly. He needed encouragement not rejection, she thought, although the habituated contempt she held for anything human edged nearer to awareness, to the point she'd reached the previous day, and fretted to be allowed governance again. Why would the boy lie about his name?

"It has a good ring about it – it's a man's name. Some names people pick these days are quite…quite…" she stopped, just in case she dug herself into a hole.

"My name is Dean Cartwright."

"Cartwright?"

"Yes. Dean Cartwright." He watched for any flicker of change in her face, but nothing came. His face brightened; she wasn't going to yell at him. Even now despite the lie she was smiling, and the smile looked like she meant it.

"Thank you for telling me, Dean Cartwright." Reaching out her hand, she gently touched his face but felt him instantly recoil.

"I'm sorry I lied to you, Miss Jones." He meant it. He was. It felt good to tell her. "I won't lie to you again." Her hand worried him reaching out in the way it did but her sing-song voice and the gentle look on her face…but wait a moment. The tone changed ever so slightly in her voice.

"I hope you won't need to. I've only got one problem with this matter, young man."

And now it was as if her face had hardened into stone and the voice was as sharp as steel. Dean flinched again; there were always conditions. *I'll love you if you're a good boy.*

"I'll probably forget and keep calling you Barry! At my age my memory isn't so good." She winked and laughed a pretty laugh like that of someone a lot younger than she was. It was incongruent, this youthful laugh from such an old face. "Actually, you're lucky I even remembered it at all!"

"I'm really sorry," he repeated. Slightly giddy from tracking such quick changes in Miss Jones he shifted from foot to foot, and tried to regain some balance in his head and body.

"My word, how many apologies can we make in a day? We mustn't carry guilt around like a tail!" She laughed again and he heard it move through the corridor to be lost among the stacks.

The old lady opened a tin of shortbread biscuits from a stockpile under the stairs and made him eat a tongue sandwich, even though he complained a little and said he didn't like cold meats. He thought to tell her he was a vegetarian, but didn't. He'd promised not to lie to her and he'd keep to it. The fact was he was starving and he actually enjoyed the sensation of being full, if not the taste of the food. Miss Jones got a thrill from feeding him too, sitting him at the scullery table, and waiting on him. It had been a long time since she'd had a role as carer, and the sudden recall made her heart ache a little. Then she'd been useful, and despite the onerous demands at least she'd had the company of someone who cared too.

When she passed a rickety kitchen cabinet she saw her reflection in the glass-fronted door, grinning as Dean devoured the sandwiches. She enjoyed the sensation of feeding him, of fulfilling some part of herself which she felt, or rather knew she didn't deserve. An absurd idea flitted around her mind, an image of herself as a nurturing mother – a *mum*. But almost as soon as it buzzed like a mosquito into her thoughts she swatted it away before it settled, bit, and drew blood.

They looked at each other surreptitiously, nervously weighing-up the moment and what it meant to an old lady and a young boy. Occasionally their eyes met and both looked away quickly, self-consciously aware that the relationship was so brittle, so fragile, it could be lost again if any slight misunderstanding appeared between them.

When he finished eating she sat across the table, groaning a little as she lowered herself in a high-backed chair. He stopped chewing for a moment and watched with a brow creasing concern. It touched her. How long was it since someone had looked that way? For a time they gazed without flinching, and perhaps for the first time they recognised, despite their distance in age and the short gap across the table, they had touched something in each other.

"I think I can trust you, young man," she said, her voice soft and yet assertive. Dean's eyes strayed from her face, though not shiftily, rather more from embarrassment. She sensed she might grow to really trust Dean. In recognising the child's response to her she drew comfort and a greater measure of certainty. It felt safer now, safe enough to let him in again. It was done in a rush of sentimentality before – foolishly premature. Yes. She could tell him now.

"I really want to tell you about my secret, to share it with you." Even as she spoke a tremulous sensation moved through her, peaked and didn't abate. Such a notion had the quality of a confessional, a quality of catharsis – a feeling released after being held onto for too long. But it felt right to reveal her innermost dreams and plans to him now. The idea exhilarated her.

"Okay," Dean nodded, not knowing how much to say. If he was too nosey she might get the wind-up again, and if he didn't show any enthusiasm she'd think him rude; especially as it all sounded so important to her. He hoped he didn't look inscrutable, as it might upset her too.

"I'm going to show you around my house, Dean Cartwright." It had such a weight of importance Dean responded with a deep breath which he held onto and only let out gradually as he followed her awkward back.

He couldn't quite get his head round the size of the place. It had five bedrooms, each bigger than the flat he lived in with his parents; a bathroom, cold despite the sun breaking through the fancy-patterned opaque glass and which echoed when he gasped his surprise. Washing was an unnecessary event for him, and to see a room this big dedicated to getting clean seemed mad. He wanted to ask her about the vast array of boxes, but he felt it better to wait until she offered him the information. He was aware that she feared being robbed, so he knew enough now to keep quiet and not provoke her anxiety and ultimately her anger. Miss Jones remained silent throughout the tour, just giving him a curious smile every now and then when she caught his eye. In each room he encountered more teetering stacks of boxes, or full-bellied bags which in some cases had torn or burst open like disembowelled bodies. It would have been entirely chaotic had not each box or bag had a mark a number or letter, or both, written on the side.

"This is my insurance," she said at last in a deadly earnest voice as they finished looking through the upstairs rooms and stood on the high walled landing. "When the inevitable happens I will be prepared. It's all in the predictions, you see. I can see the signs. You'd be a fool not to because they are so absolutely clear and yet everyone carries on regardless of what is coming."

Dean felt he must be a fool because he couldn't grasp what she told him, but he noticed the hardening muscles around her eyes and mouth and knew he would have to learn quickly.

"Look here!" she declared excitedly as she opened the door to a small room at the bottom of the stairs. Miss Jones opened a cupboard crammed full of yellowing newspapers and read gleefully from articles pasted in scrapbooks. Each one gave dark and disturbing details about the state of the world; the population explosion, global warming, global dimming, carbon dioxide pollution, super-bacteria, viral illnesses. Many pages insisted in both scientific and other more spurious research that glaciers were melting and the polar ice caps would break up and flood the world. One page, circled by thick red ink, declared the likelihood of an asteroid smashing into earth. He listened as she read to him, his skin crawling as she pronounced with absolute certainty it would soon be over. As she read her voice moved from slow and earnest to an almost gushing and gleeful crescendo. "It will soon be over for everyone. Everyone will be wiped out. Annihilated! Well…" she paused and tapped the side of her nose with an arthritic finger, "*…nearly everyone!"* She lingered on the words, and looked at him with a long searching look, before continuing to read or tell him about the coming disaster.

"There is too much carbon dioxide in the atmosphere, and it traps the heat of the sun like a greenhouse, you see, and the world is warming-up because of this. The clouds are full of muck and rubbish from years of cars and power stations producing tons of soot, and lead, and God knows what other stuff. Just now they are helping to shade the world from the heat of the sun which would make it even warmer so when they try to clean it up it will heat up even more quickly and boil over and the weather will change so dramatically the world will end! Bang!" She slapped the open pages of a scrapbook and released both dust and a terrified response from Dean. He nearly fell over. "But listen, when the changes come I will be able to survive any extreme because I've planned and planned and planned. Listen to this..." She became even more animated and unfolded an article from a magazine and read –

"Nostradamus has predicted the end of the world in 2025. A man before his *time, he predicted terrible events in* our *time and has pinpointed the global catastrophes the world faces..."*

"2025? That's soon," Dean said, his voice shaky.

"Yes, young man. 2025." She seemed to delight in the absolute certainty of it all. Then she showed him ledgers. "Do you know what these are?"

Dean blinked. "Are they sums?"

"Kind of," she replied. "These are my calculations of how much food would be needed to feed myself over the years ahead."

Miss Jones' eyes peered unblinkingly into his and he felt spooked by the intensity of her stare. Shifting under the terrible darkness of her explanations he glanced at the numbers again and tried to make sense of what they meant.

"Come and look at something," she said, suddenly pushing him towards another door, and into another room.

She squeezed between boxes and pointed to crates where water was stored in a regiment of bottles. Another, smaller series of boxes were crammed with medicines – *aspirin, paracetamol, Anusol, Gaviscon* - remedies she'd need to cure everything from headaches to haemorrhoids to heartburn. Doors barely opened under the weight of boxes shoved behind them. Eventually she took him into three empty rooms which seemed huge after the cramped conditions elsewhere in this strange house. She grinned when she told him how many more years supply they would hold when they were as full as the others.

"The only thing that bothers me is if the house will sink under the weight," she joked, heady in the rush of excitement her sharing had brought on, but then her heart skipped a beat as she caroused toward an out-of-control giddiness. She should slow down. Maybe this was all too much for the boy; perhaps she was taking too many risks in letting him know so much. She needed to slow down, sit awhile and let him speak; see what it meant to him.

"Yes," she began, taking a long breath and slowing the pace of what she said, "One day the house will disappear under the weight of all this. All my work for nothing!" The seminar ended almost as abruptly as it had started.

Dean didn't understand the joke because he really felt the house would slide away like a battleship he'd seen in an old film about the Second World War, a slow and stately tilting until it stood on end. A picture formed cinematically in his head of Miss Jones clinging on to the small flag at the back of the ship as it nose-dived and disappeared. The house *was* a cargo ship and she the weird captain steering it into a dreadful future. What could he make of it? If what she said was true and despite his difficulty with arithmetic, he made a reasonable guess he'd be young, very young, when the end came.

"The boxes and things are full of food and stuff?" Dean asked directly, wanting to clarify the situation, but he knew really and wanted to break the silence which hung over him like an angry father.

"Yes, my supplies are my insurance for the future." She was gleeful. Triumphant.

"How long have you been storing things?" he asked.

"A long time, Dean Cartwright. I've got stuff here to last me for five or six years."

"Six years?" It didn't feel long enough, he thought, six years was nothing.

"It's not enough!" she responded as if she'd read his mind. "I'm aiming to collect enough supplies to last me at least fifty years!" she exaggerated, clearly enjoying sharing her plans with the youngster.

"Fifty years!" he exclaimed and whistled through his teeth. That sounded more like it. He would be ancient in fifty years, and it occurred to him Miss Jones would be really old by then, ridiculously old, and he couldn't imagine she'd live that long.

"Yes, and when they've all been crushed by ice sheets, or died in a famine, or been struck down by awful diseases, I'll still be here in my nice little home!"

Dean watched her face dance with delight at the prospect of being a survivor. He didn't know how to feel, or what to say. If the end of the world came…if it did…if it really came, why would she want to live? What would be left?

"Wouldn't it be lonely on your own?" he said, feeling a strange sadness and an awful anxiety mixing up together.

"Oh, I don't get lonely! I've had a long training in being by myself, having to fend for me and me alone over these past years. The last time anyone…" She stopped suddenly, and smiled a smile that didn't have warmth or humour. "You can be lonely or you can be alone. I choose to be alone."

Dean didn't understand the difference. "Yes, I suppose…."

"People need to stop and think about things more, young man. There is only one world and we only have one life, and we can't afford to muck it up. It doesn't matter how clever the scientists are, how brilliant the leaders in the world, they won't make a jot of difference!" She chuckled to herself.

"But God won't let it happen," he blurted, unsure as to

whether he believed in God, and if he did, if he could help anyway. So far, despite his prayers in the past, God hadn't intervened, but Dean thought that maybe he hadn't prayed in the right way. The headmaster at school said praying was not an opportunity to ask God for toys, or sweets, or money and stuff, so Dean never did. He only asked for bad things to stop, and as God hadn't been able to help out with those prayers there seemed to be no chance at all he could do something as big as stopping the world from ending.

"God? God?" Miss Jones' face looked twisted in response and flushed a little, and she decided not to say anything more. "Would you like a piece of cake?" Her sing-song voice returned, lilting and dancing, and somehow made the awful thoughts and images fade just a shade in Dean's overworked imagination.

Five /

When Dean left the house, head and belly full of different foods to stimulate a new appetite, a different taste, he couldn't bring himself to go home directly. He'd get punished for sure. Dad kept him on a tight rein despite his lack of affection for the boy. Dean was a small part of the world the angry man could control. He couldn't shackle Patsy any longer, he couldn't contain his need to drink, and he certainly couldn't control his ever present rage. When he wasn't blowing steam it fizzed and boiled just under the surface. Despite this impending threat, Dean wanted to walk a little, to look around and make some kind of sense of what she was saying. If Dad was mad what would be different? Dad was always mad with someone or something. Dean could survive the eruptions in his world in the same way Miss Jones planned to survive the eruptions in hers.

Down by the river a stretch of land ran between the gas works and a mucky brown canal. It was here the kids met up and did stuff. Allotments edged a narrow strip running from the river to the canal side, and this land flooded in rainy seasons. It was known as Paddy's Field, after an Irishman who grew dahlias and other bright flowers on his small rectangle of land. The pun was lost on the kids who met behind the tumble of patched-up sheds and greenhouses. This was the place where a feud constantly ran on between the gardeners and the kids – a battle between creation and destruction. The gardeners' grew and nurtured the land with pride, and reacted with great hostility and loathing when the kids ripped it up. Ever watchful they patrolled their land and yet failed to prevent the vandalism.

Dean liked it here. He liked to walk between the neat pieces of worked soil and look at the rows of things growing. He'd broken windows sometimes, not from a need to rile the old men who worked among the seedlings and plants, but to give him a sense of power. It was a thing a kid did. Dean was stuck between the angry old men and the wild youngsters, belonging to neither group, and always watchful as he roamed this place, ever ready to avoid them. The old men would shout and brandish their forks or spades, and the kids would circle him on their bikes silently intimidating him. Twice he'd been done over by three youths who had claimed the land as theirs. And twice he vowed he'd come back despite them. No-one was going to stop him from going where he wanted to go, but he didn't want to do it in his dad's way – *facing them out* – Dean needed to learn the art of subtlety. And he had to learn quickly.

The sun weakened its grip as it slipped beyond the bleak vista, casting an orange tinge on the town. The weathercock on the church glinted, a brief spark against the deep blue sky, and a hundred starlings drew their huge swooping crowd into a condensed blot on the pylons towering over the railway works. Dean watched stragglers flit and flick persistently around the structure, against the dying light, squabbling for a place, until they claimed a spot, settled, and preened oily feathers. A breeze, still warm and soft against his skin, lifted the hair hanging over his brow. He felt a slight ripple of comfort spread through his body as the air warmed him. He had ached with anxiety and felt chilled and lonely. Miss Jones' vision ate away, filling his head with pictures of terrible things, but now with a belly full of cake and the last flicker of sunlight warm on his face, it seemed far away and no longer threatening.

As he looked over Paddy's Field, fringed with horse chestnut trees, it reminded him of the paintings he'd seen at school. A supply teacher showed slides of paintings, mumbled, uninspiring and indifferent, as the children sent text messages to each other in the darkened classroom despite being within talking distance. Dean liked to see the paintings. He especially liked pictures by an artist who painted melting clocks in deserts because they were weird and spooky, and he recalled an awful picture the teacher said was about a war in Spain, wherever that was. Mum had been to a foreign country but he was sure it wasn't there. The teacher said the picture predicted a terrible war, and Dean remembered the ugly faces and dismembered bodies.

Predicted.

Miss Jones predicted terrible things too. The end of the world would be like the painting – mangled and wrecked, with a face so ugly it made his stomach turn. All around the wreckage was a big, dry and empty desert and strange looking women with draws sticking out of their legs who wandered like mad monsters, arms outstretched, and faces blunt and featureless. He imagined Miss Jones as one of those women, draws stuffed with things to keep her going in an empty world. Some of the kids had laughed, but from his seat at the edge of the room, Dean stared and stared, tried to understand what he reacted to. Afterwards Dean paused by the projector and told the teacher he liked that picture best, and wanted her to tell him it was okay, it was just a painting and there was nothing to worry about. The teacher wrapped up a cable and ignored him.

Over the stretch of land a man stood upright and watched Dean as he walked between the plots. Dean glanced at him and continued to move along the dirt path, carefully picking where his feet fell. The church clock struck seven. He'd be for it when he got back. As he walked beyond the broken and daubed fence skirting the allotments, he glanced back at the old man who still stood, arms akimbo, waiting for him to move out of his territory. Dean thought about shouting something, but couldn't be bothered. What was the point? What would he say? For a brief moment he felt a surge of kindness towards the man.

They were both damned. The end was coming and they were going to die. They would be mangled up in the strange sunlit landscape of the painting, a vision, a prediction a mad artist had seen. A shiver ran down his spine as he recalled Miss Jones' story of Nostradamus.

*

Miss Jones couldn't settle after he'd gone. Her excitement abated now, and she reconnected with her feelings of self-doubt. Had she shown him, told him, too much? He'd gone quiet, and she'd observed an edginess about him. Although he smiled, he smiled without warmth. She wondered if he tolerated her ideas but deep down thought her nothing more than a silly old fool. She knew she liked him, and admitted to her great sense of joy that he'd come back. But there was something else and she couldn't put her finger on it.

Dismissing the worry she gathered up a packet of bin-liners and made her way through the tunnel which served as a stairway, and opened a heavy oak door into what had been a library. The shelves were intact after all these years and she remembered the rows of elegant leather bound books that once stood in academic loftiness along the ledges. Her father was a learned gentleman who had an appetite for the Arts, and he almost squandered a fortune on buying volume upon volume of books in an attempt to assuage his hunger for knowledge. He would bid for a rare book before he'd furnish the table with food. She loved him dearly, and after his death she vowed to keep the library exactly in the pristine order he'd left it.

Now she packaged the few remaining volumes of dusty books in the black plastic bags without so much as a glance at what lay beneath the heavy covers. A book, whatever its contents, was only a book, and there would be no use for books in the coming world. As she carefully placed a small book at the bottom of the bag, a ticket fell and floated beside her as she deftly shook the sides of the statically charged plastic to stop it from sticking to her clothes. She ignored it at first, but a second glance stopped her from scrunching it into a ball.

It was a ticket for, *The Tempest,* at the Lyceum, the old Edwardian Theatre in Crewe town centre. Immediately it brought a rush of nostalgia, so exquisite in its intensity it caught her breath, and made her eyes flicker as her memory replayed that night. The

Lyceum was a jewel in Crewe's sooty heart, and during plays trains rattled the rails and sent a deep and throaty boom along the decorated facades fringing the high proscenium arch – a well-timetabled reminder and eruption of reality into magic. Nantwich, for all its ancient glamour had nothing to rival it. Ye Olde Wyche Theatre, on the corner of Market Street, had had its day, but saw it slip away into the less than Regal Cinema, and eventual conversion into Chatwin's Bakery offices.

Well-to-do families arched well-groomed necks over the balcony of the Lyceum as they were drawn to the magnetic stage, while in the stalls below people scuffed boots on the cold linoleum and watched wide-eyed as fantasy and fiction illuminated their dark industrious lives. It was lovely; the smell of the velvet curtain; the sudden hush as it rose to reveal a light as brilliant as a full moon and a rich fulfilment the audience anticipated and craved. And at the end many hands clapped soft skin or hard segs in appreciation of this utterly amazing escape from the daily rut, the bleak ordinariness of the railway town. Miss Jones would have been twenty-two then and her father took her to a whole season of productions. She'd loved them all, but mostly she loved to link his arm and walk with him to the car afterwards discussing the play, the actors, the ideas and images.

She gently squeezed her arm, pressed her fingers against her elbow, and fancied she could feel her father's strong grip, and smell the mustiness his clothes absorbed from the ranks of books. He was *Prospero*. He was a wise but disillusioned old man moving towards his death, and she was *Miranda*, except no *Ferdinand* craved or courted her then. It would be several years until she felt such an intensity of love, and later, regret. Momentarily she recalled Father's face as he lay in her arms at the end, unprepared, exhausted and wide-eyed, as he looked into the abyss of death. She'd nursed both her parents – first her father whose decline in health was quick, his body becoming consumed with a voracious illness that quickly devoured his life. Mother lingered under the cudgel of an insidious losing of mind, body and spirit. As slow weeks turned to slow months and years, Miss Jones bore the brunt of this incapacity which ate away at two lives – the cared for, and the carer, mother and daughter. Then she wished Mother could show just a little of the spirit, a fraction of the tenacity Father showed.

"Why can't I die?" Mother would say. "Why won't you finish me off?"

The spectre of death haunted Miss Jones for years afterwards, and she fancied she could see signs of it in the eyes of people as she walked and shopped and experienced the world. How could people give up in such a way? *You had to live, you really had to live*, she thought. In contrast, Father fought death like a cornered cat, spitting and hissing his dismay and subsequent rage at the rapid decline, catching Miss Jones with his claws and teeth. Heart heavy and bristling with anxiety, frightened by his fight, she tried to turn her face away from the horror of ending, and to maintain a vision that looked away from the world of death and grief. Living was all that mattered, to make the most of every minute, to feel life coursing through her veins and to cling on to hope beyond despair. It was better never to admit to death and dying.

In a quiet place embedded deep within her, she had an obligation to live; to make up for another small life which barely came into bud, let alone bloom. Now, a flash of a face rushed before her eyes, and just as quickly she blinked and made it disappear. Many times she'd fought to banish his face from view, to let her heart rest. This time the face was Dean's. Trying, but failing, to suppress the thought, she wondered if it always had been.

"Don't!" She slapped her hand against her thigh. "Don't pursue this!" She screwed the ticket between her fingers, and the last vestiges of her father were clenched in the tight ball of paper to be thrown into the bag along with a few worn-out books. *No time for sentiment*, she thought, while at the same time recalling Dean's eyes and feeling annoyed with herself again that she held such contradictory thoughts about him. Why wouldn't the blessed boy be gone? She imagined herself thrusting him into a bag in an effort to put him away, and then felt immense guilt. He was eleven. For all the guile she imagined and invested in him, he was just a boy. Was there really anyone in the world who had innocence? Deep within her a tiny voice, a child's voice, distant and yet still strong, answered. *Yes, there is.*

His face illuminated her thoughts again, and shone with the brightness of theatre lights, but she felt deeply troubled as she tried to separate one face from another. She took the crumpled ticket, straightened it against her knee and put it in her pocket.

*

"Your dad isn't coming home today," Patsy Cartwright informed her son. "He's had to go away for a time."

Dean didn't respond to the euphemism. He was curious, but guessed he'd been done for fighting again, especially after the mood he'd been in the night before. His relief was abundant when he got home to find Mum there, and Dad out. It was nearly eight, but she didn't say anything. Her lack of reaction was due to indifference rather than tolerance. Dean looked through a couple of shopping bags for something to eat, but his mum offered him money to get a bag of chips. He shook his head, still feeling full from Miss Jones' sandwiches and biscuits. Once again, her response was low-key and unsurprised.

He sat on the other end of the sofa for a while and watched a soap with her, glancing occasionally at her profile, the still pretty nose and forehead. Her hair was a deep brown colour drawn back in a long tail. She rarely let it loose from the tight clasp, to fall around her face and frame her good looks. Dean remembered her tickling his chest with it in the days she read to him, leaning over the bed to kiss him goodnight. Watching her go from the room always filled him with such sadness, and yet nowadays he hardly missed her, or felt it better not to think about it as it filled him with such guilt. She was slight and quick, and loved to dance, though dancing was something she rarely did now; getting by took away opportunities for fun. If anything held her in thrall it would be dancers and dancing – and she trawled the TV magazines to see if something was scheduled, and then she'd sit back trying to relax but failing when the music filtered in and made muscles quiver and stretch as they ached to move in time with the beat. How many times had she grabbed Dean when he was a toddler and danced him around the living room? - though she never, ever, did when Billy was home, hunched in a hangover, or even when he was sober. It was a tacit understanding, a rule she didn't break. Her pretty face was worn down and weary and only occasionally flickered into life when something amused her. People said Dean looked like her, and it pleased him.

She yawned, and stretched her arms.

"Jesus, I'm knackered," she said, yawning again. Dean caught the yawn and it cracked his jaw when he yawned too. "I think I'm going back to bed. If your dad gets out he'll be a bastard. What are you doing?" she asked him.

"I don't know. Watch telly I suppose."

"There's nothing on worth watching." She'd flicked through *TV Quick* carefully to see.

"I'll go to bed then." He yawned again and watched her brush her top free of crumbs and then light a cigarette. "Mum?" he asked quietly, and waited until the red tip of the cigarette ceased to burn and she blew smoke through tight lips into the already foggy room.

"What, Dean?" There was a note of impatience in her voice.

"Mum…" he hesitated, unsure of what to say without sounding stupid or something.

"What? Come on, Dean, please! I'm tired." She stood by the doorway, hands on hips, eyes beginning to blaze.

He wondered whether to say anything at all, but then found himself blurting it out.

"Mum do you believe in the end of the world?"

"What? What are you on about?"

"When do you think the world will end?" It was important, he wanted to hold-out against her immediate note of annoyance and get her to talk to him, give him reassurance.

"God knows, Dean! What a bloody stupid question. Have you been doing about it at school?"

"Yeh," he lied.

"They shouldn't fill your heads with such crap. Bloody teachers are useless! Do you want me to go in and have word with them?"

"No, Mum! No, I just wondered. How would you know if it was going to end?"

"Don't ask me, Dean! What kind of question is that? Do you think they'll advertise it on the telly or something? End of the world coming for the weekend! Make sure to get your booze before it goes! Better tell your dad!" She laughed and tousled his hair. "Don't think about such things. The world will go on forever. God made the world and he isn't going to muck it up, is he?" She still had a vestige of belief, a last reliance on a Catholic upbringing. "Look, sunshine, get to bed and read your comics."

"But, Mum, what about global warming and stuff? Some people, scientists I think, say we might get hit by a big rock from outer-space, or the North Pole will crack and drown everyone. Will it, Mum? Will it happen?"

Despite the note of fear weaving through his questions, Patsy continued to walk out of the room.

"There was this man who said it is going to end in 2025. He made predictions and stuff, and he said it would be the end of the world. 2025. That's not long off, Mum."

"Go read your comics," she repeated wearily as she closed

the door and shut him out.

Dean didn't have comics nowadays, but he got up and went to his cramped room, pulled back the curtain and looked down over the town. They lived four floors up in the block, and if nothing else he liked the view. The sky was black. The moon was a shiny badge pinned on the chest of the night, and he fancied it moved, became bigger. He felt uneasy. What held everything up and together? How did the moon stay up there and not come crashing down onto earth? It was like magic and if God did that how could he do it forever? And he understood from what he'd heard that God sometimes got mad and killed everyone. Noah loomed large now in his head. The big flood where everyone was drowned was God's doing. Angels came and warned people in the Bible that bad things were coming, and God punished them, all except those who believed in what the angel said.

He wondered whether Miss Jones had information from an angel, or maybe she *was* an angel, though he'd always imagined angels were young and blonde-haired, not old and creaky and living in Wellington Road. But maybe angels were old? Who could say? Dean couldn't recall anything in the Bible that said they were young, though the teacher at school who taught them about religion and stuff said 'God works in mysterious ways,' so maybe this was one of those mysterious ways. *Miss Jones – an angel.* It didn't seem right, so he dismissed it.

Dean decided to say a prayer. He used to do that with his mum when he was little, kneel by the side of his bed and bless everyone. Maybe if he prayed hard God would take pity on the world, and even if it was bad, spare the people from dying. He shut his eyes tight, but couldn't find anything to say. A picture of Miss Jones stuck in his mind, long and thin, with legs full of drawers, and in the drawers, heads of millions of people with ugly beaten-up faces, faces like in the painting, the painting of the prediction. A new and powerful idea struck him. Maybe Miss Jones was like Noah. Maybe she was warning and saving him.

In his head her face shone brighter than the moon.

*

There was something in his voice which triggered her guilt. Patsy almost went back, but after sitting for a moment on the edge of the bath she decided not to. She really was tired, and his interminable questions might rile her. She stood and looked in the mirror, and flinched at what she saw. This was her face. How old she'd grown, how the lines around the eyes had become deeper, and the mouth more drawn-down and tight. It was the face of helplessness and impotence. After undressing, laying her clothes neatly on a chair beside the toilet, she went into the bedroom, safe in the knowledge that tonight she could sleep without defilement, without invasion and a brutal forcing of one body onto and into another. As she lay on the bed, lighting a last cigarette, she began to bathe in the dark pool of guilt; angry with herself at missing an opportunity of supporting, hearing her son. He was frightened. She'd heard that and did nothing other than diminish him further. Why wasn't she able to hold him anymore? Despite her heavy limbs and head fuzzed with a need to sleep, she couldn't switch off from the shoulder of history thundering against the door.

Looking back was a painful process for Patsy, and if she could only hold onto Dean and look forward, maybe it would be okay again. As she looked at a framed photograph of him as a sleeping infant, warm and safe, eyes tightly shut, she realised how much had slipped just out of reach, and all the aspirations she'd had in the past drifted away in the murky stream of her existence. Now she struggled to keep her head above water and away from Billy's fists.

How often she wished she'd never seen Billy for the first time, at a dance in the Civic Hall, in the days when she thought her tiny feet could trace wonderful patterns on the creaking boards of the wide floor, and where, some nights, with a good partner, she really thought she could fly. He looked like a good laugh, and after he'd asked her for a dance she laughed a lot at his awkwardness, quickly snatching her toes from under his big booted strides. Being good-looking, and having strength in his arms that thrilled her, negated the fact he lumbered along. It didn't seem to matter. But later, after a thousand promises that he would learn to dance, she began to have regrets. Much is promised, she thought, when beer coats the breath.

Regrets were something she'd tried to push to the back of her mind – just enough out of view so as not to cripple the whole point of trying to live. Cynically she believed she'd been born to suffer, and die. *Life's a bitch and then you die!* Patsy said it often enough until it became an habituated truth – one of life's certainties. As much as she'd grown to feel indifference to her needs and desires, to enjoy any little pleasure in life without having to pay for it, she looked at a picture of Dean sleeping and felt a shift in her heart, a movement towards him that she'd postponed or forgotten in the act of survival. It would have been better had he never been born, but she wondered if it would be possible to find the love for him she once felt, and make it worthwhile.

Immediately after the birth the first glimpse of the child took her breath, and pain away, but even then she recoiled at the horror of his conception. As she gazed at her son's image, she remembered the soft hair on the back of his neck, but couldn't fix it long enough before she remembered *that* night, replaying it like a bad movie in her thoughts – images, feelings, sensations taking her back to the grim reality of a less than Immaculate Conception.

After turning out the bedside light she saw the shine of the moon, pale and silvery as it sought her out through the gap in the curtains. The bed creaked as she moved and turned onto her side, and instantly pictured herself standing in the dance hall, as she usually did, at the edge of the floor waiting for him to break from the crowd around the bar. Even then, so early on in their relationship, she'd concluded that he was too fond of the drink. Mrs. Nolan, the teacher from the school above Burtons who took them shortly after they were married, said he was potentially a fine dancer and should think of taking the medal tests. Patsy knew it was just a way of making money to keep the school afloat, and then Billy admitted, acidly, 'I'm only doing it to please the missus. Examinations are not my thing.' At home he told Patsy she could stuff her dancing classes if she pressured him further. She backed-off, but determined to carry on going to the dances at the Civic Hall. He could drink; she would dance with whoever asked her.

Staring into the darkness of the room, she recalled her pleasure at a new pair of sequined dance shoes she'd bought, but knew as she paid for them she'd wasted her money. A black pair she'd had previously were completely ruined when she used them to go shopping in; the strap broke on the left shoe, and scuffs down the patent strip on the t-bar made them unfit for dancing. After saving up, surreptitiously for many months, she'd splashed out on the classy shoes she wore for the first time that night, the night of conception, and Billy didn't even notice. He'd seen her prettiness and her fragility, and it cultivated lust rather than any shred of a loving. Billy had nodded across to her and tipped his hand in front of his face. *One more*, he mouthed, and grinned, as if to charm her. Over the years the gesture became empty and pointless.

In her head, Patsy heard the three piece band playing an introduction to a waltz, the drummer beating a steady rhythm until the organist hit the right notes. Several couples walked from the dark perimeter and hesitated before striding across the floor.

Patsy's eyes narrowed as she lay against the pillow and remembered. She wondered whether to have another cigarette, but then felt too tired to smoke it. The moon dimmed, momentarily, beyond a cloud, but then seeped through, and illuminated her memories – a cold and distant landscape.

She pictured Bet and Eddie Ashton spinning from corner to corner, grinning ferociously as they passed. Big-heads, she'd thought, and moved into the shadows under the brown arch at the side of the platform. Peter from the bakery had been smiling when he came in through the glass doors. He always looked nice in his suit and black tie. He stared at her all the time, in those days, but she knew he wouldn't ask her to dance. If Billy didn't dance with her, which he hardly ever did then, no-one else would. They didn't have the nerve. Men of all ages who'd flown around the floor with this little bird, ceased to ask; they distanced themselves from her, and wouldn't risk an occasional glance. Even in the progressive dances – where at the end of each sequence partners stepped in wonderful synchronicity from one to another – Billy had pulled her hard against his hips and refused to let her move along. No-one said anything, even when the confusion spoiled the sequences.

It became an unspoken and unspeakable rule. Of course he'd go to the dances with her. He'd drink. She'd watch him drink. The bedroom darkened again as the moon disappeared behind a heaving cloud, its big chest pushing the wind before it until the window frames rattled like a drum beat.

It would have been the Bert Grange Band that night, she thought, and smiled a faint and distant smile. The drummer was on good form, she remembered, and pictured herself tapping her feet, new shoes sparkling, waiting to shimmer in the swirl of light dancing from the glitter-ball. Impatiently she'd looked across at the bar again, and saw Billy's head tilt as he drained a glass. Maybe it would be enough for now, she'd hoped, but then saw him light a cigarette and pick up a whisky chaser. The music finished with a flourish, the organ rasping discordantly before being subdued by the crash of the cymbal. Without a break they played a quickstep, the guitar plodding through the melody.

She remembered pulling a black cardigan over her shoulders as she walked around the edge of the floor and sat at a table beneath the band. It was a way of hiding, disappearing into the shadows. That near, the wrong notes mattered less too, and the vibration under her feet was near-enough on tempo. They'd get that much right at least. Some of the other bands were far worse. That night the drummer was a white-haired old boy who sat upright behind the glittering tubs and beat skins like soldiers she'd seen as a girl in parades. She'd half expected him to lift the sticks under his nose. The guitarist was a boy of about eighteen, cheeks ravaged by acne. His eyes flitted nervously over the women who sat under the light next to the toilets, hungry girls, whose eyes desired and devoured him, while the man on the organ stared anxiously at his music, sweat rolling down his neck and blooming on his maroon collar. Was it that much of an ordeal? Patsy wondered. His intensity amused her, and even now it raised a smile.

"Got you a Babycham!" Billy had said, his voice booming in her ear. His breath stank of the booze and he'd rocked slightly when he placed the bottle and glass on the table. Despite his state she'd itched to leave the shadowy perimeter and get onto the floor.

"Billy, I want to dance."

"Aye." Cigarette smoke flew into her face.

"Come on then."

"Aye, in a bloody minute." He winked and returned to the bar, slapping someone on the back as he crossed the crowded floor, not caring that he bludgeoned his way through the dancers. No-one cursed him, and even black looks were censored or controlled until he'd moved back to the bar, where there was always a deferential gap waiting for him.

Bastard, she thought, as she shifted in the bed. She would have thought it then too; the only difference now was its intensity. Peter had sat opposite and would have noticed through the dancers how she fidgeted with her silky handbag, head well down to hide the flushed cheeks. But he did nothing. Maybe she should have walked across the floor, held out her hand and said, 'Come on. Dance with me. Dance with me you bloody coward!'

A great roar had gone through the hall. She always got to hear the dirty joke later when Billy pawed her in the backyard and tried to unzip her dress. Two years of marriage and he still preferred to take her in the cold, urine and dog faeces stinking on the slippery path, the wall rough against her backside. And he'd say she wasn't a bit romantic when she pushed him away.

Patsy remembered the conversation with Mary, Mrs. O'Brien's girl from the top of the Beam Street who had sat with her, uninvited, moments after Billy had lumbered back to the bar.

"Billy says for me to come and chat with you," she'd said.

"Did he?" Patsy replied without interest. The stupid girl always twittered on about this or that lad as if they were pop stars.

"Isn't he a great looker," she started, nodding at the guitarist.

"No. He's bloody spotty."

"He'll grow out of it!"

"Men grow out of nothing, Mary, except their women."

Patsy had watched Peter take Irene Jones' hand and lead her into the fox-trot. *Lucky cow.* Even now in the dark and silent bedroom she relocated and felt the force of her anger. She'd worked so hard to feel that dance, to move in its seductive grace, and when people said how easy she made it look, they hadn't acknowledged the intensity of work she'd invested into achieving such poise and ease. It was, beyond all others, her favourite dance. *Slow, slow, quick, quick, slow.*

She'd glanced at Irene's shoes sparkling in the lights, the legs bending against his, her head thrown back like a pro's. The bitch can dance, she'd thought, watching her push her hips into his when they turned. Billy never held her like that. Never. Not even in the backyard. Patsy had made an excuse to Mary that she'd got a headache, and after making some cheap comment that Billy would be disappointed tonight, Mary got up.

"Tell him *I'm* ready to go," she'd said to Mary, leaving her in no doubt about her intention to get him away from the bar and away from the dancing. It had become too much to bear, and she'd decided never to dance again. And just at that moment, as if to deride her decision, laughter from the bar suddenly turned to shouts, and glasses crashed to the floor.

"Christ, look Patsy! Your Billy! Look!" Mary had yelled, face flushed in fascination and excitement.

Billy was punching and kicking at the crowd as they fought to get away from him. His face was contorted and saliva flirted from his mouth and over his black trousers.

"Patsy! Look!" Mary and several others had shouted.

"I can see," Patsy said, coldly. "He's only dancing."

The band played on, though the pace of the music quickened and became more emphatic as the drummer bashed his sticks against the drums. Within seconds three men dragged Billy from the hall. Patsy turned away and looked across the floor at Peter. He'd taken his hand from his partner's waist and glanced back at her. But Irene slipped her arm through his and crushed her breasts against him. He turned and laughed. As the doors banged, they talked excitedly and started to dance again.

"Bloody coward," Patsy hissed.

Outside Billy lay against the corrugated walls, blood dripping from his nose and over his shirt front. His feet twitched in the lamplight.

"Take the silly bastard home, love," the manager had said. "He's banned! This is one time too many. He needs to see a shrink or something, get him dried out!"

Patsy slipped her arm through Billy's and dragged him to his feet. Blood dripped over her shoes and spotted the white panel around the toes. He groaned and cursed, but when his eyes focused on her face he allowed her to help him. She felt his big hands heavy on her shoulders and when they eventually lumbered down the rear entry she felt them on her neck.

"Come on, Patsy." His voice was husky. He pinned her against the wall. She felt his hips grind into hers. "How about a dance now?" he rasped in her ear.

In the distance she heard the dull but insistent thud of the drums, like a heart beat, reminding her of the inescapable brutality of life. And now a seed had been planted inside her. *Life's a bitch and then you get pregnant.*

A tear trickled down her face, tickled its way under her ear and fell into a damp patch on the pillow. She stroked her long hair, and knew sleep would be hard to corner, difficult to catch. Next door she heard Dean turning in his bed and loved and hated him all in one surge of feeling. How much she wanted to hold him close and yet how badly she wanted to shove him away. *Poor, poor boy,* she thought, and regretted the planting of this bitter seed.

Six /

"It's a problem since the grocer closed down. He delivered, you see, so I could have quite a big order. Some I live on, most I put aside for the future. Now I have to fetch the stuff myself, a little bit at a time. Some days I do two shopping trips, one for now, one for later. Still. Slow but sure," Miss Jones explained. She sat next to him on a sofa, gently stirring her tea before tapping the spoon on the edge of the cup. The chink sounded like her voice, Dean thought, bright and cheerful. He wondered how she could stay so happy knowing what was coming.

"You must start to save things yourself, Dean! No time to lose, you know!"

"My mum and dad wouldn't let me."

He couldn't say the flat was pokey. He was ashamed of it after experiencing the vastness of Miss Jones' house. "I don't have any money, and they wouldn't believe me if I said about it, about, you know…"

"You haven't told them about me?"

"Oh, no! I wouldn't tell no-one about you!" Dean said, hoping not to damage the fragility of their relationship. He would keep the secret of Miss Jones' insurance policy.

"No disrespect to your parents, Dean, but they're silly short-sighted people! The writing is on the wall! It's happening already! Every day brings us closer to the end!"

The sun found its way beyond the boxes and made a carpet of light on the floor. Miss Jones put down her cup and fumbled with a length of cord, pulling it tight around the top of a box, and when she turned she saw him fidgeting, as if in discomfort. Sunlight scuffed the top of his head, and she noticed the deep brown hair illuminated in its rays. His face lit up too, and her eyes traced the deep frown embedded in his forehead.

"What's the matter, Dean?"

"Nothing."

"Dean, come on?"

"It's nothing."

"Really? Why so glum then? Hey?"

Her soft concern released something. Her gentleness reached deep down into him and unleashed his terrible sadness.

"I'm scared," he blurted. "I don't want to die! I don't! I don't want it to be the end of the world! I know my mum and dad are stupid but I love them and I don't want them to go and leave me. If they get mad it's only because of me! I'm bad. God will punish me!"

"You, you aren't bad." She looked at him strangely, and tried to tousle his hair, but he moved to the window and stared at the cars going past in the street. "Don't be scared," she said softly. "Everything will be alright."

"It's alright for you," he said, "You're old. I'm only eleven. Mum's twenty-eight. My dad is thirty. When will it come? When? Will it be 2025 like that man said?" Anger and frustration were unleashed in his words, and he fought to keep back his tears.

"I don't know, Dean." Miss Jones tried to soothe him, as she felt a pang of guilt force its way into her consciousness. It hadn't been her intention to frighten the boy. God knows, she didn't want to do that. The look of fear in a child's face was too much to bear.

"Did God tell you?" he demanded, "Are you an angel, or like Noah or something? How do you know about it? Why don't you tell everyone? It's not fair!"

"I just know." Her voice trembled, and she felt awkward under his scrutiny. "I'm not an angel. I'm not building an ark. I'm just old me, Dean. *Old Miss Jones*. Do you think I want to know these things? Do you think it's easy to see the world as it is? The world is getting to be a bad place, and it's not God who will destroy everything. It will be men and women!"

She grew stronger as she spoke, more certain. "I feel for your mum and dad, but you mustn't tell them about what I know. People will have to reach for the future in their own way, and in their own time." She peered at him, watched his face to fathom his reaction. It was awful, but Dean had to respect her knowledge and prevent them from coming along and rubbishing everything she believed in. Even his parents, even they had to be kept firmly out.

"When it comes the panic will be awful and people will turn on each other in an effort to save themselves. Why should I pay the price for their blindness? Anyway, if I told anyone they wouldn't believe me, and if they did they would come and tear my house apart, take it away from me, survive at my expense. When you get as old as me you begin to understand things, see things in a different light. I've spent too much time looking at death and dying. If people want to squander their lives and not look at what is inevitable, then what can I do? I live to save and save to live. They don't. They waste every minute of every day. They waste everything, every opportunity to heal a sick world. I can't help them, Dean. I wished I could." Her voice was passionate now, the words simmering, and her eyes fixed and hard as she envisioned and announced the awful truth. She stopped, as she caught the look on his face.

Dean wanted to cry. He wanted to warn everyone. He wanted to tell his mum and dad. He needed to. But if he did he'd be a liar. He'd promised Miss Jones he wouldn't lie to her, and yet now he felt he had to break that promise.

"Dean," she said gently, but firmly. "Come and sit with me."

He hesitated, but eventually moved towards her. He watched her face change, she became softer again, and her voice lost its edge and she spoke in the sing-song way he liked.

"I know how you're feeling. It's awful to think about it. Maybe it's too big to hold in your young head. Sit down." She held out her hand, and gently guided him next to her. "You see if people knew, they'd feel scared and bad, and they'd do whatever they could to save themselves, but in the end they'd just go back to how they were before. People are like that. Trouble is, no-one, no-one in the world will believe you, Dean. If you tell them the end is coming they will only laugh at you. Now tell me honestly, if you told your mum and dad what do you think they'd say, or do?"

He blinked hard as a tight feeling in his chest eased. He imagined telling them; even pleading with them, and then a light came on in his head. He remembered how Mum had been. Miss Jones was right. They'd think he was stupid and Miss Jones would be a nut-case. He imagined Dad swallowing the truth along with his beer and he knew instantly how he'd react. In his head he heard the torrent of abuse and the coarseness of his laugh. 'End of the world?' he'd say. 'Sod off!'

"It doesn't matter how much you love someone, Dean. If they can't or don't want to see the truth you won't change it. People only see what they want to. You know the saying – *Seeing is believing* – well I think it's the other way round – *Believing is seeing.* People only want to believe in things that are easy. *The end of the world?* Isn't that thought just a little too big to fit into people's heads? I think so, don't you?" She nodded, wisely, heard the voice of her father merging with her own. Prospero spoke his wisdom through her, and then she remembered his blue-lipped mouth, and unseeing eyes, the dreadful aspect of a life ended, and knew how much she wanted to live.

Dean blinked. He gazed into her old face and listened to the words which seemed to echo through his head. "Miss Jones?"

"Yes, Dean?"

"What if I helped you with your shopping?"

"What do you mean?"

"I could go for you sometimes, or help you to carry it."

"You could…but why do you want to that?"

"I don't know. I don't know. I just want to help."

"It helps me when you visit me and we talk, and it helps because I know I can trust you and I can tell you things and know that you're a sensible boy who wants to help an old woman."

He hesitated for a moment. "What is it like to be old, Miss Jones?"

"I have the advantage don't I?" she laughed. "I've been young and now I'm old. What is it like? Do you see the trees down by the river, with the leaves turning now the autumn is here?"

Dean nodded.

"I'm an old tree. My roots go deep. My leaves are fading, turning, and soon I will lose them. But come the spring they will be back, and I will be astonishing! I put my roots down into good soil, and they will cling on when the World shakes her back and throws off the parasites that reap but never sow. I will survive, Dean. I will throw out fresh shoots and I will go on and on for a long time yet. My roots will be replenished by the compost of humanity!" She stopped, feeling momentarily self-conscious. "Good grief! What must you think of me, Dean?"

"It's okay. I feel okay now." He hadn't understood much of what she said.

She moved towards him to give him a hug, but he shrank back, so she pretended to pick something from off the floor. Patting the creases from her patterned dress, she smiled and winked when he turned to look at her.

"The benefit of age is I get increasingly watchful of the world. I always sensed something even when I was your age. I'm not an angel. I'm not Noah. God hasn't spoken to me. I worked it out for myself, you see. I observe the world and what goes on in it, and I keep myself informed, and I make careful plans. What do other people do, Dean? They waste time. They ignore the signs even when top scientists tell them about it. They bury their heads in the sand and don't want to look."

Dean thought about what she'd said. "But if these things happen won't you be killed too? If the world ended won't it end for everyone?"

"That's the thing, Dean, someone always survives. No matter how great the disaster someone always gets through. History is full of such survivors!" she said, cheerfully.

"My teacher told us about the dinosaurs. They became extinguished…"

"Extinct," she corrected.

"They all died out because there was an ice-age or a big rock landed on them or something and they all got too cold, or crushed, and it killed them. Something like that."

"I don't know about those things, but a man called Charles Darwin… have you heard about him?"

"Don't think so. Does he live in Wellington Road?"

"No, Dean, Charles Darwin was clever man who lived a long time ago and he worked out that everything evolved over time and even we evolved from the monkeys and apes."

"What does evolve mean?" he asked.

"We change according to how the world changes, and the strongest and the cleverest survive. The weak die. Maybe the dinosaurs, as big as they were, didn't get used to the cold and they died off. We have to be smart, Dean. We have to plan for the worst, and we have to evolve. We have to change. If we don't, we'll…"

"Die."

"Yes. It's simple. Read the signs and adapt and survive, Dean." She stopped and waited to see his reaction.

His brow furrowed as he laboured to understand her, and make sense of what she said. She was old and wise, and she was like a deeply rooted tree. The teacher said trees lived much longer than human beings.

"Why have you told *me?*" he asked, his face quizzical.

"Why?" Miss Jones paused. The question went deep and lodged inside her. Her heart swelled. For a moment a poignant and dangerous feeling threatened to erupt. "I think you are a good boy," she said, her voice low and uncertain. "You remind me…"

Another face bloomed before her, merged with Dean's open, bright face, eyes wide under the mop of dark hair, a face she knew and yet dreaded. It was too much to bear and yet her mind moved to allow a distant memory to find its way into the light. Something in her shrank away, and a long established defence dissolved. She saw her brother before her, sitting where Dean sat.

"You remind me of John," she said, at last, breaking what seemed an age of silence. It was John's face. She blinked. "You are the image of my little brother."

"Is John still alive?" Dean asked in innocence.

"No. He died." Miss Jones looked away for a moment and then looked at him again.

"How did he die?" Dean asked, not meaning to intrude.

"He got knocked down."

"Knocked down? By a car?"

"Yes. A car."

Her voice was so far away he barely heard what she said, and he knew it was best to change the subject. The look on her face was strange – she stared at him with unblinking eyes, as if she could see right inside him. He didn't know what this meant – whether she was happy or sad, angry or calm. Despite feeling a strong pull of curiosity he decided not to ask anything more about John.

"Why don't you keep things under the floors?" he asked suddenly.

"What?" Her face changed instantly. "What did you say?"

"Why don't you put things under the floorboards too? Do you have any cellars? You know – rooms under the floors? You could put things in them."

"What a good idea, Dean. Could I do that?"

"Yes. I keep stuff under the floorboards in my room at home, stuff I want to hide." He hoped she wouldn't ask him what kind of stuff.

"Maybe we could do that, Dean. I do have a cellar too, but

it's a long time since I went down there. I don't like spiders, you see." She shrugged, and grimaced, and her face began to lighten despite her horror of spiders.

"Spiders don't bother me," he said, pleased she'd come back from wherever she'd been.

Just before he left, Miss Jones asked him if he was happy to keep coming to her house. Even though she'd miss him she needed to know it's what he wanted to do before she prepared to share an idea with him. He nodded enthusiastically, telling her he liked to be there, and it made him feel safe.

"What do you tell your mum and dad? They must wonder about where you are and what you're getting up to."

"They don't ask usually. My dad gets on my case sometimes, but he doesn't care really. He just…"

"He just what?"

"Nothing." He didn't want to tell her about his drinking and fighting. He felt ashamed and uneasy in case she judged him.

"But your mother must worry?"

"Yes. No. I don't know. She works nights most times."

"What does she do?"

"I've got to go now." How could he tell Miss Jones he didn't have a clue what his mother did at night?

"Listen, Dean, before you go I'd like to put something to you."

"What?" He thought she was going to tell him not to come back, and he shifted nervously from foot to foot.

"How would you like a room here?"

Dean tried to work out what she meant. "What to live here?"

"No. I want to give you a room for you to put stuff in for yourself; a place for you to prepare for the future. I can let you have one of the big rooms, or even the cellar. We can work together. Partners in crime," she laughed. "Think about it, Dean. Think about it."

*

When he reached the bottom of the street he began to run. He ran through the town centre, down Castle Street and Welsh Row, and through a short entry which opened out onto a walk by the river. He ran for ages until he reached the edge of the allotments, and out of breath, stopped and leaned against a rickety fence. He allowed himself to slip down until he sat on the path's edge. The moon was full, and so bright it burnt his eyes for a moment. He covered them and peeped through his fingers until he coped with the strong light. It hung like a big white ball and he gazed at it unblinkingly for several minutes.

Scrambling to his knees, he bowed his head and said softly, "Please God, don't let the moon drop." He looked up, and was relieved to see it in exactly the same spot and no bigger than it was before. He bowed his head again. "Please God, give me time to get my stuff, and bless Miss Jones and make my mum and dad happy. Please God. Amen." It was the first time he'd prayed in a long time, and he wondered if he'd done it right this time.

*

After pouring herself a large glass of whisky, she sat on the edge of a chair in the kitchen, looking unbalanced, uncertain, as if she were about to sit down, or to get up, caught in between two actions – a reflection of her state of mind. She hovered in this way as she sipped her drink. She didn't want to put it in tea. The heat slipped quickly down her throat and into the pit of her stomach where it relaxed and released a tight ball of inhibition, allowed feelings of fear to shrink and fall away. The heat rose up into her head, where it unpacked the memories she'd tried so hard to pin down and forget. She gulped for air, sucked her breath as she made one last stand against the dark stain of her history.

And here he was. John.

On the roadside he played under a beech tree, the long shadow obscuring his lovely face. He crouched, knees together, and examined something in his hands, probably an insect, or a flower. Maybe it had been a coin, she wondered. The smell of the Sunday roast pervaded the street – to walk along the pavement in those days was to wander among the thick aroma of good home-cooking, and the voices of families as they gathered to eat around a long table, or a round table, covered with a fine cloth embroidered by daughter, and mother, and grandmother, each in turn leaving a trace of themselves in their craft. He looked up at her; she saw the glint of sunlight catch in his eye, and the flash of white teeth as he smiled. *John,* she said, *John, come for your dinner.* How many times had she called to him across the street?

Just before the moment of impact she saw the look of fear and helplessness in his face, and that awful look of a small boy who'd felt betrayed. *She had called him. She had brought him to his death.*

No-one blamed her. Father had been wonderful. Mother had been sick for weeks but eventually began to live again. Miss Jones struggled to turn away from the last moment of the life she'd taken away.

The whisky circulated in each corpuscle, arrived in every cell, disturbed her very essence with its heat, and as she slowly sank to her knees she watched the tears drip from the end of her nose to darken the red-tiles beneath her face. Blood red spots covered the floor in the way they'd covered the street. She'd taken a life away. How much she needed to live. To die would mean she would have to see him again; to be accountable. She would have to face him and that lingering, pained expression as he stared up from between her feet and looked beyond her into the cruel blue sky.

Seven /

Outside the block of flats he watched as an old lady tugged the collar of a reluctant Yorkshire terrier. She carried a small plastic bag in anticipation of the dog dropping a load somewhere on the street. He smiled. Old people were okay, he thought. She looked funny as she tugged at the lead. She wanted to go one way, to take the dog out into the night to relieve itself, while the dog didn't want to leave the warmth of the tower. She tugged again as the dog tried to double-back and make for the entrance hall. Dean looked up at the windows, and saw a light blazing from his parent's flat. The curtains were drawn. Someone was home. If it was Mum it would be okay. If it was Dad, it wouldn't be. Hesitating by the big glass door he made a wish that everything would be alright. The stairs echoed when he ran two at a time up the steps. If he got to the door and looked hot and sounded breathless maybe Dad would see he'd made an effort to rush back. All the time Dean ran through a dozen excuses and as many voices – pleading, hopeless, helpless, begging.

The stink in the room caught Dean's throat and made him gag. He nervously pushed open the door, and hoped his dad was asleep so he could creep in and worm his way under the covers of his bed. For a moment, as he shivered under this fear, he heard Miss Jones' words. *How would you like a room here?* To be this frightened was awful, he thought, to come to this place where he lived and be terrified of entering. And who was here for him? Dad was always mad; Mum was usually tired, if she was at home. How much he would have liked Miss Jones to have offered him a room to stay in, to have meant that he could live there, with her.

Before he moved his foot into another slow and careful step, the door burst from under his grip, nearly spraining his fingers. Dad's big hand grabbed his fleece and yanked him into the room. Mum lay on the floor, face tear-stained, pale as a ghost.

"Where the hell have you been?"

"Nowhere…" he knew he'd said the wrong thing, and his dad's wrath exploded.

"No-friggin'-where? Everyone has got to be friggin' somewhere!"

"No, no!" Patsy screamed as the man shaped up to hit him. His fist fell and caught her fully on the head, and she fell stunned to the floor.

Dean was horrified. He was frozen to the spot. Was she dead? Had he killed her? Even the brute was confused as he looked through his stupor and saw the boy still standing while Patsy lay on the floor. He swayed now, his head spinning as his vision began to slide, and he fell, the exertion too much for his alcohol soaked limbs. His last effort at co-ordination was to try to hit his son again, and he missed.

Dean rushed to help his mum, who lay stunned. "Mum!" he screamed, trying to lift her. "Mum!"

"It's okay. I'm okay, Dean, Baby. Help me up. Help me up, Sweetie."

"Mum," he sobbed, his chest convulsing, his heart drumming against his ribs.

Eventually she managed to crawl along the floor and climb up onto the sofa. She looked at her prostrate husband, his face contorted as the booze relaxed his muscles. A bloom of urine spread across the front of his trousers as other muscles lost tension too.

"We've got to go, Baby. Come on, Sweetie, come on."

"Mum…mum…" Dean felt lost and confused and didn't know what to say, or what to do. All around the room stuff had been broken – glass was everywhere, and bits of plastic stuck like dangerous splinters from the rugs.

She staggered to her feet and holding the boy close tried to make him move. He was solid. His muscles clenched. "Come on, Baby. Come on."

Dad coughed. Dean felt it run through him like an electric

shock. Both he and his mum were through the door and down the stairs, and out into the streets within minutes. Outside the cold air teased her cuts and bruises and made them open up again or ache and throb. Dean stared up into her face, and watched her look directly ahead into the night as if she knew where to go, what to do. Disabled by shock he followed empty-headed beside her, and when eventually he lay down on the soft bed at Auntie Jessie's house, his chest grew so massive he feared his ribs would break. He released a massive, silent cry into the dark, stuffing the pillow into his mouth. Moonlight cut like a razor through the crack in the curtains, and in that moment he hated God, and he hoped the moon would fall down on top of everything, and wipe out everyone.

*

Miss Jones lay on top of her eiderdown not quite ready to settle under it until she finished untangling the confusion of her thoughts. Her heart had felt like it would break, and after sobbing on the cold, unyielding floor for what seemed hours, she attempted to pull herself together. For another hour or two she lingered on each button and strap and lace as she tried to undress herself, as if she'd forgotten the easy habitual sequences of a life time. All the time she watched the two faces before her, merging and parting in an ever repeating pattern. Her whisky breath caused her mouth to dry and tongue to loll, so she made herself a cup of tea, barely remembering how to do it, and in what sequence things should be done. This was madness she said to herself as she looked at her face in the bathroom mirror. This was senility and dementia. This was how a mind cracked and mucked up life in a worse way than any cancer could. This was a sickness of the soul.

Eventually the alcohol released its grip and she settled on her bed, not daring to close her eyes and snuff out the banal image of the light-bulb hanging from the centre of the room. Its simplicity and ordinariness prevented her from entering the dark chambers of fear. As it ebbed, she regained strength. Feeling stronger she searched for the splinter lodged in her heart, and discovered Dean's simple question – *why me?* In that she discovered an opportunity, and began to recover equilibrium, re-establish the weird symmetry she'd created in the past and learned to live by. Now it was time to put things in order, to mark the boxes of her memory, stack them neatly, high and wide, build a barricade. It was time to put it all away. It was simple.

John was dead.

She'd killed him.

John isn't Dean.

Dean isn't John.

She would help Dean to live.

It was simple.

She could atone for her sin.

Together, they would live and be happy and free.

She speculated on what they would do together, what they would share, and eventually what they might become to each other. Pictures like sweet home movies ran through her head and she watched scene after contented scene with a big grin on her old face. He was a lovely boy, and she was certain now he would never let her down. He was clever too. The idea about the floorboards was sweet, and although she doubted it would be of much use, she laughed at his ingenuity.

It crossed her mind that if they became as close as she hoped, she could make him the sole beneficiary of any Will she might leave, if the world did not end before she did. Whatever, the greatest legacy she had in mind for him was that he should inherit her great insurance for the future. Yes. This considerable gift might well be left to him should he become the opportunity to rid herself of the long tail of guilt she carried around with her.

When she turned off the light she caught sight of the moon, bold and lovely just above the church tower, and she hoped tomorrow when Dean came they could start to plan and build for a future, together. The moon looked beautiful, she thought, and hoped Dean could see it from wherever he lay.

Eight /

Three days later, Miss Jones stared from the window at the front of the house. Had the children noticed her they'd have seen her scowl, traditionally set to keep them at bay, had changed into a look of great despair and helplessness. The street became a dreadful vista of emptiness or false figures, counterfeit *Deans,* who when close enough for a more focussed scrutiny, became other people. The spectre of their mirth was clear to Miss Jones. They smiled, or laughed, gesticulated, walked, stood, played, and eventually tricked her into a momentary belief he had returned. And then they laughed at the old fool in the window. Eventually, heart as heavy and as cold as lead, she slumped back onto the narrow window-seat, held her head between the arthritic knots of her hands, and wept so long and uncontrollably she feared she'd cry herself to death. Dean wasn't coming back. John crawled around in the depth of her memory, waiting to confront her. There would be no redemption. No atonement. Every box and bag around her became despicable. What price survival when this loss, as damaging as anything she'd felt before, emptied every ounce of her being? Plans to survive alone in a void of a world where human awfulness had diminished and disappeared were no longer a comfort. Without the child her sense of bleakness, of loss, became monumental, and overshadowed her obsession. On the first day her annoyance rose to anger, and by the second, after a fitful night, she became embittered.

Today she began the long process of grief. In this catharsis she heard her admissions of love and desire. The words were so strange and yet somehow so familiar. Time had made her a stranger to an instinctual need to be a mother, but now this withering old woman mourned the loss of a child. How could she deserve that? she wondered. How could she hope for a child after what she'd done? Another old theme began to unwind within her grief – betrayal. She had revealed her essence to this boy, and now, had he turned his back on her? An image of him mocking her in the schoolyard grew emphatically within her imagination; only to be rendered a blur again as she tried to imagine his bright eyes and pale face peering through the mist of tears, smiling. It would not be like that, she admonished. Her lot was that of betrayal! *What goes around, comes around,* she remembered bitterly.

He would be back, she reasoned, in one voice, one attitude.

No he would not, another voice declared, viciously.

He *would* be back, the gentle voice repeated.

No he would not, the other voice said coldly.

She stood, and pulled her shoulders back, glanced towards the window before moving quickly through the room, out into the hallway, where she pulled on her coat, pinned a small blue hat to her head, clutched her stick and went out into the grey street. The chill autumn air caught her full in the face, and she wavered. Out here it all felt absurd. She steadied herself, touched the red-brick wall for reassurance before moving on. A car hissed over the damp tarmac and she paused. A child turned and tilting its head watched her through the rear window. Miss Jones caught her breath again. Everything took on a greater significance. The child would be laughing. The child would have heard about the batty old woman. Soon the street would be full of people wanting to look at her. Soon they'd come in the dark, the vandals and thieves and burglars. She turned back, then turned again, and yet once more turned in her confusion to seek him out, to chastise him, to slap him, to shout and scream at his betrayal, at her betrayal, to hold him, to kiss him. To love him. *Love.* The power of the word, the thought, the idea, the sensation, made her shake. She had found a child to love, a child in which to make amends, and now he'd betrayed her. She had been abandoned. It was ludicrous that she deserved another chance. She saw John's face before her, accusing, betrayed.

*

Patsy Cartwright traced her fingers lightly over her face and felt the tightness of skin around her eye and mouth. He'd always said she bruised easily, and at first she believed him. Nowadays she understood, in part, the lie – the transference of responsibility onto her, in an attempt at abnegation of full responsibility for his violence. *She bruised easily, and she asked for it anyway. It was her fault.*

She'd been young and Billy's reputation a decade before filled her with a strange kind of fascination and infatuation rather than love. Now she didn't believe love was possible, although as she peered into Dean's face, troubled despite his sleep, she remembered her delight at having a baby, and an intensity of feeling she'd not imagined until she held him after a difficult birth. Watching her baby grow was paralleled with Billy's increasing need to 'get wrecked' and its trigger for his remorseless and unapologetic violence. He hated the boy, was jealous no doubt, but she couldn't get her head around that. How could a father despise something as precious as a son?

When the Social Services got involved it only served to increase his animosity and rage towards the world. It would be easy to suggest that his own upbringing, some trauma of abuse inflicted on him, acted as a force now, in his so-called adulthood. But Billy came from a 'good' family, respectable, hard-working, and disappointed in a demanding and arrogant boy. Constantly in trouble he killed his father simply by breaking his heart, and now vented his wrath on the poor man for abandoning him, 'just when he needed a dad.' Patsy fell for this completely, and her renunciation of Billy's family and an avid need to create barriers in which to keep them out served as a double edge sword. It eventually swiped, cutting her legs from beneath her, and at the times when she desperately needed support, or counsel, she had none. Everyone vacated her territory and left her to it. All, that is, except her sister Jessie.

When Jessie opened the door, after what seemed an age, she blinked hard to get her eyes to understand the pathetic shapes standing in her front porch. This late at night she ensured the heavy chains, she'd installed three, were linked to the reinforced door-frame. Eventually she made sense of things and understood it was Patricia, with little Dean.

"Oh, God," she moaned, feeling her scalp tighten under a wig, "What do you want now? Is there something wrong with the boy?" She knew despite the question. She listened to Patsy speak in a pained whisper, and even after hearing the story, she hesitated before sliding the links to free the door. "If you want to stay it's for one night only! My God, Patricia, how many more times before your stupid brain gets working and gets you to shift your arse out of there for good?"

Jessie continued to chunter, and Patsy understood she meant the stay to be as brief as possible.

"I'll go to the women's refuge and take the boy with me," she hissed, feeling it constituted a threat and would make Jessie pity his plight, if not hers. But Jessie only reiterated what she'd laid out before –

"Just one night, for the kid's sake."

Patsy walked away next morning vowing she'd never go back.

Dean didn't sleep at all that night, and now, despite his exhaustion after a day moving from place to place, he slept badly. He sank fitfully into no-man's land consciousness, the bizarre and awkward stage between dreams and wakefulness, and as the manager of the refuge took details from Patsy the words were absorbed into absurdity, jumbled into ludicrous images and sensations. One moment he thought he was Barry Jones, the stupid kid, the next he was slipping into a brown mush of canal water. He fought to put his face above the stink and shout for his mother, who had changed into

Miss Jones, and she ignored him while fire fell through the sky, and the moon wobbled precariously before falling. A bright, white light woke him, and he shivered with the harsh cold of the cramped dormitory, and the flickering of strip lights that hung along the ceiling. Hearing a dirge of other children, younger than he, moaning and whinging, he fell finally into a cyclic dream, a nonsensical dream, where everything was abstract and without form or language. A constant return to the same point, feverish repeats of tactile sensations, made his muscles ache, his bones bend with an invisible pressure. A constant noise, a rumble, rose up and down from bass to high pitch, and his ribs pushed against his flesh as the sound made his body dance to its tune. It was an ugly dream, and Patsy wiped the beads of perspiration off his brow and top lip.

Nor could Patsy sleep. Despite overwhelming feelings of exhaustion, her adrenalin surged and pressed every cell into hyperactivity, especially the few brain cells which hadn't been damaged after Billy's punch-bag routine. Her watch over Dean was hyper-vigilant, almost hysterical. She couldn't take her eyes off the boy, or her mind off the inevitable visit from a social worker. Patsy dreaded having to confront her own guilt for she knew she was as bad a mother as they said she was. She was neglectful, indifferent, selfish, callous, and had put the child at risk. Often she was out late and sometimes hadn't gone home at all. Her defiance of Billy, coupled with a growing need to enjoy the childhood she felt she'd never had, served to leave Dean in a vulnerable situation. The social worker would surely tell her that again. As she looked at her boy she felt pain in anticipation of separation and loss.

Dean moaned under her touch, but didn't wake. She watched the women as they came and went in the dormitory, eyes dark, mouths drawn in thin down-turned lines. No-one spoke. Sometimes someone would nod, and try to make a smile, but as the children eventually settled and fell into a fevered sleep, even the smiles faded. They watched over the children with wide insomniac eyes.

Dean stirred from the heavy and oppressive sensation of a dream, and Patsy leapt across the harsh fibres of the blanket to catch his fall back into consciousness and buffer him from the awfulness of this new reality.

"Where are we, Mum?" he asked in a flat and heavy voice.

"We're safe here, Dean. Remember? We're stopping with the other mums and kids, Sweetie. Come on, Baby, go back to sleep."

"Is Dad coming here?"

"No. No he's not. They won't let him. He's not allowed, Sweetie."

"Why?"

"What do you mean, why?" Patsy was aghast. "Do you want to see him?"

"Why is Dad mad at me?"

"He's not, Baby," Patsy lied. Billy was mad with everyone. Billy was mad.

"I'm sorry, Mum." Dean's lip trembled.

"What for, Sweetie?" She touched his white face. "What for?"

"For making you stay with Dad. I didn't mean for you to get hit."

"Baby! You didn't do anything. You're not to blame!"

Dean knew he was. He'd heard it said so often before and she always said it when they had fights, sometimes she said it and it led to a fight. But, she always said it. *I'm only staying because of the kid.* Dean thought of Miss Jones sitting in her big, full house, and thought of the room she had offered him so he could store things too, but now it seemed a million miles away. It felt pointless and impossible; absolutely useless. He looked up at his mum's face, the pretty profile bruised and swollen, and he hated himself so much for being born and being such a bind to her and Dad, so much that he didn't care anymore if the world ended. Miss Jones was nothing more than a stupid old cow. Mum needed him now more than ever. He had a lot of making up to do, and he needed to try and get her to love him again like she did when he was small. If she could be proud of him, if she could, everything would be okay.

*

On Sunday the church bell rang and scattered pigeons across Nantwich Town Square. A street cleaner brushed cans and greasy papers onto a long-handled shovel and rammed the pile into his bright green council cart. He looked at the woman sitting under the War Memorial, staring into white hands folded on her lap. She'd been there from the moment he entered from Pepper Street, and now as he prepared to move along Pillory Street she still sat in the cold morning.

He wondered whether she was one of the poor souls from the old folks' place, on the bend in Audlem Road, a home for those with dementia. He thought to call in when he passed, but then dismissed the idea. If she was from there they'd be bound to come looking. Best leave her be, and anyway, the streets were bad today on account of some festival they'd had the night before. Real ale and stuff. The streets were splashed and stained with it. He pushed the remains of a pizza onto his shovel and red sauce ran along the stale. He grimaced and slammed it into the cart. Even the sharp blow didn't disturb her reverie, although pigeons flapped away, circled the church tower and settled along the roof of the Market Hall.

At 10 o'clock they came to church, and Miss Jones slowly surfaced from her deep and dark place of desolation. It was time to admit that Dean had let her down, and she felt a wave of vulnerability run through her like a strike of lightening. How earnestly she trawled through the events which had led her to this place – having and losing faith – gaining a soul to accompany her along the long and lonely route of life, and now she had to learn to let go again.

Struggling to keep the memory of John at bay she recalled the repugnant surrender into a whisky fog, how alcohol had loosened the long years of defence and denial. And yet despite her fall into the fog she craved another leap, this time to fall forever and never come back – like Dean had done. He wasn't coming back. He'd abandoned her to stand alone against John. Going over their last meeting she tried to understand Dean's fear, his sadness at what she'd shown him. She'd been so convinced he'd understood the importance of the way, a way that travelled beyond the trivialities of life. She thought he'd understood. No! No! She had to galvanise herself against such thinking! Hadn't she been alone and strong before he wandered into her life? He would be the fool if he abandoned her. It was no use worrying about what might happen – at the end nothing will matter, only her survival. She had to set the compass again and pull up her bootstraps. It was time to put the child away, to turn as best she could from the faces of these children. Determined now, she rose from the damp bench on the Town Square, and looked towards the graveyard in front of the church.

People walked along Churchyardside, dressed well, faces cheerful, as they moved to the magnetic peel of bells – the pull of faith. Miss Jones felt a sudden envy, but knew it would be useless. Many times she'd been into the huge cavern of Nantwich church to prayer for God to forgive her – but her prayers rattled through the rafters and drifted up into an empty universe. What use is faith? she thought. Sing and pray, but nothing will avert the end of the world.

"Hello! Good heavens! Look! It must be years, ten years!"

Miss Jones flinched. Someone strode across the uneven pavement toward her; face bright, round and red, eyes blazing with warmth, a mouth stretched into a big accommodating grin. Her heart sank. A big man approached, his waist pulling his buttoned jacket into straining bulges; his hands open, arms wide as if to hug her, face beaming with the pleasure of this meeting. His hair, thick and wavy, sat atop of his high forehead and twinkling eyes, and despite his size he was agile and quick. Malcolm Robertson, a retired Scottish librarian, often visited Miss Jones' father, particularly toward the end of his life. Both loved books and they would talk for hours about first editions and rare manuscripts, and despite a difference in age, they enjoyed a similar sense of humour and political conviction. Malcolm was barely two years older than Miss Jones, and she always believed there was a covert reason for the visits. She'd never taken to the man. He'd been overbearing at times, and expressly demanded that he be a bearer at the funeral, staking a claim for the sake of friendship, but also for a shot at status. To shoulder Mr Jones coffin was an honour many desired for its elevation of rank within the town. Bearers would be listed in the Nantwich Chronicle. Neither Miss Jones nor her mother had objected. It would have been churlish. He did have the decency, after all, to continue visiting the old man long after others had turned away from his bitter struggle to fight death and hold onto life.

"How old we are! Look at us!" he laughed. "My word, Miss Jones!" His easy quip made light of what he actually saw in her now she was so close by, or else it revealed the vanity of his reasonable health and enduring youthfulness despite the width of his stomach and hips. He prided himself on his sprightly attitude to life. 'The greatest gift in life,' he said, 'is good health and a great appetite!'

Malcolm remembered the days of his visits and his encounter with her quiet and wistful beauty. He knew the truth about John; not the malicious whispers emanating from the quiet hush of the reading room. Mr Jones had spoken of the boy and the tragedy, so he viewed her beauty tinged with sadness as a possibility – the instinctual attraction of men to vulnerable women. Young then too, but clumsy in the way of courting, he'd fallen before he'd even flown, not knowing, even from instinct, how to get to know her. His bookish attitude failed to offer her a *Ferdinand*; and despite his efforts at romance, she kept her eyes resolutely turned towards her sad vista.

"Hello," she replied with as much warmth as she could

muster, feeling, knowing she sounded hollow and insincere; one small word huge in its reluctance to have been spoken. It wasn't a good time to make small talk, to search for platitudes when a heart was heavy. Nothing had changed despite the roll of years. His walk, his face, those flapping hands and all embracing arms, his protruding belly and insistent manner, still managed to evoke feelings of revulsion. *He was a nice enough man,* she'd once told her father in response to a delicate probing of a possible match, *but he wasn't her type.* Nothing else was said, not to her at least, but after the enquiry Malcolm studiously avoided bumping into her in the town. It was far enough away now for him to celebrate the meeting. The past meant nothing. It no longer hurt. "How long is it?" the voice insisted. He wasn't going to let her off the hook.

"I don't know..."

"Well, well! Are you coming into church?"

"No. No, I've been out to take the air, to have a walk. This morning. Yes, I felt like taking the air, walking," she coldly. Her mouth chilled the words and refused to articulate anything other than her reluctance to be seen, to be known.

"Are you still at Wellington Road? In the big house?" He knew she was, but it was a starting point for his curiosity. The Electoral Role and Thompson's Almanac passed through his hands each year, and he always found himself checking who was who and where they were.

"I am." Miss Jones did not feign pleasure or interest in his enquiry. Too much enthusiasm might provoke a visit. That would be unbearable. There would be so many questions, too many to contemplate. Better to be brusque and avoid complications. Besides, there was an urgent need to bury herself in the boxes and the stacks, to pick-up the plans, write an up-to-date inventory of her life and needs. After such a short space and time spent in a relationship with Dean she really wanted to steer the ship away from the rocks.

"I can't get over seeing you here after all these years," he said, the smile fading as he guessed at her indifference.

"No. I keep to my end of town mostly," she said, her voice flat.

"Yes. Yes, indeed." Her eyes fell on his for an instant, just enough for him to catch the depth of pain. Nothing had changed, except the aged face that surrounded them. But for the first time he caught something else. He recalled the look Mr Jones had given him on the last visit; the feeble turn of a head weary with an effort to believe itself alive. In Miss Jones' face he saw that too, hardly perceptible under the weight of her frown.

"Well," he started, looking towards the church, shifting uneasily, feeling somewhat foolish in his approach to her. "I'd best be away to my prayers."

"Oh, yes," Miss Jones replied. "Yes, you must do that."

"I beg your pardon?" Something in her voice mocked him.

"You must pray, Mr Robertson. Pray hard and long." For the first time in hours she made a move to go, brushed the front of her coat, adjusted her hat, turned to look at him without smiling, then nodded and walked away.

Malcolm Robertson watched her hunched back and the awkward hobble assisted by a walking stick. *How old she was,* he thought, *how tormented.*

Nine /

First thing on Monday, Miss Jones walked to the school in Audlem Road. Dean told her it was his school after his initial deceit. A tiny, but vicious voice in her head walked with her, cultivating any seed of concern that might blossom, any sign of warmth or compassion, instilling her with only one possible perception – she was a victim, totally and exclusively. *He'd said he was Barry Jones. Fool. Remember his lie?* She had to come. She had to make an effort to find him, and have it out. Why had he not come back? Would he keep the secret? Her doubt and fear went round and round in her head and wouldn't settle or resolve. She'd let him in and told him everything, and now she deserved better than this. *He will have told his parents! His friends!* Last night had been awful. Her insomnia had aggravated her fragile mood and she ebbed and flowed between wanting to do one thing or another; but there was only one thing to do – to see him, have it out, and put it all to rest.

Several times she asked children if they knew Dean Cartwright, but they either didn't answer, being too busy on their mobile phones, talking, texting with furious thumbs; or they said, quietly and aggressively, that they didn't know him. Miss Jones was unaware of the culture, the kids' commandment – *thou shalt not grass*. She tried others, but got the same response. Every where she looked she met with indifference or contempt. Inside her both anger and anxiety began to froth and bubble. It was a world that should end, she thought. If these were the custodians of the future, dark-eyed under the hoods of their tracksuit tops and baseball caps, it would be a terrible world. Their energy fizzed with malevolence and negativity. Two boys smoked openly at the school gates, and swore persistently in the course of what seemed to be an ordinary conversation. She moved away from them, wary, feeling her age as a disability, and acknowledging how truly vulnerable she was. The context drove home the truth, and she shored up wavering defences against a growing sense of being overwhelmed. Was this the world in which Dean lived? To survive he would live like this, be like this. Perhaps she should go, forget him, return to her home in Wellington Road, close the door, draw the bolts and keep this world at bay.

A small bespectacled man carrying a briefcase walked towards the school gate. He noticed her before she spoke, and smiled pleasantly. He moved to the side to allow her to pass, but saw the earnest face, her eyes set on him.

"Can I help you?" he asked.

"Are you a teacher here?" Her voice was shaky.

"Yes. I am. I'm Mr Teal." A sensation of uneasiness stirred in him. Although she didn't look like trouble, irate parents came in all shapes and sizes. "Yes, what's the problem?"

"Do you teach Dean Cartwright?"

"Who's asking? May I ask your name?" He became defensive. It was better not to admit to anything. In doing so you increased the risk of being liable for one ethical dilemma or another. He knew Dean well, and liked him well enough. He was bright, and sometimes things caught his imagination and he went off like a rocket. At other times he sat in a slough of despond, unable to concentrate. Whether it was a result of depression or distraction, trouble or laziness, he often became withdrawn and uncooperative. With the recent turn of events he wasn't surprised by the boy's inconsistency. At one time he'd approached the lad and suggested he saw the school counsellor, but Dean had been horrified at the idea. Like so many children from the towers, it was best to let things rest and not stir-up whatever reaction lay in store if a parent found out. They would come to the school berating the staff making the usual wearisome accusations and threats. And nowadays teachers flipped, fled the classroom for early retirement, or fantasies of working on a checkout in a supermarket. *You can just do the job, go home, and forget all about it.* It became a professional mantra.

He knew of Billy Cartwright's reputation. He knew about Patricia Cartwright's indifference. In the smoky staff room he'd heard other members of staff talk about the family, often with concern, more often with dread at the effect this was having on the child. It was his final year in the school and he wondered what graduation would mean for the boy. He wasn't the most confident of kids.

"Do you know Dean? I just need to get a message to him." She tried to keep an even voice, so as not to give anything away.

"Who are you?" he asked, immediately concerned by the enquiry. There was a procedure to follow.

Miss Jones clenched her fists in her deep pockets. "I'm Dean's granny," she lied. "I need to speak to him."

"Right. Can you give me evidence of that? How do I know you're his Grandmother?"

"I need to speak to him," she said more insistently, becoming frustrated by him. "I need to get word to him."

"Can I ask what it's about? It would help to know," he insisted.

"I need to see him after school." It was obvious she couldn't manoeuvre an immediate and straightforward face-to-face meeting with the boy. "Will you give him a message?"

Mr Teal looked into her eyes trying to make sense of what he saw. She was old. She didn't seem like trouble. More importantly she only wanted to leave a message. That felt like an acceptable option. But wouldn't she have known about things? She said she was his grandmother. He made the decision to tell her, test out her reaction.

"I'm afraid Dean's not here."

"What do you mean?" Her eyes widened.

"He's off at the moment. But wouldn't you know that?" He became suspicious. "He's not been in for over a week. Look, do you want to come in and talk to the head teacher?" Mr Teal regretted having spoken so openly.

“Why is he off? Is he sick? Has something happened?” she asked breathlessly. It all made sense. He’d not let her down at all! Something had happened to him, preventing him from coming to see her again. Her heart rose and fell, and rose again. How stupid she’d been for thinking him so heartless.

“I’m sorry, what did you say your name was?”

“Mrs Cartwright.” She replied without hesitation. The lie came easily. “I’ve not heard from him and I’m worried sick. Me and his folks, well, we don’t get on, I…I…just want to know if he’s well…where he is….”

“Look, would you like to make an appointment with the head teacher? She could explain things to you.” He felt a surge of compassion for the old woman. It really mattered to her. He could see that. “I can tell you he’s okay now. He’s safe.”

“What? Safe? What do you mean?”

He felt anxious again; he might be breaking confidentiality, contravening school ethics, but he saw the pained and anxious look on her face, every bit that of a worried relative.

“Look, Mrs Cartwright, Dean is with his mother at a refuge. There’s been some trouble with his father again.”

“His father? His father? Do you mean his father has hurt him? Hurt Dean?” she demanded to know.

“I’d prefer not to go into details, but I can tell you he’s safe, and we hope he’ll be back soon.” He’d hardly finished before she turned and hobbled off.

*

She knew what a refuge was. She wondered if he meant here in this town. She should have checked, should have had the pluck to ask him more, insist on details, on places, on names. She had to find Dean at all costs, and at once; now she knew he’d been a victim she’d protect him and care for him, and give him all the love she felt in her heart. Her head ached as she tried to understand everything. What kind of a father would hurt his child, or wife, or both? What kind of a beast was he? She wondered too about Dean's mother. How could she choose to be with such an animal, and expose Dean to those traumas? Certainly now Dean would see how right she was. If his own father was a brute, a monster, how would he invest trust and confidence in anyone in the world? But he could trust her. She'd fight until her last breath to ensure his safety. They would survive. They would remain when the world ended. A sensation surged through her old body enervating and charging; clearing her mind of anything other than a singular obsession that she must work as she'd never worked before. All that mattered now was that she found him.

*

It was the culture of confidentiality that finally broke her spirit. Not being a relative meant she had no rights, nor could she lie herself into being one, despite a strong urge to do so. Finally, after another enquiry, the social worker asked Patsy Cartwright if she knew, or had heard of a, 'Miss Jones?' Patsy had no recollection of such a person, and despite Dean sitting next to her, flicking through a colouring book he'd been given and which he disliked for its babyish cartoons, he didn't flinch.

Dean had to fight now to make sure the world didn't end for his mum because the Social Services were making her cry a lot. He'd heard too that Dad had been done and was doing time. Dean knew what *cold turkey* meant. So, if he could be strong and helpful and look after everything until Dad got back, maybe they would get together and he would be loved and loving and everything would be okay and they would stay together because it was good. And Dean would stop being the rope that bound them in their misery.

Miss Jones slumped into a depression and for several weeks didn't shop. She eventually opened a box of supplies. Staring at the tins she shook her head at the stupidity of her obsession, and understood how empty the world is, and would always be. She rarely went for an hour without thinking about the boy, and her only reassurance was that he would be protected as the local Social Services service department, despite their retreat into 'confidentiality' had given away inadvertent and yet sufficient information in their responses for Miss Jones to know he was a 'client.'

Now, she told herself, all she had to do was to get over it and start to enjoy the few years she'd got left on this miserable planet. There was nothing she could do other than let go.

One day she found herself upstairs in father's old library, and she wept at its emptiness and her broken promise of many years before to keep it in the way he'd left it. For a moment she sensed his presence in the room, and she fancied she smelled the 'Brilliantine' he sometimes wore on his hair. Had she forgotten him so completely? Had her constant doubt about the world dimmed even him, the man she loved so much? She'd given away his books and manuscripts and now looked across the empty room and felt a deep sense of regret. She smiled sadly, and fell quickly into tears, her face crumpling as she felt a deep sob rise from her breast. How much she missed him now.

For many weeks she sat or slept, and allowed the moods to shift between the languid and the restless, but eventually Father had supplanted Dean, and she knew he'd come to ease her loss. When Dean came to mind, she diverted her anxiety, anger and sadness by conjuring Father. In the evenings she moved through the house, resisting the temptation to stare from the window in the hope Dean would appear. She walked between the boxes, the stacks, the rows, stopping every so often to touch them, to push and pull, realign and restructure, and gradually resumed control of this small piece of the world, the only piece she had control over.

Soon she moved with more vigour, and at one point she

caught herself humming. She smiled. It wasn't so hopeless then? she thought, but felt a shiver of doubt too, which sobered her for a while. Before too long she noticed her resurgent energy again and eventually allowed a smile to stay. She could do it; she was getting over things. As long as she stopped any thoughts of the boy she would cope. She remembered what her father had told her. *I don't know anyone who copes as you do,* he said during the crisis of his diagnosis, knowing she'd be there to help him through the coming uncertainties. He had understood her distance and silence to be strength. She carried the words like a curse. In her silence she hid her guilt.

She stopped her bristling, efficient work, as she remembered his words, and sat for a moment looking around her home. She decided then she would fill the empty rooms, and starting with the library she would banish all other things from her life. She was going to survive. It was an unbearable thought that she would look into John's face again. Whatever had happened she had to trust no-one. She was the one who would cope with what lay ahead, and as much as she missed young Dean, she needed to return to how it had been. And besides, hadn't this episode served to underpin what she already believed, what she already knew? The world was a bad place, a terrible place, and foolishly, in a weak moment she had let it right into the core of herself, allowing it to unleash the spectre of John, and now she needed to reclaim her life. It was her destiny to be alone, and to resume a direction of sight which took her eyes away from the faces of children.

After Mother died, she'd searched for meaning in her life. For a time she'd gone to chapel, a little Methodist church in Welsh Row, secretly hoping for answers, but longing too for someone to be there for her, someone to help her cope, she supposed now. Despite not being close to her mother in the way she had been with Father, Miss Jones sought companionship to fill the emptiness of her life, but met with disappointment. People were shallow.

They spoke of forgiveness.

They spoke of redemption.

They couldn't know.

They didn't see the look on John's face.

She attended coffee mornings and meetings, even became a member of a discussion group, but eventually despised them all. No-one called on her after she retreated from the chapel. It was her destiny to be alone, she reaffirmed, feeling a subtle joy in her knowledge.

As is the nature of dreams, one night, Miss Jones dreamt about the end of the world. It was strange that despite being preoccupied with these thoughts for many, many years, in her conscious life, she had never once dreamed of such things. After waking she lay for an hour or so, revisiting the images and sensations. It had been real, the deep sense of panic and despair, and she watched the hopelessness of people as they paraded through her bitter dreamscape. The dream took the form of a journey, and she was surrounded by a crowd of people. Wherever she looked she saw panic, fear, desperation, while others seemed resigned, and while some doubted it with their tongues their eyes betrayed them. It *really* was the end. She recalled how a group of foreign women, dark-eyed and dark haired, had thrown themselves from an aeroplane in which they were travelling. One by one she saw them fall dutifully to their deaths, pushing their children before them, tightly holding onto their babies. She heard their screams. It was better to die this way, than in the apocalypse that was coming. Along a road she saw thousands packed, rushing and trampling on the weak as they fell. Cars ploughed along the roads until they congealed into motorways where in desperation families abandoned them. All over the landscape people teemed like ants, black trails of a million lives, meaningless and without direction or sense. In one moment she flew above the world, in another she pushed through the streets. She watched faces without pity. A crash startled her, and she turned to look back at a parade of shops, places she'd known all her life, and through the people she saw her reflection in a shop window. Standing by her side was a dark self, her shadow. An angel of death.

How would it be, how would it end? Throughout the dream now, she talked, not with Dean, or her father, but with the dark, familiar aspect of herself, split-off, a faceless presence that watched and waited. The journey moved to its climax when the menagerie of travellers stood at the end of everything, and she jostled the crowd so that she could stand before them, look into their faces, and feel victorious.

And then it was over. The landscape shifted beneath her, and she fell upwards into a blue sky, and she was alone, absolutely alone. In her dream she thrilled that she was alive and conscious, and when she looked to find her other aspect, to call out, to shout gleefully that she was alive, she understood she had reunited with *herself.* She felt quietness within, a sense of perfection.

Would it be like that? She speculated in the dark room, retracing every moment now of her life, trying to make sense of it. Would she meet the end with such curiosity and certainty? What had life been? She thought about the dark aspect of herself, watching quietly, stilly, as she herself had done for years, watching the world and waiting, without fear. She remembered the overwhelming sense of stillness and completion. Resurgent feelings filled her mind and body. *She would survive.* The dream said so. When everything and everyone declined she would continue. The dark self had walked into the light, and merged with her. She had triumphed over death, and hope and energy were rekindled.

She would be fine now.

She would be okay.

Now, she was back on track.

Ten /

"Did Dad buy it?" Dean asked, his eyes alight as he saw his present in the porch. He was twelve today and felt really grown up and wanted a grown-up present, not toys and stuff. He didn't expect this though. A bicycle was beyond any expectations he had. In all the birthdays he could recall, nothing had been like this. It was a stonking gift! "Did Dad buy it?" he repeated.

"No," Patsy replied, feeling disappointed, tugging a smile across her face to hide it. She wanted to remonstrate with the boy but didn't feel it was the time to burden him with her annoyance. Her maturity had come at a cost. Life had changed dramatically and everything that once stood as a grim certainty had become a discordant note somewhere in the cacophony of her past life. Billy was off the scene, for sure, and no matter how much Dean speculated on him and desired to see him, that's how it was, and he would come to accept it. He'd have to. It always gouged deep into her new found stability when he spoke of his dad, and she couldn't understand his need to talk about him, not after the terrible time he'd given them. She speculated and questioned and conjectured, until a child psychologist told her it was probably guilt. Dean felt guilty.

"What has Dean done to feel guilty?" She demanded to know. "Guilty? I can't get my head around it!" At that point she'd closed her mind to its possibility and Dean was left to struggle with his need to achieve the reconciliation of the irreconcilable.

They'd moved now, and the work she got meant she could be at home more, and although she found it hard to keep the Social Services happy, Dean was a good boy and made few demands. His quietness and reserve pleased her, although the new social worker, Mark Tomlinson, felt it was unnatural for a boy of his age. He suggested Patsy got Dean a bike – it might encourage him to get out and about and make friends. He'd hardly left her side when she wasn't working. The social worker explained it as *separation anxiety* after the trauma of Billy's attack on her.

"He feels responsible for you, and needs to protect you," he'd said, over coffee in the kitchen of her new house. But still she couldn't let the notion seep through; it all seemed upside-down and back-to-front.

"Come on, Mark, how could a kid see it like that?" she asked. "He knows he couldn't do anything to stop Billy slap me!"

"Exactly!" he said, and laughed gently, not wanting her to think he was taking the Mickey, but still she didn't see the point. He liked the fact she called him Mark. He'd insisted she could from the first time they met, but until now she'd always called him Mr Tomlinson.

After a few weeks cutting down on cigarettes and other things that made life tolerable, she made a first payment and looked forward to the thrill of seeing his face. And now he nearly spoilt it by thinking Billy had bought it.

"Bet Dad got it for me!" His face was feverish with excitement. That would have been the fulfilment of a dream. It would have been the first stage of being a family again.

"I got it for you Deano! It's got nothing to do with him. Are you pleased then?" Once again she struggled to subdue the disappointment in her voice. The past year had been an agony of uncertainty; everyone had chipped in with what they felt would be best for the boy, and Patsy fought hard to hold-on to the love she developed for him, fought to maintain her sense of direction after being lost for so long.

Billy had several months to go before release, and during the time spent inside he'd dried out. On several occasions he tried to contact her, to tell her he was a new man, and had become an *abstinent* alcoholic. Patsy pushed ahead with plans to divorce him and refused to respond. An alcoholic was always an alcoholic. He was out of her life and that's where she wanted him. No apology would seduce her into reconciliation. No amount of grovelling and meaningless promises. She'd heard it all before, experienced every angle he'd come from.

"Wow! It's wicked!" Dean held the handlebars and played with the brakes, pushing the bike forwards and feeling how they grabbed the wheels and held them firm. "Great brakes, Mum," he enthused. "I like the seat." He didn't notice the strained look on her face or the note in her voice. He'd got a bike all of his own.

"You be careful on it, Baby," she said softly, her aggrieved feelings melting away as she responded to his enthusiasm. She touched the back of his head, ran her fingers along his neck, and patted his shoulders.

"I never had a bike when I was a kid. My Dad didn't think I needed one," she laughed sarcastically, thinking of the bike she eventually managed to straddle. Billy had a motorbike in the early days of their relationship, and riding pillion on the back of Billy's motorbike had been wonderful both in the exhilaration of speed and danger, but also in getting one over the mean old man. Her father might have moaned to her about it, but when Billy was present he shuffled warily around the council house as if he wanted to be invisible. Billy had real presence, but even then it was dark and spooked her sometimes. Why hadn't she the sense to see it?

"Can I go for a ride?" Dean asked, the question so sharp in its anticipation and enthusiasm Patsy couldn't refuse.

"You be careful, Sweetie," she smiled. "You don't go too fast, will you? Come home before it gets dark."

"Thanks Mum." Dean turned to hug her and the bike slipped against his side and crashed against the wall and onto the floor. His face crumpled. He looked to see whether it had scratched or buckled, and carefully lifted it up. The front wheel spun slowly as he held the crossbar and inspected the forks.

"It is okay, isn't it?" Patsy asked, concerned more for Dean's sudden rush of anxiety than to what had happened to the bike.

“I don’t want to spoil it. I want it to be perfect for when Dad comes home.” Dean struggled to hold it while he reached for the door, and Patsy quickly grabbed the handle, frowning as she did so. Just as she was on the verge of telling him to stop talking about Billy, Mrs Anderson, her new neighbour stuck her face through an open window and shouted after them.

“What was that awful commotion? Was it you?”

“Sorry,” Patsy said, pulling her cheeks and mouth into a tight expression of apology. Dean was oblivious as he pushed the bike down the path.

“It used to be such a quiet place round here!” Mrs Anderson chuntered, and closed the window with a bang – just as noisily as Dean’s accidental crash. “Never known an estate go down hill so fast!” she whinged, eyes like burning coals in her flushed and sweaty face.

Patsy watched him ride unsteadily down Queens Drive and towards the busy junction at its head. “Be careful, Dean!” she shouted, and turned to see Mrs Anderson watching, face thunderous, from her seat by the window. “Nosy old cow,” she hissed, and nearly gave her two fingers but thought better of it. It was time to settle down now. Billy was out of her life. She was getting sorted. Despite her bad feeling and self doubt, her deep belief that she was, or had been, a lousy mother began to change and she felt she could be okay if pressure was kept at bay. *No, she wasn’t useless, or neglectful.* Mark told her that, even insisted she needed to look at herself in a more positive light. He said he wanted to help her build up her self-worth and self-esteem. She was rediscovering the thrill of being a mum again, and now she found time and energy and wanted to be with Dean more and more. Despite her doubts about the Social Services, they’d been okay. She’d been allowed to keep Dean as long as she looked hard and changed her life, and without Billy on the scene she knew it was possible. The boy may well have longed for his father, but she would fight tooth and nail to keep him away.

Something deep inside had changed. Billy could break her bones, but he wasn't going to break her spirit.

*

It was the freest and most wonderful moment of Dean's life. He cycled around Nantwich and looked at the world from his new vantage point. Sitting astride his birthday present he felt taller, and stronger, and certainly quicker. He'd had a bike when he was younger, but that didn't count. It was a kid's bike, and had silly stuff on it, flowers and rainbows and things. *This was a proper bike.*

The town was quiet after the congealing school-run-cars had unclotted and trickled back into the suburbs, and now the streets only had a few late shoppers straggling their way home along Beam Street. The shelters along the bus lanes were empty except for the K48 destined for Crewe. A woman rattled keys as she locked the main door of the library, looked up at the modern faced clock, before walking towards an entry and into Cowfields. The bus coughed black smoke and gears ground as the driver forced the reluctant engine into motion, and slowly moved off.

Dean stopped for a moment outside the Civic Hall, parked by a bench, and without dismounting he placed one foot on the seat and balanced while he admired the shining chrome and enamel beneath him. He felt like he was a man now, resting there after the ride, sitting tall in the saddle like a cowboy on the prairie. Or better still, he had made a pit stop. No time to get off. The mechanics whizzed around and did their bits, refuelling, tweaking, shouting above the roar of engines, and stepping back smartly as he, Dean Cartwright, revved his grip on the handlebar and with a surge, pushed away and sped along Beam Street, where beyond the Alms Houses, tall lime trees bordered an expanse of grass and rose beds. He imagined the nodding blooms as a sea of faces packed along a tight stadium, every eye watching the kid zip along like a devil. He heard the roar of the crowd. He wondered how fast he was going. Could he catch the bus just ahead turning into Millstone Lane? Yes, it slowed and pulled in at the stop by Potter's Yard where timber stacks sent a woody fragrance along the road, and Dean slipped past with a neat swerve right and left, a slight tilt as he slid along, and the rush of air making his hair stand up on his head. He gently touched the brake, changed gear, pushed the revs up and up, heard the engine rise and lower in pitch as he worked the gearbox into red-heat. He was going to win. Just a turn here into Crewe Road, a quick dash up the incline and down towards Mount Drive, the poshest place in town, to a tight bend where he could lean, knees brushing the tarmac, burning his leathers, to pass the boy's club, and swing back into the straight length of Park View and more tall limes bending in approval of this mad devil of a speed freak, and look! The finishing line was in sight. Back into Beam Street, keep up the pace, and keep them at bay! The crowd of roses rocked and rolled, and there he was again, foot resting on the bench outside the Civic Hall. But now he was on the podium.

He was the *Champion!* Dean laughed breathlessly. His face was red, and little beads of perspiration formed on his top lip and under his hairline. What a race! What a bike! Now for a slow ride around the circuit to hear the cheers, the applause, catch the bouquets and wave to his adoring fans. *Dean Cartwright Champion Motorcyclist. British Champion. World Champion. Champion of the Universe!*

He dismounted and sat down, while holding his bike so that he could see it. He traced the angle of the frame and smoothed his hand over the seat. A speck on the shiny chrome wheels came away easily when he touched it, and he vowed he would always keep it this clean. When Dad came home, after the cold turkey, he would be better, and he would see how carefully the boy had looked after it and would be really, really pleased. He wouldn't need to start drinking again. A lovely picture ran through Dean's head. Dad and Mum together in their new home. Dad would be pleased about that.

He hated living up a 'bloody chimney stack.' It was a proper home on the ground with a backyard and a porch at the front. Queens Drive was nice, running to the edge of the town, and there were trees along the pavements.

Mum didn't talk about Dad anymore, but Dean knew deep down she would be glad to see him. When he tried to talk about Dad, she changed the subject, and whenever the social worker called she saw him on her own and behind a closed door. The social worker called him in a couple of times and said he hoped he was happier now, as if he had been unhappy, or bad or something. Dean was good now. He must be because Mum said she loved him, and so Dad would love him too. They'd be married again and happy and it wouldn't be Dean who tied them together. It would be happiness and fun and they'd *want* to be together. This was surely the best day of his life, so far. When Dad came back it would be even happier. It was great thinking like this. It was great.

Some big lads from the Comprehensive appeared from the side of the Civic Hall, smoking and guzzling cans of strong lager. They saw Dean on the bench but before they had time to harangue him, and probably wreck his bike, he quickly mounted and sped away towards the Town Square and under the church. He hesitated at the top of Pillory Street, by an old Victorian Library, red-bricked and ornate, but then pushed on towards Wellington Road. At the railway crossing the lines angled awkwardly and he dismounted to go across. He had an image of the front wheel being caught between the tracks and buckling, or worse still, to slip between the shiny lengths and be thrown head over the handlebars onto the wooden stretches between the rails. He hesitated again. Miss Jones' house was just up the road and he had an urge to go and show her his bike. What would she say; maybe she'd be mad that he'd not gone round before? It was a really good day and she might like to know it was his birthday. She might even give him a present. But it was getting dark and there were no lights on his bike. He would be going too far away from home. He paused a moment longer, recalled the stuff she'd said to him and felt a mixture of fear and sadness and yet affection for her. Maybe he'd go back tomorrow, or another day.

He turned for home.

*

Just at that moment, Miss Jones moved towards the window at the front of her house. The street was empty. She looked one way, and then the other, though not with any *conscious* intent to see if Dean was there. Such are the workings of the mind. It had been a long time since she last used a small amount of alcohol or acts of distraction to keep her focused, and her pain at bay. Wind rustled the trees and caused branches to sweep the low grey sky. Several leaves fell and swirled in circles over the wall and into the road. A car rushed by, whipping them into more frantic motion. She watched, transfixed by their movements, their light and shimmering dance, and felt herself to be heavy and tired. What a sad world, she thought. Look at all these stupid and misguided people doing all these ridiculous things to the planet. What fools. Even if God blazed down from the sky and the Devil rose up from the earth the people would idly watch a silly programme on the television, munching crisps and chocolate, without a care. God help them when it comes. What will they live on when the polar caps melt, and the rivers run dry, and food can't be eaten because of the weird genetic manipulations of plants? Everyday she read or heard more of the impending consequences of meddling and ignorance. Where will *they* find food and water? she wondered, glancing backwards into the tight room, crammed with her insurance.

Miss Jones didn't feel smug. The empty street chilled her. There was no-one there for her. She was, and always had been alone, and there was no use or mileage in worrying about it. Father had praised her for her ability to cope. When the end comes there will be no time for such silliness. The empty street will be how it is. There will be no-one there.

Right. There was much to do. If her calculations were right she still had space for supplies to last for at least another three years in the library, three in the top bedrooms, and if she pulled up the floorboards as Dean once suggested, there might be an unexpected richness of room. Her arthritis had become a problem and she found herself struggling to carry bags from the supermarket. Tins and bottles had weight too and the plastic handles pulled into tight strings which cut into her skin and joints. Taxis were expensive, but she found several obliging drivers who carried the groceries to her step and one polite young woman offered to take it inside the house. Miss Jones resisted. The less they saw, the better. She'd read in the local newspaper how several houses had been targeted in the town, and that old people were especially vulnerable to bogus officials. Miss Jones also calculated how quickly the end would be. She'd seen the seeds of change early on. At Mother's funeral she looked tearfully into the sky and strange cloud formations towered above the high sandstone tower of the church. The vicar announced 'dust to dust; ashes to ashes,' and she knew. Staring into the grave she saw the end of everything. All around friends and family watched indifferently as another life, a good life, sank into nothingness, her soul rising into an empty universe, and Miss Jones knew she had to hang onto life at all costs.

This was it. This is how it was.

*

Dean wiped bread over the centre of his plate and swept the sauce aside into a neat and shrinking blob. Patsy watched and smiled. He ate well nowadays, and she didn't palm him off with a pound for the chip shop. It was nice. Here they were in a new home, and despite the old bag next door it was wonderful. For the first time

Patsy felt life was on the up. After surviving Billy, the hostel, and Social Services, she had increasingly found her own way, her own mind, and it was exhilarating. For many years she had lost the ability to love, sometimes doubting she'd ever experienced it. Her mother left her when she was little and she had to bear the brunt of her father's wrath and misogyny. No wonder when Billy came along she was swept up by his madness and his motorbike. But the best moment of her life was in seeing Dean's bright blue eyes for the first time – as blue as the sky. A nurse in the hospital said he should be named Gabriel for he was certainly an angel.

Even the intensity of her love for him tarnished and diminished under the weight of living, and now, remorseful but with growing optimism, she felt they'd make it. Her only concern would be Billy's return. The few months he'd spent in prison would be over one day, and although she lived in a fair sized town, it wouldn't be difficult to find her. She'd started divorce proceedings but knew Billy would hold such things in contempt. Her hope was that now he was dry his perspective would be as hopeful as hers, and he would change for the better. Deep down Patsy doubted such an eventuality.

"Was that nice, Sweetie?" she asked gently, lovingly.

"Lovely, Mum. Thanks."

"Do you want anything else?"

"No thanks. Can I have some lights on my bike?"

"Lights? Well I'd rather you didn't go out at night."

"You used to let me."

"That was before. It's different now."

"Why's it different?"

"Because I want to keep you safe."

"I would be if I had lights."

"I'll think about it." She started to clear the dishes from the table and watched Dean as he moved into the small hallway to look at his bike. "Giving it another coat of looking at?" she laughed.

"Yes. I love it." Dean felt a surge of sadness. "Do you think

Dad will like it?"

Patsy didn't answer. She turned on the tap and splashed water into the pans. It was strange cooking meals. She hadn't bothered in a long time. After she left her father's home she didn't care to. He'd expected her to do everything Mum had done, and she fought against some of those expectations with tenacity. Cooking was something she didn't want to continue, and Billy's diet of booze and roll-ups usually suppressed his appetite anyway.

Dean wandered into the tiny kitchen. "Do you think Dad will like my bike? Mum? Why won't you talk about Dad?"

"Don't pester me, Sweetie, I'm busy." Patsy's annoyance grew, but she wanted to hide it.

"I'm not. I just wanted to know if…"

"Look, Billy, don't spoil everything…" She wasn't conscious of the mistake.

Dean was. He seized it immediately. "Mum. You called me Billy!" He felt a mingling of surprise and hope. *She did remember him.*

"What? I didn't!" she protested. Her temper rose quickly as she became frazzled and forced into an uncomfortable corner.

"You did, honest. You said *Billy*. You called me *Billy*."

"Okay. I'm sorry. I just don't want to talk about him. You've got to understand Dean he's out of our lives now. He's gone. We don't want to see him." She was on the verge of tears.

"I want to see him. I want him to see my bike."

"He can't. He can't come here, Dean. He's banned. The police won't let him."

"Why?" Dean was horrified.

"Don't you remember what he did? Do you want him back after that? He's dangerous, Dean. He's mad. Crazy. One day he's going to kill someone."

"He's had cold turkey! He'll be okay now, he'll be better!" Dean pleaded, his chest tight and eyes burning. How could he make her see?

Patsy wiped her hands on her dress and moved towards him. He was frozen to the spot, too distressed to move. She wanted to whack him and she wanted to kiss him. He looked so small and yet his needs were so big. How could she tell him she'd fallen out of love? How could she make him see beyond his childish blindness? How could anyone love such a brute? And yet she had loved Billy too, a time ago, she'd fallen under his spell. How could she help Dean to understand?

"Dean…I…I don't know how to explain to you what I feel. I thought your Dad was wonderful once, a long time ago, but sometimes we grow out of love with people. I was just a kid when I met him, and he was so exciting." She put her arms around the boy, and hugged him to her. His hair moved above his ears as her breath caught it while she spoke. "It was exciting but it didn't last. He changed a lot. He spoilt things, Dean. Don't let him spoil what we've got now."

Dean felt like he was locked up in his head. Although his mum held him she was still on the other side of a glass window. It would be okay now if Dad came home, it had to be. They would be okay. After the cold turkey everything would be okay. Dad would want to stay and make it better and he would do everything right if he knew Patsy still loved him, and Dean was a good lad, really, who behaved brilliantly. Dean no longer wanted to be a burden, the rope which tied them together. This was a chance to be a proper family now. He couldn't understand why she felt like this, and no matter how hard he tried he couldn't make her see it. Frustration bubbled and exploded and he felt the lock break in his head, and a rush of words rattle from his tongue.

"Dad will be okay now! I want him back!" Dean shouted, and tried to push her away. "When he comes back he'll be better. He'll be cured, Mum!"

"No, Dean! Don't make me laugh! Do you think he's going

to change just like that?" She snapped her fingers. The muscles cracked in her legs as the tension rose. "Don't you think he's stopped before? Good God, Dean every time he gets done he stops and then he's right back on it at the first opportunity! He can't help himself, Dean! He's an alcoholic! He can't change, but we can! He'll kill someone some day or he'll kill himself. God wouldn't it be a blessing!" She was furious. Her voice became gruff with the tightness in her chest. "You can't cure an alcoholic, Dean. You can't!"

Dad had drunk for as long as Dean could remember, and sometimes he was nice after a few drinks, but more often he was nasty. One thing for sure, Dean knew Dad didn't like him more often than he did. He was always saying – *Everything was alright before the bloody kid came along!*

The boy sobbed, his head a confusion of frustration, sadness, anger, and an intense longing, a yearning for something he knew deep down was an impossibility. The more he yearned for it, the further it went away, until it became a speck, a bit of dust in the eye, pricking , scratching, making the face burn with tears as he tried to work it out and take the pain away. Patsy couldn't hold him and she watched him as he flew into the hall. He kicked his bike.

"Dean! Stop! My present! Don't damage it!"

"I don't want it! I don't want it!"

"I got that for you, not your bloody father! Don't!"

Why didn't she understand? Despite what Dad had done, he was still his father, and even though sometimes in the past he wished Dad was dead, those awful times when he had been cruel and violent, Dean still wanted him to come back. He wanted so badly for Dad to tell him he *loved* him. Heavy hearted, Dean couldn't recall any time in his life when it had been like the stuff on television, on the adverts, mums and dads and kids having a great time in the full sunshine of life. He so badly wanted it to be like that. *It had to be*. Other kids had proper families, and he wanted one. Other families were good mates and wanted to be with their kids. The confusion of feelings began to distil into one tight, hard-edged, red-hot sensation – rage.

“You’re stupid!” he spat, “You’re sodding stupid!”

Patsy snapped. She slapped him. He stopped dead. “Oh, Baby! Sweetie! I’m so sorry!” She was shocked at what she’d done. It was his birthday and she’d hit him. Everything she wanted to be, everything she’d imagined fell apart. Maybe she’d phone the social worker and tell him, ask him what to do. “Baby, it’s your birthday,” she said weakly, and slumped to her knees.

Dean didn’t move. He was rooted to the spot.

“Baby…Baby…” She tried to reach out and hold him, but he moved quickly now and avoided her outstretched hands. “Don’t move away from me, Dean, please don’t.”

“I hate you,” he hissed, feeling the stinging flesh of his cheek. It began to burn as his anger simmered. “I bloody hate you!” He saw an image in his mind of him destroying the bike, taking it to a cliff and throwing it down, pushing it under a train, dragging it onto a motorway. He saw it smash and tangle, heard the wheels strain and heave as they buckled. He could never have a family. Never. He wanted to smash everything up.

“Please come over here,” Patsy pleaded. “I’m so sorry! I shouldn’t have hit you.” She was as bad as Billy. At least he had the excuse he was drunk when he lashed out. “Dean, Baby, please say you’ll forgive me?”

Dean moved to the door. He looked at the bike, and then at his mum. He would take it out and he would wreck it.

Patsy sank back on her haunches and held her head in her hands. “They’ll take you away from me, Deano. They’ll take you away. I’m crap!” She felt a wave of exhaustion. What was the point of dreaming? She didn’t have the capacity to love anyone. She knew now for sure.

When Dean flung opened the door and crashed his bike out

through the porch, she didn't move. She heard Mrs Anderson outside shouting something abusive to him, like a screeching cat, but Patsy couldn't respond. There was no point. It was his birthday and she'd hit him. It was unforgivable.

Eleven /

"Hey, you little bastard!" the man shouted as he walked unsteadily outside the Bowling Green Public House. Dean rode perilously close, nearly sending him flying before he cut through the blue brick path of Monks Lane and down towards the North Crofts – a clutter of houses surrounded by cinder topped roads. Despite having no lights, and some of the town's streets were badly lit, he didn't care about his or anyone else's safety.

If the bike got wrecked it wouldn't matter.

If he got wrecked it wouldn't matter either.

For a time he stood on the River Weaver Bridge in Welsh Row, and thought about chucking it over the side, along with the tangle of supermarket trolleys already sinking slowly into the silt. Cars started to queue behind him waiting for the traffic lights to change so he decided he'd go the canal, by the big Comprehensive School at the top of Welsh Row, and after clambering up the rubble path by the aqueduct, he'd let it role into the thick and muddy water.

When he got there, some kids were messing about dropping stones onto the cars as they passed underneath and he turned quickly as they spotted him, yelled like banshees, and threw them after him as he retreated. It was getting late. The cold began to bite hard. *Let it bite*, he thought. There was no going back. He was smart enough to avoid his mum if she came looking. He wouldn't go home, Dean was sure of that. No matter how cold it got he'd stay out all night. In fact he might never go home again. What would be the point?

Crossing the Barony Park he noticed the vicar from St Mary's Church walking under the rank of limes on Barony Road. He regularly sought those night-birds who wandered the town in a stupor of alcoholic or depressive insomnia whenever he wasn't presiding over church meetings or giving dubious blessings to someone. The vicar always had a big smile on his bearded face, and looked a little like Father Christmas. Dean wondered how awful it must be to have to smile like that all the time – non-stop, day in and day out. Dean wanted to avoid the smile, and he wasn't in the mood for hair tousling. He wanted to steer clear of any questions and prayers. He wondered if the vicar knew about the end of the world, if God had given him a glimpse of what was going to happen. Surely the vicar would know, being so close to God – surely he'd be in on it in some way. Deep down Dean didn't think so. He wouldn't spend so much time blessing people and smiling; he'd be more like Miss Jones, and the vicarage was hell of a big house with masses of space in which to store things for the future.

Glancing repeatedly over his shoulder to ensure no-one else noticed him, Dean made for the cricket pavilion in the middle of the park. He hoped there were no couples tonight having a snog. If it was empty it would be a good place to sleep; well out of sight from passing cars, and apart from highly-charged sexual encounters, and of course seats for the local crowd supporting the cricket club, it was rarely used. It was getting desperately cold, and the sky brooded and threatened to mix snow in with the biting wind. Occasionally, from behind the bank of clouds, a frail slice of moon struggled to give Dean an awkward smile, an apology of a smile compared to the vicar's, but Dean pulled his collar up over his ears and turned away. He parked his bike against the white fence, and made his way up the dry and splintered wooden steps to the back row of the pavilion where he sat on a hard bench and felt the shock of cold on his backside. There was nothing to smile about, and deep down he had the conviction that no matter how much the moon beamed it would fall one day and batter the world. It was a false smile. And it would be a matter of luck then if anyone survived, even Miss Jones. Her face came to mind and Dean wanted to push her away, turn her off like a light. He thought about her tucked up in her bed in Wellington Road, in the big grey house, along with the rows and rows of boxes. He remembered the stacks of food; beans, mushy peas, beans with sausages, carrots, curried beans, every type of food imaginable; she had sacks and boxes of stuff he'd never heard of, and some of the labels looked old-fashioned and faded.

If the end of the world came, he thought, there would be no electricity or gas or anything, so how could she cook stuff? Then he remembered. She could light a fire, of course, like the boy scouts did in the Wesleyan Sunday School in Hospital Street. They'd been outdoors in the big rear yard, gleefully rubbing sticks together or using magnifying glasses to concentrate the sun's rays, setting fire to pieces of paper and wool. But then a tapestry had been damaged when they overzealously practiced the craft, indoors, during the scout master's brief comfort break. If he were Miss Jones, Dean thought, he'd make sure she had plenty of boxes of matches, or packs of lighters like the men sold at the back of the market, five for a quid, and she should keep them in a tin so they didn't get damp or anything. She was too old to rub sticks together. If he lived after the end of the world he could do that. He'd be able to make a fire. The idea only served to increase his sore skin's reaction to the creeping cold.

He looked at his bike. The chrome glinted for a moment as the moon tried one last time to break through a big bellied cloud. The cloud looked to be full of rain or snow, dark and heavy, and frowned at Nantwich town hunched on the wide Cheshire plain. Mr Teal, a teacher at school said Cheshire was unfortunate as the Welsh mountains disembowelled the bellies of the rain clouds as they passed over from the west, and spilled their waters on the land. *It is good for the cows because it makes the grass lush and green, but it's not so good for the people who grow lugubrious when it rains all the time.* Dean asked him what lugubrious meant, and Mr Teal replied, 'You, Cartwright. *You.*'

The cold bit deeper. His fingers hurt and his feet ached. He yearned for his bed. The cold made his muscles cramp and teeth chatter. The cricket pavilion caught the brash wind full in its face.

Dean decided he had to move before he froze to the hard unyielding bench. It would be best to ride around the town again to get warm or to find somewhere warmer, but he ached so much he struggled to get his leg over the crossbar, and when he did he nearly fell off his bike. His muscles were rigid and unmovable and couldn't be corrected sufficiently to help him compensate and balance; in time, picking his way carefully and slowly, they unfroze enough to become responsive.

Eventually he retraced his previous route and found the Town Square was nearly empty of people. A few drunks spoke in loud voices, and a tall, thin man relieved himself in a flower bed by the War Memorial. Dean was unnerved when someone shouted at him. "Give us a ride, kiddo! Give us your bike!" He sped off down Pillory Street and found himself in Wellington Road.

Miss Jones' house looked eerie in the dark. The shrubs at the front and side of the house looked like hunched figures, and a tall oak groaned when the chill wind scraped its branches. Dean fancied it writhed against the cold, almost imperceptibly. An owl screeched and frightened him, and somewhere, out beyond the edge of town, a vixen screamed. Dean thought it sounded like a woman being murdered.

Should he bang on Miss Jones' door? Would she let him in? It had been months now since he walked away, and maybe she'd be like Auntie Jessie and put on a face colder than the night. No, it was better not to disturb her. She was old and old people got spooked if someone knocked on their door so late in the night. He turned to go, the front wheel crunching the muck in the gutter by the side of the road. He was too far away to notice the light go on in the front bedroom or Miss Jones' shadow cross the curtains as she made her way to bed. Slowly and reluctantly he rode up Wellington Road, carefully crossed the railway tracks, peddling hard to prevent the wheels slip into the deep ruts of the rails, and made his way back home. Despite his anger, the knuckle whitening prospect of seeing

Mum and having to face-up to her after she'd ruined his day, was outweighed by the sharpness of cold invading his clothes and hugging him until it caressed every crevice and crease.

*

"He's run away," Patsy said, breathlessly, worrying about the phone call, and yet he'd offered, he'd said it would be okay. He'd given her his mobile number after all, and that stood for something, she felt. There was no sense of shock or hostility either when he answered, none of the distance she'd met before in every, so-called, caring professional. "We…we had an argument. He was going on about his sodding father again and again and I just snapped. I told you I was useless! I am such a bad person…" The silence unnerved her, and she stopped until she heard him make a small sound of acknowledgment and then she started again, berating herself, beating herself up. "I don't know what to do. Shall I report it to the police? I don't think he's coming home. I'm really scared. It was his birthday and I slapped him. He was so mad. I'm really scared." The voice became reassuring, soothing her, and she listened intently. "It's late. You can't do that," she said at last, but hoped he meant it.

After she'd put the phone down she looked at herself in the mirror hanging at an awkward angle on the living room wall, and despite her anguish, she still found time and motivation to straighten the mirror, hair, and make-up, in readiness for the new social worker to call. Weird it may have felt for her at this particular time, but she needed someone to come and hold her, in every sense; to take away her agony of doubt and make it all right again. Dean came back to mind, and she looked in the mirror again and hoped she looked fretful enough for when Mark Tomlinson called.

*

It was a lovely floating feeling, being so tired and lingering in-between sleep and waking. A good day's work had been done to the point where her limbs ached, and as the night progressed and her energies became thin and tense with the cold, she found solace in the depth of comfort and warmth in the big bed. The cold spot under her feet soon warmed until the whole of her basked in the sensuality of a body relaxing, yielding, unwinding. There would be no trouble in achieving sleep tonight, she thought, no need for a small tot of whisky or hot cocoa. Outside the wind suddenly growled and made the gutters rattle.

Now there's a thing, Miss Jones thought. How would she repair her home in the years to come? How would she do such things as climbing ladders, hauling bricks and cement? Sleep dropped away like a falling garment as she returned naked and vulnerable to a prickly consciousness, fretful and exposed. Instantly she thought of Dean, a young boy grown into a strong and able lad, but equally as quickly she dismissed him from her mind. Whenever he sprang to mind she became either maudlin or euphoric, both unwelcome in the way it unsettled her and stimulated thoughts and ideas. Tonight it felt possible to slip into the darkness and sombreness of the former rather than the latter, so, it would be better to think of other things, and after all, if the world was empty she could take any house of her choice. She smiled, as she diverted her attention away from the boy, and thought about the newish houses on the Broadway. Yes. One of those would be nice. Very nice. It would be possible to inhabit any house she chose, use the big house in Wellington Road as a store – a kind of distribution centre for her needs. She realised the notion released more space. If she didn't live here the house would be capable of holding even more stuff. She drifted towards sleep, slightly fevered, head still counting tins and making calculations. Her body felt incredibly heavy as she imagined herself… imagined herself… imagined…. but the thought didn't form and express itself as she fell into a deep and welcome sleep. The moon briefly struggled to throw its small and fragile light through a gap in the big bellied clouds, and superimpose its smile onto her gaping mouth.

*

The cold made his fingers stiff and Dean found it hard to let go off the rubber grips on the handlebars. Tugging with the front gate the black and rusty iron latch pinched the side of his palm, and he winced and swore, though tried to keep it under control so as not to aggravate Mrs Anderson who even now stood with a face like a gargoyle as her mean eyes patrolled the street. The bike chain smeared grease on his jeans, and in this moment he felt such discomfort all he could do was think about how wonderful a bed was, and a duvet, and pillows. Looking over the bike he saw it gleaming still in the half-hearted moonlight, and the less generous street lighting. That was good. Mum wouldn't go off on one, and deep down he didn't want to trash such a treasure. It was probably the best thing he'd ever had, and it seemed weird now that he'd wanted to wreck it just a few hours ago. Dad would have done things like that. Once he'd got so mad and drunk, he picked-up a video recorded and smashed it over a television. They'd gone for two weeks or more without them until he thought up a scam to get them replaced, and boasted, to anyone brave enough to be near him, about his deceit and victory over an insurance company.

When Dean opened the door, quiet as a mouse despite the agony of cold and stiff limbs, he didn't expect to see Mark Tomlinson there with his mum. Did social workers work nights, he wondered, and sit next to mothers, with arms around them, letting heads fall on shoulders? Patsy leapt to her feet and threw herself towards him.

"Oh, Baby! Baby! You're okay! Thank God! I'm so sorry! Come here!" She held his head between her hands and felt his icy ears, blue and sore. She pulled him into a hug which hurt his back and arms it was so tight. "Oh, you poor thing! You're so cold. I'm sorry, Dean, Sweetie! I'm so sorry. You must be frozen!"

The social worker stood sheepishly in the background, glancing at the boy, an enigmatic grin on his well formed face. He cleared his throat several times before saying he'd have to go, trying to sound matter-of-fact, that tonight had been *par for the course* – the outcome qualifying the intervention. He wouldn't, however, mention the time of contact, merely the details. The social worker stopped briefly beside them, looked intently into her face, and then down at Dean. He was about to say something, but then felt it better not to.

"Thank you, Mark," Patsy said in a quiet voice, "for being here for me." There was an attempt to emphasise her feelings, stress the words, but her relief at having Dean back home outweighed, in this moment at least, her need to communicate…something.

Dean thought Mark would say something nasty, tell him off for doing this to his mother, and turned away, not wanting to listen, but the social worker nodded at Patsy, in a strange acknowledgement, eyes wide and ablaze, and quietly slipped out through the front door.

The curtains twitched at Mrs Anderson's window, as his engine coughed into life. Whatever she said merely clouded the glass, and softened the sharp contours of an aggrieved face.

Twelve /

After sleeping deeply for a few hours she had another early bout of wakefulness, and now Miss Jones struggled from her bed. Today she had a heavy sensation, a dull and grim feeling in the pit of her stomach. Her arthritic hands throbbed more than usual, and she would have difficulty dressing. She'd listened to the birds at the crack of dawn, and at this time of the year they sang less as winter approached and dimmed their spring songs of sexual prowess and territoriality. Her focus was arrested by the unpleasant caw-caw of crows, and squabbling of magpies. She listened for an age, too seedy to do anything other than languish in her bed. Their noises mocked and jeered, and she resented their vicious energy. It was day; time to get up. Her image in the large dressing table mirror was white and ghost-like – dark rings under her eyes, and hair tangled like wire-wool on this night worn face. There was much to do today, she thought, shopping, and checking-in, making a list of what to get, making another list of where it would be put, in which room, in which pile or stack. Her mind was more active than a poorly responding body, but she gathered determination along with her flouncy nightdress and pulled herself out of bed. The wooden floor made her wince as her feet touched the hard wood impregnated with late autumn.

A cup of tea, stronger than usual, and a half-hearted untwisting of cellophane on a loaf and its quick re-twisting, was her breakfast. She caught the yeasty smell and it made her heave. When she opened a box to seek out some aspirin she spilled the entire contents on the floor and crushed some tablets under her unsteady feet on the floor boards, the place where just the day before she stripped a piece of linoleum away, when her thoughts momentarily flitted back to Dean's idea about using the void as a storage space. It wasn't practical. Edwardian builders and subsequent contractors, had left rubble over the years, and dust had fallen between the cracks and settled on the unsightly deposits; to clean out the space would have been too much trouble. The very idea today, as she tried to brush the fractured and powdering aspirin between the gaps, and add to the muck, was overwhelming and made her head spin. She'd clear what was left of the mess, later, when she felt up to it. As it was Friday she had to carefully make a list of things she needed, and traipse down to the supermarket. Thoughts struggled through her porridge head, slow and thick, and when she wrote down an item she immediately scrubbed it out and felt frustrated by her inability to make a decision. More energy went into this exasperation than into her motivation and intent, and all she wanted to do was go back to bed, but eventually she managed to create a sufficient list of needs, and a modicum of activity to get her going. She hesitated by the door, peering through the coloured glass, making decisions as to what to wear to face the day.

Outside the day was dull and squally, the sky overcast, and so she tied her plastic rain-hood tightly under her chin. It covered a small blue hat; she wouldn't go out of the house unless she wore one. It would be too exposing, almost indecent, although she didn't trouble to understand why. It was habit. Father always wore a trilby, a neat hat with a wide brim and black band, which he wore on a tilt over his 'Brilliantine' hair. *If you want to get ahead, get a hat,* he'd say as he adjusted the angle in a mirror by the front door, winking at her as he did so. The memory served to warm her and inject feeling back into her limbs as she unlocked, unbolted and opened the heavy door. She sniffed the air, wiped her nose on a tissue, and carefully walked down her blue-brick path, holding her stick. At this time of the year it could be slippery, so she went with caution until she stepped onto the tarmac footpath. The wooden gate scraped over the brick-path as she closed it, adding to a thousand other swipes, scouring an arc deeper into the surface. She noticed a section of paint on the gate had flaked away and the rotten wood underneath exuded pin heads of orange gluey stuff, causing her a transient feeling of concern. Repairs meant expense, and she needed to carefully watch her spending. Everything was aimed toward future survival. Was the gate really so important, she thought dismissively, for who will use it in the future except me?

The street was nearly empty except for a red-faced young woman in jogging pants and a sweat bloomed top, who ran around her, struggling to catch her breath. Mr Bryant, a neighbour, nodded to Miss Jones as he pulled a wheelie-bin to the front of his house. It was merely polite and without warmth. They had lived in the street for several decades and this was the only acknowledgement they admitted to. Her smile in return was quickly extinguished as she passed. An electric milk-float rattled over the uneven surface of Wellington Road, clattering as it jumped over a high grid covering the water-mains in the middle of the street. Miss Jones watched it pull over and a young man in a woollen hat step out, grab two bottles and whistle his way across to Hill View Place. His whistling depressed her. It seemed relentlessly cheerful on such a dank morning, and her head ached despite the two aspirins she'd taken. It was a struggle and she wondered what was wrong with her. Despite the close proximity of the supermarket every step was proving to be difficult, and she imagined herself as the sweaty young woman labouring to keep going, to achieve the challenge despite the face full of agony and a shirt heavy with sweat.

Resting for a moment against the barrier surrounding the trolley park, she decided she'd have a sit down in the supermarket café and order a coffee or something, just rest for a moment in the hope her sloth would subside. Having a coffee was something she'd not done before; feeling the cost in time and money was too much, and to have to face the crowds of shoppers hunched in the tight café filled her with dread, and not a little contempt. How she hated shopping, and to feel unwell on top of it was too much. She was cross with herself. Perhaps, she admitted grudgingly, she was doing too much, becoming too obsessed. She conceded and admitted to obsession, but felt uneasy that it was becoming dangerously like an addiction. Father called himself an 'addict.' He had an addiction to books, he said, which wasn't as dangerous as drink or drugs, although it was just as costly. Books make the brain blossom, booze makes the brain wither, he asserted. Miss Jones felt her brain was withering today, it felt too small and too tight to hold thoughts, or too addled to make words, do calculations.

No more, must get on, she said under her breath, and crossed the car park, hesitating while a huge lorry slowly negotiated the quick turn on the supermarket mini-roundabout, its brakes hissing when it stopped to allow her to make her way across to the entrance. The supermarket was busy, and her heart sank. Farmers and their wives came into Nantwich on a Friday for the market, and it seemed they'd all crammed here in the warmth. They queued at the checkouts, pushed and shoved down the aisles with their full trolleys. An annoying babble of music played in the background constantly interrupted by announcements. The long strip-lights burned overhead, as bright as daylight, but brash and troubling in the intensity of their illumination. Somewhere a child cried bitterly as a mother denied it a toy or some other novelty, a cry that turned heads in disapproval and condemnation. After the sudden and emphatic change from a chill day to the overwhelming heat of the tight aisles, Miss Jones felt claustrophobic and feared she'd faint; so she immediately made her way to the café. She had to sit down, it was urgent now, and not consider where she sat and if the place positioned her near to anyone. An empty seat was only a moment away, but her head spun so violently she grabbed someone's trolley to steady herself.

"Are you alright, love?" a man asked, his ruddy face creased with concern. "You look awful."

"I'm fine," she said, breathlessly, her head pounding now. Miss Jones felt silly. How foolish she was.

"Do you want to sit down?" he asked, moving to her side. He held her under her elbow, and tried to move her, but she resisted. "Shall I call someone?"

"No, really! Thank you, I'll be alright. I'm going to have a drink in the café."

"Here, let me take you across," he insisted, and she relaxed her grip and allowed him to park his trolley and walk with her. "Shall I get you something? Water, tea, whatever?"

"No, no. I'll order in a minute when I catch my breath." It was really too much, feeling like this. Her stomach knotted and she thought she might be sick. She watched the man return reluctantly to his trolley, his face full of concern and sympathy. She wondered if he thought she was drunk and felt deeply ashamed, so she tried to smile pleasantly, wave to him. He disappeared into the fruit and vegetable aisle, and was gone. Trying not to look conspicuous, she held a hand under her chin, propped an elbow on the table and let her head fall on this temporary support. Closing her eyes she took several deep breaths, believing they would settle her. All around the noises seemed to increase and it was difficult to concentrate sufficiently to facilitate a sense of relaxation and a subsequent settling into well-being and no matter how hard she tried her attention was inevitably pulled towards the cacophony. Added to this was her wretched sense of awkwardness and embarrassment.

She opened her eyes when a young woman approached her and said it was self-service.

"Pardon?"

"It's self-service, not waitress." The young woman smiled, and pointed to the stack of trays at the end of the stainless steel counter. "You have to help yourself."

"Oh, right," Miss Jones responded awkwardly, feeling another surge of tension and a blood-rush blooming on her pale cheeks.

"It's just over there, Madam," the girl repeated.

"I'm sorry, I'm not feeling too good," Miss Jones apologized, keeping her voice low as rose to her feet; but she moved too quickly, too determinedly in trying to avoid a scene of any kind. She steadied herself against the table top.

"I'm sorry, I didn't realize. Look, can I get something for you?" the young woman offered kindly, but feeling a transient insecurity at her mistake. The old lady looked a little bit like her Nan, and recently she'd attended a customer relations programme which awoke and inculcated a sense of direction in her. This was her first job. "You sit back down, and I'll take your order. Go on, it'll be okay. Do you want me to call for a doctor or a relative or someone?" It gave her an odd sense of validation to help like this, to offer support in such a way to the old lady. Kindness and assertion became muddled in an unconscious drive for her to be seen as efficient and effective – professional. Her voice rose and she moved with certainty, as she attempted to attract attention and let the public, and her supervisor supervising from the till, witness this expansion into a new role, her role, as rescuer, as kindly soul, as a hard-working woman.

"Oh, no, no need to send for anyone, please. I'll be fine with a cup of coffee." Miss Jones smiled weakly and fumbled for her purse. She wished the well-meaning girl would keep her voice down and not make her the centre of scrutiny.

"Pay me after you've drunk it and you're feeling better." Her voice was direct and firm. "Coffee, you said? Espresso, Cappuccino, Latte, Americano, Macchiato?"

"Oh, just a plain old coffee. With milk and a little sugar."

"Instant, you mean? Just instant?"

"Yes, yes. That will be fine, thank you so much. Look I'll come and get it when it's ready," she offered, quietly, hoping to divert eyes.

"Oh, no! I wouldn't dream of it. You just stay where you are and let me run around for you. Treat yourself! Would you like a pastry with it?"

Miss Jones stomach turned at the thought. "Oh, no thanks. Nothing to eat." She felt utterly miserable. Several customers turned to look, and two women across the way spoke behind their hands, and darted surreptitious glances at her. When the young woman walked by them towards the counter, one touched her arm, stopped her, and said she thought it was self-service.

"It is, madam. The old woman is not very well so I think we can make an exception, don't you?"

"Oh, really? Yes, of course," she flushed slightly and glanced at her companion before they resumed their whispered conversation. At the till the supervisor said something to girl, and they both smiled, though the young woman's smile was triumphant.

Even after she'd sipped her coffee Miss Jones still felt queasy and light-headed. She knew she'd have to get up soon and go. Many people had come and gone, tables emptied and filled and as they filled again she felt guilty she took up a table to herself. The young woman was kind despite her efficiency, and told her to take her time, but Miss Jones felt herself to be a nuisance and would have to go. She wondered whether to ask the girl to get her a taxi, she would offer to pay for the call, obviously, but the young woman was blooming now, confidence high, and was, as a consequence, making herself very busy. Miss Jones decided she'd already done enough. No, it was time to move. She'd manage to get outside and walk to the ranks. It wasn't far to her house, but she didn't think she'd be able to walk back that far unaided. On seeing her rise the young woman came across and took her payment.

"Are you sure you are okay?" she enquired. "If there's anything else I can do?" Miss Jones gave her a 20p tip, and the girl smiled graciously despite her disappointment. She walked with her to the exit, and reiterated her offer to help further, but Miss Jones declined and walked carefully towards the automatic door, and into the cold, damp air outside. The young woman walked across the café a good few centimetres taller. A good deed for the day had been done, and it enhanced her sense of worth no end.

*

When he woke the next morning Dean stretched his muscles and tugged and shrugged until the duvet slipped and left his arms high and exposed. He shivered and pulled them in again. He'd slept well after the tearful reunion and Mum telling him it would never, ever, happen again, and he could trust her now. Mark Tomlinson was mentioned several times, which made Dean feel uncomfortable. Getting into bed had been wonderful, and all the time she'd showered him with tears and promises, he longed to get away and shrink into a hot ball of sleep, and no worries. And now it was day and he wondered what it would bring. His stomach felt heavy and he didn't want to do anything in particular. Yesterday had been another disappointing day in his life, so there didn't seem to be much point in feeling enthusiastic. He remembered it was a Friday, a school day, and decided he'd bag it off. Somewhere downstairs he heard his mum vacuuming, and the noise of the cleaner took him back to the times he stayed with Auntie Jessie and Uncle Ralph, just a few years back before the illness crept into Uncle Ralph's bones and ate him up, from the inside out. Uncle Ralph would have been good at living at the end of the world, Dean thought. He kept ferrets and he went fishing, and he boasted that he could live off the land. He was always showing Dean strange looking stuff, giant puff-ball mushrooms, and tiny white flowers which had bulbous roots, pig-nuts, which tasted good when he pushed them into his mouth and broke them with his young teeth. Yes. Uncle Ralph could survive, Dean thought, sadly, hating the cancer that stopped him. Uncle Ralph was a giant of a man; tall, face angular and firm; hands as big as spades, and boots like barges. It was shocking that such strength could be sucked out of him.

Dean had been fishing with him many times, though Uncle Ralph declined to take him rabbiting. He thought the sport too cruel for the boy, and wanted to delay any exposure to the bloody efficiency of spitting ferrets, and rabbits crying like babies when caught in the cruel jaws or purse nets. It's Nature, he'd say, but understood how brutal Nature could appear. He didn't want to disturb the boy and secretly hoped Dean would grow up to be a *decent man,* different to Billy, but not one of those wretched vegetarian-new-age-pansies he so abhorred.

When things were bad at home Dean had been able to stay with Uncle Ralph and Auntie Jessie, and things were bad so often he sometimes pestered and pleaded not to be taken home when the troubles had apparently settled. His Aunt and Uncle never blamed him or accused him, and he settled into short moments of bliss before returning to long term passages of guilt and worry. Uncle Ralph had shown him so much too, and he thought, with some pride, that he'd be able to look after himself if things really got bad. He wondered if Miss Jones could catch fish and skin rabbits, and if she couldn't how boring it would be to live on tinned foods?

Dean thought about fishing and the joy he'd felt when Uncle Ralph took him along. Some years before, after school on a lovely hot day, warmed in part by his remembering, Dean recalled a magic time and pictured himself running like mad down Queens Drive. He'd dug for bait early in the morning, under the grass cuttings behind Mr. Simpson's garage where Uncle Ralph told him to dig, dropping red brandlings and slimy lobworms with bristles on their bands, into a dented aluminium tin. And then he pressed waterlogged bread into balls for ground baiting the mere. Earlier, in the maths lesson he'd weighed golden, wide-eyed bream in kilograms, while Mr. Hughes, the maths teacher, monotonously described arcs and tangents on the blackboard.

It would have been his third trip, he remembered. The roach he caught in the canal on his first shone like silver and whipped its pale red fins against his palms; cold, sad-eyed, the scales in neat rows like polished chain-mail, the small jaws, and the gills gaping to show fine pink frills. He'd seen nothing so beautiful. He wanted to keep it, but Uncle Ralph laughed and said there'd be bigger and better, like the huge tench in the glass case in the Wyche Anglers Club, in London Road – *Yes, even as big as that.* The second trip produced nothing. But Dean gazed over the brown river and dreamed.

It was really hot that day, he recalled. Tar trickled on the road as he shot up the bank by the police house, his trainers sticking in the soft stuff, and Mrs. Wilson, an old lady from next door, a neighbour of Uncle Ralph and Auntie Jessie, smiled and waved.

"You're in a hurry, young man."

"Going fishing with my Uncle Ralph!"

"Fetch us one back!"

"You make the chips then!"

She laughed and heard the side gate crash against the wall as he ran until his lungs ached and dashed indoors.

"Hello, Dean," Auntie Jessie said warmly, not with the indifferent tone Patsy used when Billy was around to play down the arrival of the boy.

"Hi! Did you put my big jumper out, Auntie Jessie?"

"Yes. And your jeans, the blue ones. I've patched the knees."

"Cor, thanks. Uncle Ralph says it's okay? He's still coming isn't he?"

"Yes. He rang to say he'd be here at five, so that'll give you time to eat!"

"Alright!" he shouted as he disappeared up the stairs. Dean adjusted his baseball cap and rolled up his sleeves while he waited on the wall that bordered the council houses. He felt the heat in the bricks burn the back of his legs. His Wellington boots were soft, and the tops were hot where they touched his skin. It would be a good night, he thought, and daydreamed about the fish dozing in the cool mud, waiting to bend the rod tip until it poked circles in the water. Men had spoken in hushed voices on the canal towpath and said that monsters lurked under the waterlillies at the far end of Marbury Mere, blowing bubbles as big as a man's head. Ten years ago a man had his arm bitten off by a pike. Flap! Snap! Gone! They laughed.

"I'll take you there next time," Uncle Ralph promised, and Dean imagined great fish being gaffed, water boiling under their gleaming bodies, bigger than those in the pictures in *Mr. Crabtree Goes Fishing,* a book Uncle Ralph had given him for Christmas.

He heard the car horn at the end of the lane, bang on time as usual, and saw the sun glint along the polished black body of Uncle Ralph's car. He grinned behind the wheel and leaned to push the door open.

"Shove your tackle in the boot. It isn't locked. Auntie Jessie all right?" he asked, before sliding from the seat and going indoors just to say hello, kiss her cheek, say goodbye, and rejoin the boy. He was as enthusiastic as the child, and she knew it.

"It's going to be a good night, Uncle Ralph."

"The night of the big buggers! They'll be jumping out to sunbathe and all we'll have to do is keep our arms open and our gobs shut!"

"I shouldn't have bothered with the worms then!"

"We'll eat them, son. I'm partial to worm butties!" he joked and tousled Dean's hair.

The corrugated seat felt cool on Dean's back, and air whistled through the quarter light window and rippled his shirt front.

"What are we going to catch then, son?"

"Bream? I've brought my lead weights."

"Aye, and those big ugly tench. Shove a lobworm on and those big lips of theirs will suck it out of the mud like that vacuum cleaner of your Auntie Jessie's. Bloody good fighters are tench. Scrap like wild cats. Good job they haven't got claws or else they'd drag half the mere out with them, or half the anglers in!"

The mere shone like a mirror lying in the grass, bouncing sunlight back up to the heavens. Dean peered across the silver surface through half-closed eyes, and Uncle Ralph rummaged in his pockets for his sunglasses. The trees bordering the far side shimmered in the heat, and a heron, on the sandy stretch by some willows, stood absolutely still. Dragonflies tapped against the rods and the whirring of their wings along with the lapping of water around the tree roots made Dean feel drowsy.

Uncle Ralph sucked a cigarette and let wisps of smoke curl from his nose and coil about his head. A bluebottle fizzed around Dean's face, and when he flicked his hand the waft of air was hot and heavy. Sweat beaded his top lip and trickled from under his baseball cap and down his neck. As he stood in the mere the water pushed his boots against his legs while the mud gripped the treads and cooled his feet. He felt like a stone statue slowly sinking beneath the surface. He shifted slightly and cracked the reflection, sending it dancing across his vision, making him feel giddy.

"Coffee, kiddo?"

"Uh?"

"You'll have to be sharper than this when the pike's nibbling your arse!"

"Sorry. It's so hot."

"Keep your eye on the rods while I get the drinks."

The sun hung above the woods and a train blew two shrill notes against the final blaze of orange sky. Bats began their trawl for moths, their shrill pips making tiny, high-pitched explosions in Dean's ears. He thought about the fish nuzzling among the weeds and circling the worm knotted on the barbed hook. He beamed his thoughts down the fine nylon line, sent radio signals surging through the black water, until he imagined the fish, like sharks, pointing their blunt faces and snatching the bait.

"Must be too hot for them."

"Can we wait a bit longer, Uncle Ralph?"

"Ten minutes and then we're packing up."

"Aw!"

"Now then. I don't want your mum and dad chasing me up the road saying I'm keeping you out late. Anyway, it's school tomorrow. You'll be gonking in the back row with your gob as wide as a trout. Ten minutes."

"Okay."

Ten minutes later Uncle Ralph sighed, shook his head and waded back to the bank.

"Come on, son. Draw sticks and let's be off before it gets too dark."

Dean reached for his rod, and felt the cork pulse.

"Uncle Ralph!" he hissed.

"What?" He saw the boy poised, eyes wide, breath short, and fingers fumbling with the spool on his reel. "Wait, lad, wait. Feel anything?"

"Yeh. Like a knocking."

"Wait a bit. It might be your knees! Whoa. Don't pick it up yet. Hold tight, wait until you hear the line zip and then strike like buggery!"

For long seconds Dean ached to grab the butt. The reel ticked and stopped, ticked and stopped. Suddenly the tip whipped, nearly touched the water, and the line tightened and twanged like an elastic band.

"Now! Go on! Now!"

It was like hitting a brick wall. The rod bent double and he felt a dead weight, the fish arching against the pull, coiling in response to the barb, and then, zip! Droplets fell like rain from the taut line, and spattered on the still mere. Zip! Weaving one way, then the other, doubling back, dipping, ducking and every move became an electric throb through the warm cork in Dean's knuckle-white grip.

"Again! Pull against it! That's it! Play it, my lad! Play it!"

"It's a big one!"

"It's a monster! Look at the rod!"

"It'll snap!"

"Never! Play the bugger, play it!"

"I can't hold it! I can't!"

"Don't panic. It's yours for the taking! A caser, it must be. Look at the bloody rod!" Uncle Ralph slapped his sides, tilted his head back and laughed at the darkening sky. "Just a bit more! Just a bit more, son, until it tires!"

Dean wrestled with the reel, dragged the rod up and down like in the manuals. Up and down, slowly and surely. Would the top hold? Yes. Easy now, easier. Not so heavy, not so hard. He listened to the line, felt the water flick from the spool over his hands, like cool lubricant. You're mine, he wanted to shout. You're mine!

"I've got the net and the gaff. No! Don't look at me, look at your fish. Any second now and you'll see him, see his big ugly snout!"

"Yes! Look!"

The fish broke the water, twisted, exhausted, a foaming 'v' under the rolling head, a white belly now, then gone, then back. Big eyes bulging, red eyes, huge fearful eyes, and a wide mouth, worm hooked under the lip like a moustache, and now a broad back, green back, heavy back, then the fins flush along the sides, feeble, flapping fins, one last flick when the net shoved under the belly, hissed through the water and dragged the dead weight out onto the bank.

In the failing light, Dean watched Uncle Ralph rip the fat lip when he pulled the hook through, saw the shuddering gills when he played the torch along its side, saw the milky white cloud dim the deep black eye, saw gasps erupting blood under the slime and the fins tangle in the net before being torn off. Dean's tongue stuck to the roof of his mouth, and his chest ached. He'd done it. He'd done that.

"It must be a ten pounder! Christ! This bugger's a caser. What about that then? Third time out and you've wrenched a monster tench from Mrs Marbury's belly!"

"Is it dead?"

"Dead? Why?"

"Put it back…"

"What?"

"Put it back…"

"Back?"

"Put it back in the water. Please!"

"You're soft! It's a club record, Dean!"

"Please!"

He shone the torch at Dean, blinding him for a moment, but he must have seen his white face, wide-eyed and fearful. He lumbered into the water and held the flaccid fish upright between his boots. He let go and the fish sank slowly into the mud.

"Is it alright? Is it alive, Uncle Ralph?" Dean shouted from the bank.

"Yes! Can't you hear it?"

Dean listened as Uncle Ralph flapped his hands in the water, turned, and waded back to the boy, giving him a big wink, trying to reassure him. Dean knew Uncle Ralph had lied. Dean killed the fish. He couldn't be brave and strong, and he knew he'd let Uncle Ralph down. He should have been stronger. And then Uncle Ralph died, and left him full of sadness and another sense of failure wouldn't shift and go away.

Light played on the bedroom ceiling, crept around the base of a round paper lampshade, and revealed cracks in the plaster. It wasn't easy to kill things, he thought. Maybe Miss Jones was right. If the world ended it would be better to eat from tins. In his mind he saw her old face again, and wondered what she was doing right now. He guessed she'd be counting tins and stacking boxes, and it made him smile.

*

The taxi rank was near, and she stood for a moment breathing in the fresh air. Maybe she'd be okay now, she thought. Just take a minute or two and go back in and get this infernal shopping done. It was an unrealistic idea, she knew immediately. As soon as she turned and looked through the big glass doors at the crowds, she knew she wasn't up to it and she needed to get home and sleep off whatever it was that took her in its grip. When she approached the taxi rank and stopped by the leading vehicle, she realised the driver was a young lady who had offered, some weeks before, to take her shopping down the path and into the house. Miss Jones had declined, feeling insecure and suspicious.

"Travelling light today," the young woman said, in a voice that was quiet and gentle, not what Miss Jones would have expected from a taxi driver. It was usually a gruff and indifferent, *where to?*

"Pardon?"

"No bags. No shopping today?" The old woman looked troubled, and the taxi driver felt sympathy for her.

"Oh, no. I'm sorry. I don't feel too good. I'll have to come back when I feel better."

"What's the matter?" There was genuine concern in her voice; she moved closer and looked into the strained eyes set in a pale face – ghastly in its exhaustion.

"A cold or something fluey, I think. I'm not so good." She felt like crying at her own pathetic state, and was worried by the strength of sadness running through her, in union with the lethargy pulling her down.

"There's a bug going round. Have you had the flu jab? You ought to," the taxi driver said as she opened the door and helped

Miss Jones into the car. "You sit in the front with me. Do you feel sick or anything?" It occurred to her that she might throw-up and the stink would linger for days, but she felt guilty for asking. "It doesn't matter, you just sit there and relax and I'll get you home in a jiffy."

Inside the car it felt warm, and safe, like a little cocoon against the day and the crowds. Miss Jones thought how much she'd like to slip back in the comfortable seat and allow the warm air blowing around her legs to lull her to sleep. A crucifix dangled from the driver's mirror, and swayed gently, hypnotically, as the taxi driver opened the door and climbed in, adjusting her skirt as she did. Miss Jones glanced at her profile as she fiddled with the keys and started the engine. She was lovely. Despite being slightly overweight she had a pretty face, and her hair had been carefully grabbed and wrapped in a clasp at the back of her head. Her eyes were quick and intelligent, brown points in clear whites, and she bit her lip as she shoved the gear-stick and moved off.

Miss Jones had been like this once. She remembered the way her hair had been and how she dressed it, the ribbons and clasps she herself had worn, so different from the thin grey hair stuffed under a battered old hat, which in turn was held in place by an ugly plastic rain hood. Mother had brushed it for her, when Miss Jones was a child, celebrating its shine and thickness, brushed her daughter into a trance-like state, wrapped in affection and contentment, eyes fixed on the beautiful reflection in the mirror, each stroke announcing how pretty, how precious she was. To be loved in *such* a way, she thought, and then to lose it. How she ached for her mother's touch after John had died. But it stopped, and slowly, her hair became brittle and grey.

"You relax," the taxi driver repeated, "You just sit there and relax." Her voice was quiet and soothing, and she gave Miss Jones a sideways look which was full of warmth and compassion. She reached over and touched her hand, gave it a squeeze. The bones stuck through the thin skin; the old woman's hand was icy cold. The taxi driver felt her flinch slightly, as if to move, but then didn't. The quick pulse, the sudden tensing of muscles, indicated more than the taxi driver would ever know.

Miss Jones felt a deep surge of tenderness. In her head she formed the words and then the sentences and repeated them over and over again to herself – *If you were my daughter I'd be very proud. I would brush your hair. I would brush your hair.* Miss Jones' eyes filled with tears and her chest heaved under her heavy coat. The plastic rain-hood had slipped forwards over her face, enough to obscure her burning eyes, but in this moment she didn't care if the young driver saw her pain, her sadness. She would tell her. She would speak it out loud. She turned to look at the taxi driver again, watched her glance through the side window as she weighed-up the speed of traffic on the roundabout. She was lovely. If only she could reach out to the young woman and give her a hug. A moment later the car pulled into the side of the road, in front of Miss Jones' house, and the young woman got out and quickly moved around the car to open the door for her. She took her arm, and gently guided her through the door.

The moment was lost.

"Soon be home! Now you get in make yourself a nice cup of tea and get to bed. Shall I call the doctor, for you?"

"What's you're name?" Miss Jones asked, reaching for her purse. "I'd like to know your name."

"Tracey. I'm Tracey. Look put your money away. This is on me." It was no distance at all, and it would be churlish to charge her.

Miss Jones felt like she'd crumple and fall into a heap on the pavement. She didn't dare move. Tracey held her, linked her arm and asked for the key so she could get her indoors, inside, and out of the bitterly cold day. If this is what it is be like to be old, to be so vulnerable and lonely, it is truly awful, Tracey thought, and hoped someone would always be there for her, in love and support.

Miss Jones wanted to tell her about how lonely she felt, how empty, wanted to tell her something about betrayal and loneliness and love, but the words became scrambled in her head, and all she could do was look at her, and shake her head. Looking into Tracey's face she saw her own reflected, and once again looked into the mirror. She didn't resist as Tracey took the key from her purse and opened the big front door. Tracey didn't seem to notice the boxes and the tins, or if she did, it didn't matter to her.

"Shall I make you a drink?" she asked, not wanting to leave the old woman.

"No..." It was all Miss Jones could do was to summon enough strength to speak. It hardly mattered that Tracey stood in the house, was confronted by the secret, the insurance.

"I don't like to leave you like this. Can I get someone?"

"No...no, I'll be alright in a minute. I feel so foolish." Suddenly feeling bewildered something moved inside her, a crawling, creeping recovery, rising to act, to defend and protect, slowly galvanise her strength and power. She had to get control of herself and the situation.

"Foolish? You can't help being ill. These new super-bugs are so bad nowadays and you know, antibiotics are useless my doctor says. You get to bed. Shall I help you?"

"I'll be okay. Please let me pay you, Tracey."

"No. Honest. You just get well." Tracey smiled and gave her a hug.

Miss Jones felt her hair against her cheek, and wanted to touch it, to stroke it.

"Look, I must go. My boss will be on my tail if I don't. Are you sure you'll be okay?"

"Yes. Thank you so much for your kindness, Tracey." Miss Jones said flatly, and looked despondent. Control was back, but possibility shrank and withered.

Tracey moved towards the open front door, but she hesitated, and turned to Miss Jones, giving her a huge smile. "Look! What good timing. There's someone to see you. I think your grandson has come for a visit and a bit of pocket money. He'll look after you!" she joked, pleased with the outcome, a good reason to retreat in the knowledge the old woman would be safe now. She squeezed past the boy and his bike, tapping his shoulder, giving him a huge, warm smile, so warm it took the edge off the wind that enshrouded and tried to shrink them.

Standing by the gate, hand on the post, Dean looked sheepishly at the young woman as she got into the car, wondered what she had been doing here in Miss Jones' house, but before having time to ask, to check her out, he was caught by the face appearing at the door.

"Who?" Miss Jones rushed to the door now, a sudden burst of energy surging through her. "Who's there? Who is it?" She knew. She knew who it was.

Dean looked bright and perky, and without a trace of self-consciousness he announced, "Hello, Miss Jones. Look. I've got a new bike."

Thirteen /

Nothing had changed.

The walls were less visible now, as the stacks had got higher and wider too, along the stairs. It was like a tunnel, and Miss Jones laughed as she showed him around and nearly had to walk sideways at the top of the stairs. "If I put anything else here I'll have to sleep downstairs," she said, her eyes wide with joy. He had come back. Dean was here again in her house. All the heaviness and lethargy had dropped away. It was miraculous, she felt, that in seeing his face again she was rejuvenated. There was not a trace of confusion or doubt, and nothing stirred unpleasantly inside her; it was an utter delight to see him. How he'd grown too, his face filling out a little, and his eyes quick and bright as he showed her his bicycle.

Dean felt strange, a sort of dreamy feeling, like he was there but watching it all through a glass box. Miss Jones hadn't changed much. The face was just as he remembered it, white and old and fragile-looking; as if it would easily tear or bruise. The knotty hands made him shudder, and yet he was fascinated in how they articulated, undoing knots, opening boxes, strange movements that looked impossible and yet always achieving their end. He still felt funny about her, especially when she tried to hug him. He didn't like it; it was suffocating. She wanted to make him cups of tea, and she offered to open one of the boxes of special treats she stored away in her wardrobe – tins of chocolates and stuff, but he said he was full on account of the big birthday meal he'd had the day before.

In truth, he wasn't hungry because his stomach churned with resentment still. Even this morning Mum had tried to soft soap him when he didn't get ready for school. She pleaded with him saying it would look bad on her, and she'd get the blame for everything he did. When Dean tried to discuss stuff about his dad, tried to explain how he felt responsible for the way he made them miserable, and how it could be better, she didn't hear, but went white and talked through clenched teeth, saying that Mark, *her* social worker now, not *his,* felt the same as she did; Billy was bad news and it would be best if he kept away from them. He was a disturbing influence, and anyway, if he came back they might have to remove Dean to a place of safety. Dean wondered what that meant because it sounded like a threat. It all seemed so far away and daft now as he stood in the room darkened with piles of boxes, even though the room was just as ludicrous in its own way – reflecting another adult's odd and aberrant ideas. The stomach eased, but he still declined Miss Jones' food.

"How old are you, Dean?" she asked, face close to his, scrutinising him, as if the years were written across his forehead.

"Twelve. I'm twelve," he responded, averting his eyes from her's.

"Well, I'm blessed! And I haven't got anything for you!"

"I didn't expect anything," he started, but quickly decided not to be too resistant to any offers she might make.

"When you get to my age you stop counting," she smiled, straightening her crooked back.

"Yes," he tried not to show a lack of enthusiasm in knowing that, but it was the sort of thing old people always said, until they got to an age where they'd tell everyone, everywhere, everyday, how old they were. He imagined Miss Jones saying, '*and do you know I'm eighty-three!*' or whatever age she happened to be. He wondered whether to ask, but then decided not to. As he watched her moving gracelessly around the shrinking spaces he felt a sudden and unexpected surge of pity for her. She was like him – sad and lonely really, he thought. Neither of them got on with others very well it seemed, and both of them didn't like fuss and stuff. Dean didn't have grandparents around, Nan and Grandpa, like he heard other kids talking about. He knew they lived somewhere but Billy's parents had disowned him, and Patsy's father sounded like he was a mean old man. Dean reflected sadly that no-one had sent him a card other than

Auntie Jessie, who for the first time didn't mark it with a kiss or enclose any money, and of course, his mum – though Dad was not a signatory. He'd hoped that some sort of birthday miracle would happen and Dad would be there on the doorstep, bunch of flowers for Mum, parcel under his arm for Dean, bathed in a quiet flare of soft backlighting, face smiling in a way Dean could only guess at. Dad rarely smiled unless he was well gone on the booze, and then it was sarcastic and wounding.

Miss Jones' grunts and shuffling snuffed out his day-dream as she steadied herself against the big, black, ornate mantelpiece in the front room. "I do get a bit light-headed," she said, and smiled at him. As it didn't seem to worry her, Dean didn't worry either, but watched her as she rummaged in a stack of yellowing newspapers in a brass box at the side of the hearth.

Deep down he wondered what all this meant to him now.

"You can still have the space I promised you, if you want it," Miss Jones enthused. Despite the light-headedness her headache and nausea had completely gone and she kept telling Dean he was just the tonic she needed, chattering excitedly, her voice gaining pitch and speed in her joy of the moment. She looked at him as he stood in the front room, dwarfed by the high ceilings. He was lovely. His mop of hair was even moppier, and his thin little body needed a lot of love. She poked the fire furiously, stirring the embers, before throwing several large pieces of coal onto it. A swirl of bright sparks rushed up the chimney, and pin-pricks of red-fire caught the sooty black back-boiler, flickered and danced like the fibre-optic lights they sold in the supermarket at Christmas.

He was motionless, deep in thought, and Miss Jones suddenly worried that she might be going too fast, too soon again. She'd hardly asked him anything about himself, and what had happened between now and their last meeting. In a rush of nervous energy she'd been caught up in wanting to incorporate him back into her life. Taking a deep breath, holding her hands against her stomach, she bowed slightly and tried to contain the hub of enthusiasm turning inside; and gently applied the brakes. Calm down, she thought. *Calm down.*

"Would you like to come and sit with me so we can talk and catch up on everything? I'd like to know how you've been and what's happened." Her voice was quiet and more thoughtful, and he responded.

"Yes, okay. Yes."

Dean didn't know what to say. He decided it would be okay to talk more, and she shoved a tray to one side to allow him space to sit in a winged armchair by the fireplace. The black grate was dusty and once colourful tiles on either side were dulled by smoke and soot. Dean liked sitting by a real fire. Before Uncle Ralph died he'd enjoyed toasting bread on a long twisted fork in front of the mock-marble surround in his house, and despite the fire being merely *coal-effect* it still seemed like it was a real fire. And certainly the toast always tasted good. He watched the flames flicker, and heard a hiss as gas escaped from a cobble of coal.

"You can scc pictures in a fire," Miss Jones remarked, observing the expression on Dean's face. He looked thoughtful. "Do you see anything? What can you see?" she asked.

"Nothing. Nothing, really." He didn't want to say. Just that week he'd been shouted at by Mrs Anderson who'd told him to *go to hell and burn with the wicked people!* Dean imagined the flames were like those in hell where the devil lived and tortured people. It was where demons were. All sorts of terrible things happened in hell. Being burnt must be awful, he thought.

"I'd sit for hours with my father and look at the pictures in the fire," Miss Jones reflected, deep lines appearing on her face as the light played across it. "He used to be so creative in what he said he saw, and sometimes he told me very long and unbelievable stories which I knew he couldn't possibly see, but I liked his stories. I loved them." She paused for a moment. Dean looked a million miles away;

remote, almost unapproachable somehow. "So, it was your birthday yesterday?" she announced cheerfully again. "I wish I'd known. I would have got you something." It seemed important to engage with Dean and listen to what he'd got to say instead of waffling on with all her stuff.

"Thanks."

"I like your bike. Who got it for you?"

"Mum and Dad."

"I thought so. It's wonderful. I expect you'll be thrilled."

"Yes. I'm really pleased." His tone of voice betrayed him. He wanted to love it again, to keep it shiny and new, but he saw the pictures in his head of when he tried to wreck it. It was a good bike. But he wasn't thrilled anymore. It was too much like hard work, he thought, trying to hold onto enthusiasm. Dean looked at her from beneath his tousle of hair. She looked older in the soft light of the fire, more frail, and she had a sad face now, sadder than he remembered.

"How are Mum and Dad?" she asked brightly, noticing his gaze, trying to hide the concern she felt, acknowledging that she too felt some anger and hostility toward his parents. Keeping her curiosity in check, she waited, hoped he trusted her enough now to tell her what his life was really like, so that she could respond and offer him a new life, an enduring life.

"Okay." His voice was flat, but he understood the question well enough. He suddenly remembered he was twelve now, near enough a teenager, and he should feel grown-up and talk like a grown-up. His last school report declared that he was – *a somewhat immature boy for his years* – and Dad had laughed, 'What do they bloody expect? He's a bloody kid isn't he?' It was time to be a man now, Dean thought, to be able to look after himself.

"Okay? Good," Miss Jones responded, without pushing it.

"You came to look for me, didn't you?" He glanced at her, his eyes intense. He would take-up the challenge of having a proper conversation, and not being a kid anymore. He would tell her what it was really like for him.

"Oh. How did you know?"

"I heard a social worker say that you were asking after us, me and Mum."

"Yes." There was no point in hiding it. The boy knew. "Yes, I did. I thought something terrible might have happened."

"It was fine. We're okay now." The resolve crumpled instantly within him. "My dad and mum are back together and they like it better now," he lied. He didn't want to say more. An opportunity had passed and he wondered why it was so hard to speak, to tell her about things. He tried to dislodge a weird sense of loyalty and a foolish hope, and he failed.

"Good. I'm so glad. Families should be together."

It hurt him when she said that, but he wouldn't show it. He knew what she said was right, but his family would never be together. If Dad came back Mum would go, and if they did get together he'd be taken away anyway, so what was the use? It was all stupid.

"Do you want to tell me about what happened, Dean? I'd like to hear." Miss Jones' voice was firm, almost directive, but she felt his hurt, saw a flicker of pain darken his eyes, and made an empathic connection which cut her to the bone. She carried his pain and anguish and as much as she wanted to reach out to him she knew he'd flinch and retract, mind, soul and body, from her touch. She knew what it was to carry a burden, and to be lost and lonely in the world. John stirred within her, began to seep through the layers of consciousness she'd gradually put in place again. It would be better to leave things alone.

"It's okay now. It was just…nothing. It was nothing." She'd taken him off guard – being so direct. But how could he start to say? What could he tell her? Who would understand the love, and hate, he felt for Mum and Dad? Who would understand the shame, the rejection, and the repulsion, the aching need for those he loved and yet despised when he didn't understand it himself?

She looked at the expression on his face, the bright flames of the fire reflected in his big sad eyes. She wouldn't push it. He would tell her in his own time. He looked lost, but at least he'd found his way back here.

"Dean, will you keep on coming to see me. I can't tell you how much it means to me."

"Yes." His voice was hushed, flat. He looked up quickly, and turned away again, eyes fixed on the fire. "Yes. Okay."

She was content with that. "Look, Dean, you come round whenever you want to. We've got to make plans, as you know."

The future was good again, and both knew if they worked and worked *and worked* they could distract themselves from the torture and torment of impotence.

*

Over the next few days, Dean called every day, sometimes after school, once or twice before school, but more often instead of school. Miss Jones didn't think to question it. Why would it matter ultimately? she thought, and dismissed it from her consciousness. His visits filled her life with light, and his enthusiasm blossomed. Dean was always thinking up new things to do, and ways to do them, and she didn't want to discourage him.

He remembered his idea to use the space under the floorboards. He was pleased that she listened, and despite their difficulties in getting the first board free, once it had been removed the rest were relatively easy. Miss Jones laughed when she saw the dust and dirt beneath the planks again. It was better to suffer the mess rather than disappoint or hurt the boy. As they shovelled and brushed dust and muck into a bucket, they coughed and spluttered, and Dean said most of the dust in a house was human skin. A teacher said that, told the class, and they shuddered and winced in comprehension. Miss Jones laughed when Dean said dryly that with so much dust they could add water and make another person; someone else to help them out.

"Just look at that, Dean," she exclaimed, holding a cigarette packet between her thumb and fingers, shaking dust from the creases. "My father used to smoke these when I was girl. We didn't know it was bad for you," she chuckled. "Some old adverts even said smoking was good for your throat!" she laughed. She enjoyed telling Dean about her visits to the theatre with her father, and how in those days everyone smoked in the audience and sometimes it made the actors cough.

Everyone smoked these days too, Dean thought, recalling the stink in the flat after Dad watched football on the television. Mum smoked too, chain-smoked through tedious programmes where people argued and cheated on each other, and said she loved to watch soaps because they were an escape from life. She sucked nicotine and blew clouds until they hung heavy in the room. The school nurse once expressed concern that Dean had got a 'glue ear' due to the nicotine and tar.

"If you find any money it's mine!" Miss Jones laughed again, her face dancing with delight. She felt so happy now he was back. They decided the space under the floor downstairs was good enough to store things, especially heavy tins, but upstairs, where old electricity cables crazed in a bird's nest over brittle plaster, Miss Jones thought it best to be cautious and put nothing on the crumbling joists.

Dean made other suggestions over the weeks. Why didn't she unpack some of the boxes and store the tins in tighter rows? The packaging was too bulky, and took up rather a lot of space. Miss Jones was delighted and rewarded his efforts by letting him have a wardrobe in a front bedroom. He brought some of his belongings from home, and smuggled a few cans and bottled water. It was a start.

Over the weeks she allowed him to read her scrapbooks and cuttings, and it was clear that she was right. Nostradamus predicted the end of the world; Dean knew his name now. The engraved picture of him, dressed in a funny hat, with a long white beard, made him look like what God would look like, Dean thought. He looked like someone who would know when the end of the world would come. She read him an article on HIV/AIDS, and other diseases which threatened to spread like wildfire throughout the world. In Africa the population was being decimated, and they looked at photographs of children with sad faces and eyes full of tears and fear. Another magazine showed bodies being buried in a long, wide grave – a mass grave; bodies wrapped in crumpled sheets, bodies indistinct under the bonds of tape and rope, lying in terrible rows along the bottom. Then he read a piece in the *National Geographic* magazine in the school library. It said on the front that ants would inherit the earth. Carefully he ripped out the pages and stuffed them in his pocket when the school librarian slipped outside onto the fire escape for his usual unofficial and unscheduled smoke. He told Miss Jones as soon as he could that they needed to buy *Nippon* and *Deathlac.*

"Why? What harm will ants be?"

"They get in the foundations. They could wreck everything. Look!" He pulled the crumpled pages from his fleece and showed her the article. "They make tunnels in the cement and mortar, and over time they carry out every speck of sand until the building falls down." A cinema in Wisconsin had collapsed and fifteen people had been killed. She scrutinized the photographs of serious officials pointing to holes in the brickwork and foundations, and she agreed. After checking her budget she considered her income would meet the extra demand.

"We need to check its sell-by date," he said earnestly, recalling his mother saying the same on the few times she went shopping, dragging him with her. Sell-by dates were important.

"Yes, of course. Smart boy, Dean," she praised him.

Smart boy. He liked it. It was good to receive her approbation. He liked it when she said he was smart, or clever. Once she said he would be a wise man like her father, and he felt embarrassed. He was glad she didn't know him that well. How could anyone think him wise? He'd been the downfall of his parents, and teachers at school didn't see any particular merit in what he did, or who he was. In his mind's eye Dean saw himself as useless. Miss Jones offered him some small measure of hope, but she was old and probably addled, so it didn't really count. But still, it was good when she praised him. No-one else had done that since Uncle Ralph died.

"How do you think it will end, Miss Jones?" he asked.

"How? I don't know. I can't imagine. I feel pretty sure that when the global warming gets really bad crops will fail and water will dry up and go. I read that. It said this country would have long and terrible summers, droughts and massive storms, driving the land to dust, and then in the winter there would be awful floods. If the sea-levels rise some parts of the country will disappear. We're lucky here because this part of the town is on a hill, and this house is nearly at the highest point, so if the land floods, we'll be safe and dry up here. If the food runs out, we'll be able to eat. And when the droughts come, we'll have this store of water."

"But think about the millions of people who would be wiped out." Dean added, trying to imagine what the devastation would mean. "Think of all the bodies!"

"We'll have to keep ourselves shut in here for years to avoid the diseases," Miss Jones said in a matter-of-fact voice that troubled him. "In time we'd be able to go out again, but until the world settles down again we'll have to sit tight."

"Yes. Yes, we'd have to." His voice was deep in his chest, weighed down by an indistinct and uncertain feeling stuck on the verge of being expressed.

"But we've heeded the warnings haven't we? Like Noah and his Ark. We've seen the signs and took notice. When the rest die we'll survive. I sit day after day and watch them you know, from my window. And I can tell by their faces the end is near!"

That night Dean watched his mother as she chain-smoked and stared at the television. Her face, blue in the harsh light, was unblinking and deathlike. She was already dead, Dean thought. She wouldn't even notice if the end of the world came, she'd be too busy talking to the social worker, who he had to call Mark now, or watching her *favourite* soaps; though to Dean it seemed she indiscriminately watched every single episode of all the soaps nowadays. Her short-lived fondness for him had withered and retreated and she relapsed into what she was before, indifferent and distant, only now Billy wasn't there to squabble and provoke and eventually rage until they poured more emotional paraffin onto their destructive fire; leaving Dean, in the past, to carry an inevitable feeling of culpability.

*

"Tell you what we could do," he said one day as Miss Jones let him in. "We could build sheds in the garden and orchard!"

"Sheds? We've got the outhouses."

"No, Miss Jones. Sheds as well. I was thinking about it all day. When I leave school and if the world hasn't ended, I can get a job and with the money I save we could buy sheds from *Handy Jack*. I'll put them up. It'll give us a lot more space. How many more years would that be?" He danced from foot to foot in his excitement. He had the idea clearly set in his mind and saw a picture of himself sawing wood and banging in nails.

"You are as smart as my dear father, young man." She moved to hug him, but he stepped aside and turned his back to her as if to go outside or something. It felt funny when she tried to get close to him. Miss Jones understood, and pretended to straighten her belt buckle.

Over tea she asked him about school and home, more from a need to be pleasant and supportive rather than from the morbid curiosity she'd felt before. She rarely asked about his mum and dad; they'd developed a tacit understanding that the subject was better left alone, and Miss Jones was well able to recognise times when the boy had been affected by something, and tailor her approach toward him on those days. He didn't say much as his head was usually buzzing with ideas, and it made him restless. Besides, there wasn't much to say on either count. He hardly attended school and felt it was a waste of time now the world was ending, and the social worker made yet another visit to see his mum, the sixth that week, and Dean overheard him asking her, despite his whispers, what *they'd* do when Billy got out. It didn't occur to Dean that the social worker referred to himself and Patsy. Dean wasn't really included in their dealings, as he appeared to be happy, settled, and mostly, out of their way.

Dad coming out of prison didn't seem real now, it had been so long since his incarceration, and Dean rarely thought of him. He'd gradually grown to understand the uselessness and futility of hope and aspiration when it came to his parents – and yet despite that, he increasingly became inspired by the notion of survival. It would prove him to be a man, strong and true, like Uncle Ralph. When Miss Jones encouraged him to grow and to express himself he flourished into maturity. And yet, he felt a need to be distant and still, to watch and to wait in the way Uncle Ralph showed him, when fishing at the side of the mere – but in that he acknowledged the end wasn't always what you expected it to be and you had to work hard to get through it. Young as he was, Dean looked out onto the world and knew he'd survive now, and he'd survive everyone. He felt powerful for the first time in his life.

Fourteen /

Mark Tomlinson was on his case, and after threatening Dean with the inevitable 'place of safety' stuff again – this time because missing school constituted his being 'out-of-control' – Dean decided it would be best to make a few appearances in school until it all died down again. It was tiresome hearing constantly that he was affecting his mum by his behaviour and ironic too since her behaviour wasn't being taken into account anymore. The only time she became animated and sincere was when the social worker made his ever increasing visits. Now, in the echoic classroom, the boy reached into his place of stillness and tranquillity and watched and waited.

Dean looked out of the window. The teacher droned on and although they should have been working in small groups, Mr Smith liked the sound of his own voice and tried to get the children to listen to more of his stories. Dean thought about how many tins of food would be eaten in a day, then a week, and finally tried to multiply it in his head into a year, but he couldn't. He wondered too if tins would really last for years, but compensated his anxiety when he thought he might be able to trap food, rabbits and things. Uncle Ralph had kept ferrets before he died, and he was always going round to Mum's offering her 'a couple of fresh conies.' Mum hated them. After he'd gone she threw them into the wheelie bin. 'How the hell does he expect me to eat them?' she'd say. 'I can't cut their heads off! My God, and take their insides out!' Dad laughed in his sarcastic way, but didn't offer to do it. But would there be any rabbits? Dean thought. Wouldn't they all die too? He would ask Miss Jones later.

When Sandra Roberts asked to go to the toilet, Mr Smith paused for a moment, frowned, and reluctantly allowed her to go. *Toilets. Yes, toilets,* Dean thought suddenly, as if another light had been switched on in his head. If the world ended there wouldn't be anyone to work the sewers and things, and maybe they'd be damaged anyway so they wouldn't flush. How would they go to the toilet? He tried to imagine how he could make a toilet work – but finally resolved that they would have to do it in a bucket or something. He thought of Miss Jones squatting in the back garden, and of himself peeing into a grid, and he became uncomfortable. A rush of anxieties made him hot and flustered. What about washing, bathing, his need to be private? How would he ensure she didn't see him when he needed to do those things, or worse still, if he saw her? Dean's unease grew into panic, and he fidgeted in his hard wooden seat, began to crease the paper in front of him. There were so many worries, so many things they'd have to get straight. He didn't hear Mr Smith at first, his mind was too full, too noisy, but he felt the hand on his shoulder.

"Are you paying attention, Dean Cartwright?"

"Yes…" Dean jumped, felt a shock like electricity run through him. Everyone turned and looked.

"What was I saying?" Mr Smith asked quietly, but there was a threat in his soft voice.

"You were talking about when you…when you…" Dean tried to recall some of Mr Smith's stories, but none came. His mind emptied of everything and he felt like his skull would implode into the vacuum. "I don't know, Mr Smith."

"You don't know. Fine. Don't I deserve a little bit more respect than that, Dean?"

"Yes, sir." Dean retreated into his blankness – blank face, blank feeling – just be, just do, just say what they want to hear. It was safe there. He could face him out.

"Perhaps you'd like to tell us about the important thoughts and daydreams which occupy you. Maybe you'd like to tell us why they're more important than your lessons."

"Yes, sir."

"Go on then, Dean. Share them with us."

"What?"

"Tell us what goes on in your head, what shifts behind your inscrutable face."

"Nothing, sir."

"Nothing? You mean you're just an empty head?"

The children laughed, though some shifted uneasily behind their laughter.

"Yes, sir." Dean thought about the end. It was coming. When it came Smith would be dead, so no matter how difficult the other problems might be, he'd be able to solve them. He'd be alive. He fought with a compulsion to smile, to shout out the truth and laugh. But he'd keep the face on. Be blank. Stay blank.

Mr Smith moved away, walked slowly to his desk in the corner. He cleared his throat and resumed his story. Dean stared at him, eyes fixed on his face, gave him what he needed, gave him attention, and as long as he could keep staring, he'd be okay, he could resume his reverie, bathe in the luxury of knowing he would live and Mr Smith would die like the rest of them. But something he said triggered a different kind of listening and woke Dean up to his words.

"Yes, as I was saying, it is crucial to understand what will happen when the world warms up. We have to start taking care of the environment now, and it's your generation which has to carry more responsibility for the future. You have to fight. You have to take care because I'm afraid the previous generations have let you down."

"What about the asteroid thing they say will hit us?" someone asked.

"The comet, you mean?" Mr Smith corrected.

"Yes. I think so. Will one hit us, sir?"

"There's been a bit of speculation about the possibility. Certainly comets orbit the sun in the same way the earth does, and as their orbits get closer then there's a profound possibility a comet will collide with the world."

“When, sir?” another voice nervously asked.

“I don’t know. Recently Jupiter, the largest planet in our solar system was struck by a comet. Do you remember the work we did on the planets? Come on, anyone? I’m so glad you use my lessons to catch up on your sleep!” he said, voice edgy and sarcastic.

“I remember, sir,” someone said quickly from the back of the classroom. “We did that stuff about a rock-thingy hitting the world and killing off all the dinosaurs and stuff.”

“It was a spectacular sight. The comet broke up and hit Jupiter several times causing massive ripples in the atmosphere, and sending huge flares into the surrounding void! It was caught on film, and the discussion around it revealed just how unsafe the solar system is, and maybe some time planet earth could be struck by a comet or an asteroid – the *rock-thingy* to use your erudite terminology. Better keep your heads down when that happens!” he laughed, somewhat cruelly as he scanned the frightened faces before him.

“Yes, but we could nuke them couldn’t we, sir?” another girl asked, looking less anxious than her peers. “We could send rockets up and blow them apart before they strike the world. We could do that couldn’t we? My dad says scientists have all the answers and we’ll be okay.”

“Much as I respect your father’s view, it would be incredibly tricky to do that. A nuclear explosion might break the asteroid or comet up and send lots of small, but equally lethal pieces hurling earthwards. It would be a scatter bomb causing incredible devastation. Now, it has been argued nuclear bombs could divert the direction of the offending piece of space junk, and send it packing into another direction – but the jury’s out on that one.”

“But is it going to happen, sir? Will one hit us? Will it be during my life? I don’t want to die.”

The class took a collective deep breath, and shuddered at the possibility of death. Thumbs fidgety from texting became still within clamped and clammy hands, as dread filled their hearts and minds. One girl frowned so much and looked so troubled, Mr Smith felt a sudden, though transient guilt, and thought it best to rescue her. He didn't want grumbling parents at the Head's office door.

"Maybe it will be in your lifetime, maybe it won't. I honestly think you need to consider the heating-up of the planet to be the greatest threat to humankind and if the climate changes the environment will suffer horribly." Despite his effort to soften the blow a zealous little preacher sprang stridently into his mouth, and inevitably laced his words. It didn't help the girl at all. She was on the verge of bursting into tears.

"What will happen?" A nervous voice reiterated the insidious fear creeping over the children.

"There will be famine and water shortages – great droughts in some places, awful floods in others. Even now as I speak there are glaciers which are disappearing and they'll never come back. If the ice-shelves melt the sea-levels could rise dramatically, so there will be less land for an already overpopulated world. Too many people in a small space could lead to wars as they fight to hold onto, or claim new territory!"

"Is it too late?" a child asked in a small voice. "Is it too late to change?"

"No, that's the thing. It needn't be!" Mr Smith enthused. He'd hooked them in, but after frightening them it would be better now to offer hope, despite his own entrenched misgivings that it was already too late, and the generation sitting here before him faced cataclysmic changes in their lifetime. "If we take really good care of the planet, if we recycle, start to work on problems like transport, cars and the like…" His words felt hollow and insincere. He was glad he was near to retirement, and he planned to sell up and live in the mountains somewhere in Portugal.

Dean wasn't listening now. He felt a deep satisfaction. They wouldn't plan. They would go home turn on the telly and forget.

Miss Jones had seen it and she planned and did things in readiness for what was to come. He wanted to run out of the class and ride like mad to see her and maybe even give her a big hug. She was the wisest, most brilliant person in the world because she knew. When everything ran out they'd be okay. They'd survive. They had a future.

*

No, it wasn't right and Dean knew it. Mark shouldn't have been there. It wasn't his job to be in the house so early in the morning, or so late at night, and again now when he returned home from school. Dean knew he lied when he said he'd come to check everything was alright, and he was concerned that both he and Patsy were coping. "It's my job," he said, but Dean saw him wink at his mum and he didn't like it.

"You don't need to come now," Dean snapped. "We're fine!"

Patsy looked different nowadays too. When she was alone with Dean she slouched and smoked and didn't bother about how she looked, but when the social worker visited she was dressed-up, made-up, and had a sassy look about her – the kind of look girls had in the top year of the Comprehensive School in Welsh Row. The room smelled of perfume. Dean knew it meant something, but didn't want to think about it. It would be awful to picture them doing stuff to each other.

"We're fine on our own!" he snarled again. "Why don't you leave us alone?"

"Don't be so rude, Sweetie," Patsy said with horror in her voice, "After everything Mark has done for us."

"It's okay," Mark smiled and tried to tousle Dean's hair, but the boy pulled away from his outstretched hand.

"Dean! Don't be awful!" Patsy shouted.

Mark flushed, but ever so slightly, and said he needed to get to work anyway. "Give me a ring if you need anything," he offered, his eyebrows high on his forehead and he held onto Patsy's hand for a moment too long, his fingers lingering on hers. He winked at the boy, trying to make his face look unconcerned and distant, like the faces professional people adopted when they messed you about, told you what was best for you. Dean wasn't a fool. He understood. He'd go and see Miss Jones, try to rescue something good out of the day, tell her about the stuff the teacher had been saying, and that she was right. She was the only person in the world who was doing something about it, except for one more now – him, Dean Cartwright, the inscrutable boy, the lugubrious boy, the blank boy.

She welcomed him as she usually did, but noticed immediately the darkness in his mood despite the note of enthusiasm and affirmation in his voice. He said one thing, but felt another. Though struck by his incongruence, she decided to leave it alone; he would tell her if he needed to. They stuck to the rules of silent acknowledgement. Knowing but not saying.

Despite the onset of winter, the sun was bright and illuminated the gloom of the ever-shrinking capacity of the house, and often, they worked in silence as they moved through their allotted tasks. Sometimes, when they took a break, sipping tea and sucking on the dunked ginger biscuits, they stared at the world as it made its way beyond the window. The station crossing was undergoing repairs, and for some time a temporary traffic light controlled the flow of cars, buses and lorries. Wellington Road was a busy enough street, but now the cars thickened into a clot as they queued to move into the town. Miss Jones pointed towards the line of gleaming paint and chrome, not in admiration of bodywork or engineering, but because of the fumes curling up between the branches of the denuded beech.

"If you were in a car like that, but in the garage, doors shut, with the engine running, you'd soon be overcome and then you'd die," she said, quietly. "And every day the roads get locked under the strain of ever-increasing traffic. I went on the motorway once, the M6, and we got stuck in a jam so big it stretched out as far as the eye could see, in front, and behind, and up the slip roads. All those cars, mostly with one person in each; and all those fumes. And where do you think the fumes go?" She moved her head upwards, eyes rising under lids, and pointed a long and gnarled finger to the sky.

Dean smiled in acknowledgement of her truth. She was probably the cleverest person he knew. He gazed at her old face and fancied that through the shallow and translucent skin he could see her wisdom. Her cleverness was deeper and better than even that of the teachers, and the politicians he sometimes heard speak on the television. They used loads of words and said nothing, nothing at all. When Miss Jones spoke he listened now.

*

Several days later he heard them talking in the kitchen. They hadn't realized the boy was in the bathroom and pretty much heard everything they said despite their lowered voices. He caught more than the gist of a troubled conversation. Over the years he'd grown into a hyper-vigilant boy, learnt to walk on egg-shells, and be wary of mood and tone and pitch of voice. He peeped through the crack in the door too, and saw their reflection in the hall mirror as they moved in the kitchen. Mrs Anderson had reported Mark. She'd said he was showing an *unprofessional interest* in Mrs Cartwright. Dean felt pleased. He knew Dad was going to be released in the next few days, and if Mark got out of the way maybe there'd be a chance Dad would come back home. Dean's biggest fear was if he came home and found the social worker with his mum, he would kill him and would end up in prison again.

“We’ve got to cool it. I could lose my job,” Mark said, trying to distance himself from Patsy. “The nosy old bag has stitched me up.”

“But Billy’s coming out!”

“I can’t get involved. It’s too precarious, Patsy. The police know. You’ll be okay.” He waved his hands, made funny little motions with his fingers, like he was trying to shape something.

“No, Mark, don’t say that. It sounds like you’re finishing it. Please don’t talk like that.” She tried to touch him, reaching out for his arm, but he shrugged her away. For the first time in years she’d felt that someone truly valued her, but now she fell into the old residual mush of past emotions - the previous negative expectations and devalued hopes, trundled and trampled by the boots of bitter experience. She struggled to defy the thoughts, the profoundly energetic but negative feelings announcing that she’d been used and abused. But it was useless. They were too powerful, too possible.

“Look if I end up being investigated I’ll be for the chop. I can’t risk it. I can’t,” Mark said, coldly.

He confirmed it. She had been used. He was looking after himself now.

“If you leave me I’ll report you myself. I’ll tell them everything!” Patsy was angry now in her desperation. Her voice rose, and she suddenly stopped, glanced through the open door and spoke more quietly. “You can’t bloody well dump me Mark! I need you more than ever!”

“Okay, okay! Let me think. I can’t think!” He panicked. “Let’s cool it off for a week or two and then…”

“No!” she screeched, and slammed the door to.

Dean wasn’t quiet when he left the house either. He clattered his bike against the doorway, and pushed the kitchen door open. He wanted to let them know he’d heard. Patsy looked at him with shock on her face, but Mark turned and stared out of the window. She tried to look normal, but her face was streaked with tears, and despite dabbing them with a towel she still looked terribly upset. "Baby, where are you going?" Her voice was shaky, uncertain.

"Let the kid go out," Mark said, gruffly.

"Where are you going?"

"For a ride, I'm just going for a ride."

"Be careful, Sweetie." She tried to hug him, but Dean was too angry for that.

Outside he saw the curtains move at Mrs Anderson's front window – the eye to the world – the eye that saw everything. He smiled and waved at first, but then pulled his face into an ugly and vicious expression, before finally sticking his fingers up at her. He wondered whether to drop his trousers and show her his bare backside, but then thought that would be a good one to save for another time, another day.

The dim, but ample shape of Mrs Anderson retreated into the gloomy room, fizzing and popping and buckling under her wrath. "What was the world coming to?" she hissed, and cursed the nasty boy. But inside she felt vindicated. Next door voices rose further, and quietly she pressed her ear to the wall and listened. Give people enough rope, she thought, and knew she was right. Someone, somewhere, had to take responsibility.

Fifteen /

"You go and find whatever you think is suitable, Dean. You have such clever ideas, and I can't tell you how much happier I feel knowing you're with me in this."

Miss Jones touched his face gently, and for once he allowed her to. "Do you know, young man, I suppose you are like a son to me," she said softly, a powerful feeling welling up inside.

"Am I?" He was a bit nervous; first the touch on his face, and now this. He didn't want to be her son. Just now he didn't want to be anyone's child.

"You certainly are. You are the son I never had."

"Why didn't you, Miss Jones? Why didn't you get married and have kids and stuff?" Dean peered into her face. He thought it better if she talked about the kids she might have had, instead of trying to make him into one.

Her eyes looked beyond him, as if she peered into some distant place where her memories resided. "I did have a couple of young men who courted me. I wasn't so bad looking, you know," she said, trying to remind herself of what it was to be young and attractive. "There was one young chap who had a shock of ginger hair. He showed a great deal of interest in me for a time. He worked in the railways as a clerk. I played it a bit too coolly though, and he got married to my cousin. He became a top man in the works, and they had three children. I was Godmother to one of them – Bethan Grace – the most beautiful baby you ever saw. She was a stunner. That was the nearest I ever came to motherhood. She's grown up now and probably has children of her own." Miss Jones shook her head, and gently touched her chest, as if trying to feel her heart, but then she smiled, suddenly. "There was someone else, but it never really got off the ground." She thought of the librarian, Malcolm Robertson, and felt it best to say nothing more. He was well known in the town, and Dean may well have known him too. "I suppose my greatest love was my father, Dean. He was a good and handsome man. You're very like him." She wanted to touch his face again, but felt it would be too much. "I was a daddy's girl, you know. I was. I thought the world of my father, and he of me. I think it scared a lot of men off. My father was a wise and compassionate man who had the capacity to forgive anything. They couldn't hold a candle to him." Her voice dropped and she spoke almost in a whisper, and now her face changed and sadness crept across it. "Anyway, what about you? Do you have a girlfriend?" It hadn't occurred to her before, but she felt uneasy in asking. It could be tricky. She'd not considered the implication of that.

"No," he said abruptly, not through embarrassment, rather through a lack of opportunity or interest. He didn't see himself as boyfriend material, and his steady growth into adulthood so far precluded any great desires in that direction. He liked girls, especially the older girls who walked through the town after school, stopping to lounge on the benches surrounding the War Memorial. They smoked and laughed while they played with their mobile phones. When Dean rode over the uneven pavements they paid him no attention. He was a kid. Once he sat across from four young women and watched them from the corner of his eye as they laughed and gossiped and he so badly wanted to grow-up and have someone as pretty as they were to love him. He'd never treat a girl like his dad had treated Mum. Dean would be loyal and sober and loving. He would never hit a woman. Ever.

Miss Jones folded sheets of brown paper and placed them into a box. "It's a sad world, young man. You never know what's going to happen. I wanted a family, and it didn't happen, well, not then. Look now! I've got you. You are like a son to me, and I'm so grateful you're here. We'll be best pals forever, won't we, Dean."

"Yes." Dean felt awkward, a bit uncomfortable. He felt as if she was going to take him over or something, like he had become too important in her life, and she would love him to bits and it scared him. It felt okay when they were busy doing things, packing, shifting, carrying stuff into the house, but when she got smoochy like this he felt faintly disgusted. Occasionally when she wasn't looking he watched her. He was fascinated by her age, the wrinkles on her face, and the knobbly hands which looked like they couldn't work, and yet they did. He watched her now, smoothing the brown paper, the knotty fingers still weirdly articulate. Her eyes were dim, and the whites yellow, and her face sagged somewhat, the skin under her chin loose and papery. Once she bent over in front of him and he couldn't help but look down the gaping neckline of her dress. Her withered breasts were dead white, nothing like the breasts he'd seen on the girls in his dad's newspapers, or of those who lounged around the benches on the Square. Miss Jones smelled old too. She had a sour fragrance, a musty smell like old books, or damp clothes, and when she touched his face and tried to hold him, which she did increasingly, Dean shrank against the odour. It made him feel bad, guilty, and ashamed. Hadn't she been so kind to him? She wanted to give him the gift of life, to ensure his survival, just like a proper mother would.

"I'd best be going," he said, his voice strained under the heavy thoughts. "I've seen some stuff at the back of the Civic Hall, and I think there are some wooden boxes behind one of the sheds on Paddy's Field."

"You make sure they don't belong to anyone, and don't say what you need them for if anyone asks, Dean," Miss Jones reminded him, though trusted him to be careful and not bring attention to their plans. She watched him wheel his bike along the path, and waved to him from the front window. What a beautiful boy, she thought, my beautiful boy.

*

Dean decided that time must surely be running out now, and he renewed his efforts to seek out and find anything which may be useful. He made lists in his clumsy handwriting, and drew-up plans to ensure their survival. He got excited and his keenness made him sleep badly and worry a lot. When he attended school, which he hardly ever did, he listened carefully to what the teachers said, especially Mr Smith, who had knowledge of important things. But it was never mentioned again. The end of the world was coming and they'd talked about it for a moment, and then forget it again, probably by the time the bell rang and ended the lesson. Miss Jones said people were shallow, and Dean understood her comments. For them every day was an opportunity to gather and to strengthen their plans, ensure their survival, and gradually Miss Jones obsession rooted into the core of Dean's heart and mind. The house creaked and groaned under the weight of supplies, and since they'd opened-up a deep and damp cellar, something Miss Jones had previously avoided, more space became available and was ideal to store water. It was cool and dark, and Dean filled every hole he could find in-between the bricks with *Polyfilla* so that rats and mice were unable to enter the store and nibble at the countless plastic bottles containing their supply of drinking water.

"This is your domain!" Miss Jones had exclaimed in her sing-song voice. "I can't bear the thought of all the creepy-crawlies! You look after this place, young man!" Gradually, she gave him more duties, allowed him more space for himself, and eventually dropped any pretence at boundaries. What was hers was his too. She knew he was integrated with the work and the shaping of a future. She trusted him.

*

"What are you doing?"

He was startled and dropped his load. He'd been getting

cardboard from the skips at the back of the Civic Hall. It was good stuff, clean and rigid, and someone had taken the time to fold and press it so that it filled less space in the skip. It was ideal for carrying, Dean thought and weighed-up how he'd attach it to the crossbar of his bike.

"What are you doing'?" the voice repeated, this time more inquisitive in tone.

He turned quickly to see a girl, legs straddling her bike, face bright and curious.

"Mind your own business! Sod off!" His reaction of hostility surprised him; but he'd grown in his need to be cautious, defensive. She looked harmless, and yet, she was a stranger. He had to be careful.

"Charming! Do you always speak like that?" She grinned as she spoke.

"Yes! Go on. I'm busy!" By now Dean was pulling at a length of clear plastic, trying to dislodge it from beneath several boxes in the middle of the skip. One strong pull released it and he scrutinised it for tears or punctures. He could wrap it around the cardboard now, and later, and find a use for it in the cellar, possibly to line the floor and protect stored items from damp. He glanced at her again, and decided to ignore her in the hope she'd lose interest and go away.

"What do you want the plastic for? Making a fish pond? My Uncle Stan made a fish pond with plastic like that. It's dead good and he's got goldfish in it, and some frogs. They had frogspawn last year, and some baby newts and a heron got his fish too, speared one with its long beak, right through its body, and stabbed it to death, so he got a net thing over it…"

"Big deal!" Dean was irritated that she'd not gone.

"You come with me an' I'll show it you and you can get a good idea of how to do it. He only lives up the estate," she persisted. "Where'd you come from?" She lifted her leg over the bike and moved towards him. The gears clicked smoothly. She fiddled with the brakes, all the time looking hard at him, not moving her eyes away.

Her persistence bothered him. He didn't want to talk just now, just to think and plan. She was getting on his nerves.

"I'm busy!" he snapped, but to no avail.

"Want a hand?" she said, head tilting, mouth breaking into a huge smile.

"No!" Dean was aghast. The last thing he needed was a girl interfering. This was important work; secret work. He turned briefly to scrutinise her but couldn't place her face. Did she attend his school? He wasn't sure; but if she did there was nothing remarkable about her. She would've been just another face in the playground, just another girl. The fact he hardly attended school didn't help.

"You live round here? I'm sure I've seen you before, at school. You go to my school, don't you? Are you in Mr Barlow's class? He's nice. I hate Miss Davenport and Mr Smith, but Mr Teal's alright, and Mrs Blackburn. What's your name?"

"I don't go to your school," he lied. "I don't go to school because I've got a job."

"You do. I recognise you. What's your name?" She teased him now, she did know him, and she knew his name too. He was the quiet boy who bagged it most of the time, and some of the kids reckoned he was on drugs or something on account of him looking far-away all of the time, and they said he was a loner. "Go on then, tell me your name!"

Her laugh was gentle, not sarcastic or caustic. She liked the look of him, his hair and eyes, and the way he hid his face made her sure he was attracted. She wanted to play with him, string him along. Certainly, he didn't look like a kid who was spaced out and freaky. Sometimes she followed him at school. He was unaware of this, and the prodding girlfriends who pushed her into close proximity. He never knew, so it was a rich moment now having cornered him.

"Come on, what's your name?" she joshed again.

"Noah!" he barked as he dipped into the skip, shoving more boxes away so he could see what lay beneath them.

"Noah? Honest? God, what a great name. I don't know anyone called Noah, not in real life, anyway," she teased, wanting him to look up and see her. "I know about Noah's Ark and stuff, when the animals went in two by two and the rain came and drowned everything in the world except for Noah and his things."

Eventually he stopped and looked up at her again. Despite everything he was intrigued by her persistence. No girl had ever shown this much interest, and something stirred in him. She folded her arms under her small breasts and tilted her head. Under her denim jacket she wore a pink t-shirt with something written on it in sequins. He suddenly felt uneasy; embarrassed that he'd so obviously looked there. His face reddened, and he quickly turned away and dipped into the huge container. He'd climb inside it in a minute if she didn't go away. "You're a bloody pest!" he hissed, hoping she'd go and hoping she wouldn't. She didn't.

Her long brown hair was swept off her face in a pony tail, held by two pink bobbles, and her eyes were huge and dark. She liked pink, Dean thought. Actually, now he looked properly she was pretty and the way she stared made him blush even more. He pulled himself up onto the edge of the skip, scrambled his foot up onto its rim, and hauled himself over.

"I'm Mickey," she said, and waited for him to look at her again. She understood his anxiety. Girls knew stuff like that.

"That's a boy's name!" Dean scoffed, feeling she'd be offended and would go, at last, but then regretted saying that and risking her annoyance.

"No it isn't! It's *my* name. Well, anyway, it's my nickname, not my real name, see. My real name is Maureen, but I hate it, *Maureen,* so everyone calls me Mickey! My second name is Marsh see, so I'm Mickey Marsh! Get it? Mickey Marsh?" She laughed, but didn't wait for Dean to respond. "Do you like your name, Noah? Bet your parents are religious, hey? Bet they go to church, don't they? They must be religious, mustn't they, because Noah was in the Bible, wasn't he?" She teased mercilessly now as she pushed the bike nearer and looked over at him, still smiling sweetly.

Dean felt cross and stopped fiddling with the boxes and the plastic for a moment and thought about saying something really unpleasant, about how she was going to die and he wasn't. He was going to be okay, while she would definitely die; *definitely*. But he remembered the secret and he could tell no-one. He grimaced at her, which only served to bring her closer. "Go on, bog off, pest!" he hissed unconvincingly.

"I know! I am a pest!" She laughed. "And you're Dean Cartwright!"

"Why did you bloody well ask me then if you knew?" He felt annoyed, and intrigued by her.

"I was joshing you, Deano." She remounted her bike, and leaned against the skip, turning her pedals backwards making them whir quictly. "What arc you doing?" she asked.

"Nothing."

"Oh," she said, "then why are you being so busy if you're doing nothing? When I do nothing, I don't do anything. Strikes me you're really busy, Noah."

He stifled a laugh. She was mad, he thought, really mad. "Do you ever stop rabbiting?" He tried to sound annoyed, or something, but his voice was light and he started to work intently again so as not to let her see his red face and betray the fact that he quite liked her. Her fingernails were painted pink too, he noticed as he surreptitiously glanced up again. Yes, he thought, she definitely liked pink. He clambered out of the skip, and stood for a moment looking at the collection of bits.

Mickey dismounted, put her bike carefully down on the tarmac, and moved towards him. "What are you going to use this for,

Noah?" she said, and offered to help him. She moved to his side, and crouched when he did.

Dean didn't move now. She had a nice smell of scented soap. It smelled good and he began to enjoy the sensation of being close to her. He noticed the whiteness of her legs under the short skirt, perfectly rounded knees, and her long fingers manipulating the plastic sheet. The pink varnish had been inexpertly brushed on her nails, and a thin ring of silver wire formed into a knot under a bony knuckle. He swallowed the saliva filling his mouth when her hand touched his as she helped him.

"What's it for?" she repeated.

"It's for lining my Ark," he joked but then felt guilty, and awkward. He had an image of Miss Jones, and he heard her words in his head about keeping everything secret, and here he was saying such stuff. But he felt guilty too that he'd lied to Mickey. She was nice. Pretty. Very pretty. Yes. She was really nice. He wished he'd seen her in school. She would have been someone to talk to. "It's a secret!" he blurted, his voice gruff. He felt stupid, like he'd confessed to something. Miss Jones face was in his head again, and she looked annoyed.

"A secret? What kind of secret?"

"I can't say." Dean didn't want to offend her now, didn't want to hurt her, and he worried that she had been. He glanced at her again, but this time for longer, trying to make out how she felt. Suddenly it mattered. He felt gawky like his body was too tight a fit. She knelt next to him, thoughtful and quiet for the first time. He liked it. He liked her near. She smelled good, and she looked good.

"What's so secret about this rubbish? What can you possibly do with bits of plastic and old cardboard boxes?" She laughed and came alive again. "So it's for your Ark, hey, Mr Noah? If it is can I come on board when the rain starts?"

"No. No girls allowed," he joked, relieved she was okay, not mad with him or anything.

“You’re a sexist pig! You’re going to need a woman on your Ark, to help you out. Bet you can’t cook and clean and sew!”

“No, I can’t,” he laughed.

“No, me neither!” She punched his arm playfully. “But I can look after the animals while you steer the ship. See, you’ll need a woman!”

“I’ve already got one!” he laughed, but went cold as he said it. He thought of the old woman sitting in the high-backed chair reading her cuttings and he felt a surge of disappointment shoot through his heart. She was old. It really hadn’t occurred to him before, not like this. He quickly wrapped everything up, and stacked it on his handlebars and seat. It wasn’t heavy, just awkward. The heaviness was in his head.

Mickey screwed up her face, frowning, as she watched him push his bike toward the main street. She grabbed hers, and scampered closely behind him. “Is she pretty?” she asked in a little voice, girly, but pointed.

“What?” Dean asked, blankly. Mickey broke into his thoughts. He felt lost.

“Your girl? Is she pretty?”

“No. No. I was only joking. I…I don’t have a girlfriend,” he said, unsure of what he said, and why he said it. It felt like he was free and trapped all in the same moment.

“Are you coming round here again, Noah?” she asked.

“Might do.” He didn’t know what to say or what to do. He wondered if she meant she wanted to date, or something. He felt stupid, not being able to say anything for sure. And yet inside he wanted to stop here and not move until they talked more and he could fathom what it was about her that pulled him like a powerful magnet.

“I might see you then,” Mickey responded coolly. She wondered if he liked her. “Might see you then,” she repeated, hoping he’d say more. “I’m usually around town,” she said finally, disappointed at his inability to respond. But deep down, she hoped he'd come looking for her.

At the corner, as he cranked reluctant feet against the pedals, he glanced back over his shoulder. Mickey glanced too, and waved, wobbled, and nearly struck the pavement with her front wheel.

*

"This looks useful," Miss Jones commented as he took the stuff off his bike and wrestled it in through the back door. "What is it going to be used for?" Dean was always good for ideas, and she trusted he'd started a new project.

"It's for… it's…" he stammered, unsure as to why he'd brought it here. He wasn't thinking straight now, his thoughts were bending towards the encounter he'd had an hour before. Mickey may well have ridden away, but she stayed firmly in his head. "I'm going to line the floor under the bottles in the cellar," he said at last, anxious that the old woman would not persist in a cross examination. His mind was fragile and unfixed for the first time in a long time.

"I'm going to make tea. Would you like a cup?" she asked, eyes narrowing. She sensed something different about the boy, and it unsettled her. "Are you alright, Dean?" she asked directly.

"Yes," he said firmly, feeling her question was issued to root beneath the surface of what he wanted to show her. "Look, I'll take this stuff down to the cellar," he offered, needing space to think about the day, and the meeting with Mickey. "I can sort it out down there."

"Right." Miss Jones peered intently at him. "You haven't taken it or anything?" she asked, observing his unease and discomfort. She thought he looked shifty, though disliked herself for thinking it.

"No. It was just rubbish. It was in a skip behind the Civic Hall." He felt anxious in even telling her where he'd been, as if she'd have eyes to trawl into his thoughts and see clearly into his mood.

Miss Jones decided to dismiss it as a problem at home, again, and felt it better not to go there. If Dean wanted to keep something private that was fine. She'd accept it. And yet, deep down, she felt something odd had happened and she began to fret a little.

In the cellar Dean squatted against the wall, a rounded back arched against the cold bricks, his arms wrapped round his legs. It was dark and quiet and still. So far under the house he heard nothing as Miss Jones mashed tea in the scullery above. He contemplated the confusion of ideas going around inside his head. It felt good and bad, wonderful and awful, and he either nodded his head or shook it. Sometimes the thoughts became feelings and he couldn't understand why they thrilled him. Mickey was lovely. She was. He went over every word, every action, regretting this moment, celebrating the next. Was it possible that she liked him in the way he liked her? And then Miss Jones walked in on the scene and pointed the way forward – pointed her gnarled finger toward the sky where a huge black cloud hung, pregnant with a million tons of storm. And he imagined sailing on an Ark, Mickey at his side, faces bright against the rising sea, bright and hopeful, and young. He wondered for a moment whether he'd fallen in love with her. Was this how it was? He imagined how others would see it – their scorn and derision, and yet he couldn't pull back from the huge feeling threatening to push him over the edge and into a mysterious freefall. Was it love?

The withered breasts hung before his face as Miss Jones perpetually offered him a cup of tea, and he caught the old scent and wondered if that is what death smelled like. He peered into the dark and knew he sat in a tomb where there was no sound, no light, and no hope. Something would be different about him, from this day forward, he would realise and understand choice, and in this realisation he would have to make the biggest decision of his young life. He had to choose – death or life.

*

That night Dean's mind was so charged and full of her he couldn't sleep, and he was certain he could smell her nice scented smell, but no matter how hard he tried he couldn't remember what she looked like. Fragmented images and fractured moments flitted in and out of his mind. He could imagine her eyes, her hair, her mouth, but couldn't put them into a complete picture. It thrilled him when he remembered all her pinkness, but now it blurred and became foggy and he realised he had to speak to her and tell her things so she could become stable and permanent – fixed in his head so he could really see her. She'd listen; he knew she'd understand. She would listen and smile and talk, and maybe she'd hold him and make everything alright. He wouldn't mind that. He'd like to hold her close, feel her skin and taste her breath. When the end of the world came he'd just stare at her face.

*

How long an hour is, how eternal a whole day; clocks stop at every glance, and sweet anticipation is set at a maddening pace, a heavy weight of gravity holding the fingers fast. Dean watched the time drag and ached to be free. Later, after school and every other chore stacked like an obstacle course, he returned in the hope of seeing her. But at the rear of the Civic Hall it was deserted. He waited for nearly an hour, until the cold day began to fall into colder dusk, and then he rode around every estate in Nantwich. He asked two girls sitting in a bus shelter if they knew a girl called Mickey, but they giggled and ignored him. It would be best now to leave it alone. Riding around in the hope of seeing her seemed pointless, and anyway, whatever she'd said, maybe she didn't really mean it. Maybe she didn't want to see him again. He decided to go home before it got too dark. His heart was heavier than he'd ever known;

more heavy than the guilt he bore for Mum and Dad; heavier still than any act of betrayal he might enact against Miss Jones.

The church clock struck the half-hour and pigeons flapped from the Square, rounded the tall War Memorial, and landed on the flat roof of the Bank, where they cooed and preened, and watched people park up and walk into the chippie and take-away, waited in anticipation of a crust of pizza, or the crumbs of a hot-dog dropped by the late night drunks. Dean glanced down Welsh Row, and in the moment of distraction nearly ran into Mickey who peddled like mad from the narrow entry in Castle Street.

"God! I'm glad I've seen you!" she laughed. "I've been all over looking for you!"

Dean was pleased. Really pleased. His heart pounded until he felt the blood pulse in his ears. She was more beautiful than he remembered, and her face fell into perfect symmetry after the tribulation of trying to piece her together had maddened him all the night before.

"I've been looking for you too." It was hard to shape words and speak them.

"Where have you been?" she quizzed breathlessly.

"I've been all over. We must have kept missing each other."

They straddled their bikes, moved them between their legs nervously, tilting the bright frames one way then another, fiddled self-consciously with the grips on the handle bars. Mickey's bike gleamed in the last light of the flaring sun.

"Is this a date?" she asked, impishly.

"'Spose," was all Dean managed to say. It would be good if it was. He'd never had a date. He'd never even thought about dating until now, and suddenly dating became the most important thing in his life.

"Great. I like that! A date! What do you want to do!" she smiled.

"I don't know? Go for a ride?"

"Yes. Okay. That would be good."

It wasn't long before they gravitated to the big park at the end of Beam Street and away from the centre of town. Without speaking, or making any awkward contact, they rode toward the cricket pavilion. It would provide them with time and space, and an opportunity to be together, alone. Dean's heart thumped, and his palms sweated. He wanted to hold her hand, but he worried the clammy skin would put her off, so when she looked away he surreptitiously wiped his palms against his coat. She parked her bicycle against the wooden rails bordering the cricket pitch and followed him up the dusty aisle to the back seats under the flaky white walls of the locked and boarded pavilion. How many times had he been here, by himself, to seek refuge from the war at home, respite from the battlefield of his parent's marriage? He remembered the desolation of his last visit, his determination to stay out all night and punish Mum for slapping him on his birthday. The pavilion was different tonight, despite the cold, it offered shelter.

Before he had time to sink into a sad reverie, Mickey flung her arms around his neck and kissed him. It was awkward, noses colliding as they tried to decide who would angle their head one way or another. But as soon as their lips touched it came to them as easily as breathing. Slowly he put his arms around her waist and pulled her toward him. Bodies touching they felt each other's heart pounding. Her fingers played with his hair, and touched his ears in such a gentle way it thrilled him, sent a shiver running through every fibre of his body. He'd never kissed a girl before.

As they pulled apart, Mickey smiled at him. He'd forgotten what it was like for someone to be this close – hugging-close. It felt good. Everything felt good – the smell of her, fresh like lilac blossom on a spring day; the taste on her lips, as sweet as chocolate, and a taste which lingered on the tongue and made his body crave for more; the warmth of her body on his, like a gentle sun stroking him back into life. At that moment he understood more than the years at school could prepare him for – an instinctual knowledge of the bliss this contact held for him – so powerful everything else in the whole wide world ceased to be important. Looking into her eyes changed everything about him. He felt taller, stronger, quicker, smarter, and happier. A grey world slipped into oblivion, a serious world, a desperate world, as his pupils dilated to take in every part of her. And for once, he felt young.

"You're really cool," she said, a broad smile announcing her pleasure of the moment. "Some of the girls really fancy you, and I'm the one who got the kiss!"

He couldn't understand how anyone could like him, not like that, to be *fancied.*

"You're joking," was all he could say in response.

"Joking! I'm not," Mickey protested. "Lots do!"

"Yeh." His voice stuck in his chest, and sounded gruff.

They kissed again, lips pressing hard against their teeth, tongues caressing the inside of their lips. In-between each series of increasingly intense kisses they talked and laughed, made silly jokes and called each other daft names. Mickey still referred to him as Noah, and he reminded her that she was Mickey Mouse. And then they kissed again while hands became more confident as they stroked each other alive.

"Tell me about the stuff you get?" she asked, eventually, still curious about his strange habits.

"I can't really. It's a secret. I promised not to tell."

"What? Even me?"

Dean felt torn. He wanted to tell her, but he struggled with letting Miss Jones down. He'd promised so often that he'd never tell; never reveal the secret of their insurance. He moved his face toward Mickey, wanting to kiss again and put an end to the questions – the dilemma.

Mickey moved away, craned her head back, and held him at arms length. "Why's it a secret? You only go around collecting rubbish. What's secret about that?" Her eyes widened, and he fell into the deep blue depth of them. "Why won't you tell me, Dean?"

Nerves jangled. Mickey would dump him moments after she'd kissed him. It would be a first and last date. His heart missed a beat. He thought it would stop. "I promised never to tell anyone, Mickey. You don't grass."

"*Grass?* You're just a big kid!" She was angry.

"It's the rule. You don't grass on your…" He didn't know what to call Miss Jones, how to describe her. She wasn't a *mate*.

"If we're going to be an item," she said, trying to sound old and wise, "we shouldn't have secrets. We should be honest with each other about *everything*."

"Yes, okay," he responded, feeling bleak. Could this be the end so soon? What ending of the world could be more painful than this?

A tall man, hunched against the incipient dark, walked a big dog over the field, whistling and calling when the dog bound away towards the busy road bordering the park. The dog stopped, turned, then turned again and ran over the tennis courts and disappeared into Millstone Lane. The man cursed so loudly the children heard him.

Mickey laughed, and broke the tension of the moment.

"I'm sorry. You can keep your secret. I don't mind," she said suddenly.

"I'm sorry too." He really was, and wanted to blurt it out to her now. He felt stupid. A child. A big kid.

"Want to kiss me again?" Her voice was that of a girl barely out of childhood, and yet it had an attractive power that he responded to like he was a man. He would let her in. Everything changed now. He was a man, not a silly kid.

"Yes. I want to…." Dean's voice said, almost imperceptible under the wave of passion.

"Yes?" Mickey smiled warmly, her head tilting, her hair falling over her shoulder. "You want to what?"

"I want to tell you…."

"Come here!" she demanded gently and kissed him. Pulling her head back for a moment, as if to draw breath, she whispered, "Just keep kissing me, Noah!"

Everything stopped. The night wrapped around them and he felt, for the first time, he was safe in the presence of someone – safe enough to allow her this close so that every cell responded to her warmth instead of recoiling at the lightest or the briefest of touches. He wanted to open up to Mickey to tell her everything. It was as if everything he feared dissolved, and whatever was to be didn't matter now.

"Do you know about the end of the world?" He stammered as he moved his face away, let his lips loosen the hard-coil of his fears.

"What?" Mickey pulled back from him, and grinned uncertainly. "What do you mean?"

"Do you know about it? Do you know about the end of the world?"

"Yeh. You mean when that thing hit the Earth and killed all the dinosaurs and stuff? You mean that sort of thing?"

"I've been preparing in case it comes. I've been getting things…" He stopped. Mickey frowned at him. "I've been collecting stuff ready for when it comes."

"What? What do you mean?"

"I've been…" It sounded foolish. It was insane now, here so close to Mickey's life and heat. "Aw, nothing. It's just something I've been helping with. I don't believe it anyway." He shrugged the idea away, and hoped Mickey would too. "I've decided I'm not going to do it anymore. It doesn't matter."

"You've been getting stuff in case the world ends?" Mickey's faced darkened for a moment as she tried to suss him out, catch what he really meant.

“Not me. Er…I was helping someone. A woman. An old woman.” He hoped she would accept it. “She’s dead old and a bit crazy. She thinks…”

“Well,” Mickey said her voice sure and steady, “It seems mad to do that. If the end of the world comes you’re dead anyway so it’s stupid to get stuff. When you’re dead you’re dead, and if you’re dead you won’t need anything. I think you’ve got to enjoy everything now because you know you’re going to die one day so you might as well enjoy today, this moment, just in case you snuff it tomorrow.” She nodded emphatically, her eyes wide as she appealed to him.

It was like a light had come on. Dean laughed.

“Do you think I’m stupid?” she asked, frowning, as he nodded his head in his joy.

“No. You aren’t mad, Mickey Mouse! It’s me – I’m crazy! I’m stupid! I’ve been worrying about the end of the world. Me! I’ve been worried sick!” Mickey had given him permission to let go, and in her presence nothing else mattered. If the end of the world came now, at least he’d be blissfully happy.

“Well, stop werreting and give me a kiss, Noah!” she demanded.

Dean looked into her eyes. Laughter subsided, and they edged nearer until their lips touched again, more expertly now, noses angled, faces moving and tilting in a wonderful choreography; in their embrace everything stopped. High above them the moon froze in its orbit. Clouds dragged to a standstill over the sandstone tower of the church in the town centre. A police siren blipped for a second then hushed. Even their hearts ceased to beat as they dovetailed into an endless moment. Dean felt at peace for the first time in his life. What did it matter now if the world ended?

Sixteen /

When Dean and Mickey discovered the brightly coloured vans waiting along Wellington Road to gain access to Brookfields Park, they knew the fair had arrived in town. They were thrilled. It usually came during the Carnival in the Summer, but every so often it appeared during the Autumn, and though neither had much money they couldn't wait for the swarthy men and run-away lads to erect the brash Waltzers and Big Wheel. Miss Jones had commented in an irritated sort of way about it, and was troubled by Dean's distance. She hoped she hadn't overstepped the mark again. He was a child, and children inevitably loved fairs. Once upon a time she had, until her images had been shattered and she no longer cared to look back at what it was like to be a child.

"You're far away, young man," she ventured. Dean looked oddly at her, but said nothing. "Are you alright?" He'd made her feel uneasy from the moment she'd seen him.

"Yeh," he shrugged, and continued to push tins under the stairwell.

Mickey hadn't pushed him further, but Dean struggled and wanted to tell her more stuff, how deeply unhappy he'd been, how much he'd felt lost and useless, and Miss Jones had offered so much then; now he didn't want it. He felt uneasy. At last he found someone who he wanted to be close to, and yet he felt an agony of doubt that he may hurt Miss Jones. The more he thought about it the harder it became, so, for now, he resolved to say nothing to either and to continue in the best way he could. But he was increasingly troubled by the close proximity of both. He wanted Mickey to be closer than his own skin, and Miss Jones wanted to be too close in a way that made his skin crawl. For one he felt a powerful and compulsive attraction, for the other he felt a profound repulsion. Both made him feel guilty.

"Will you be around later?" Mickey ventured.

"When?" Dean asked, knowing he'd made a commitment to see Miss Jones and pull the plastic sheets until they stretched across the cellar floor and he could pin down the edges with meat skewers.

"Later!" she rebuked gently, but sensed his unease. "Are you going to see the crazy lady? I thought you said you weren't going to go anymore?" She asked.

"Yes…no…She's not crazy," he said guiltily. "I've got to go. I need to tell her."

"So you are going then, Noah?"

"Yes. I could see you after…"

"What time?"

"As soon as I finish my jobs."

"What jobs?" she pushed.

"Oh, just things I do to help her."

"Is she ill or something? Do you help with cooking and things? Is she really serious about the end of the world?"

Dean felt awkward. He wished he hadn't told her. "She's not crazy. She's sort of…I don't know. Sometimes it makes sense, you know, the stuff she says. Sometimes I look at everything and think she's right."

"What things?"

"The world. People. Everything really."

"You can't do anything about it. If the world ends we're all going to die, Noah!"

"I promised not to tell anyone about her."

"Why what does she do?"

"Promise you won't tell anyone? Not a soul?"

"Of course! Who would I tell?"

"She keeps food and bottles of water. She keeps everything. The house is full of stuff. It's like a supermarket, only everything is packed up in boxes, under the floors, and now we're putting water bottles in the cellar."

"It's mad!" Mickey laughed. "She is crazy!"

"She gave me space to keep things for when the world ends. She wants me and her to survive. First she gave me a room, and now she wants to share everything with me, and if she dies before the end of the world she's leaving it all to me so I can survive."

"Lucky you! What about me and everyone else? Doesn't she care?"

"I don't know." He did, but he couldn't bear to say.

"Will you share it with me? Will you Dean?" Mickey smiled.

"Course I would."

"But not if she was still alive. Then it would be just you and her!" Mickey laughed.

It hurt Dean to think of it. He knew then he had to stop it.

"What about the fair?"

"Yes, I know. We will go, I promise, but I need to do the jobs. I need to see she's okay."

"Can I come and help too?"

Dean was thrown by her request. His face flushed, and he turned away from her gaze. The scrutiny made him feel stupid and helpless.

"Can I come and help?" she repeated, though with no malice. She was curious.

"No. Best not. She doesn't know you."

"Right," Mickey said, dismissively, and changed the subject. "I want to go on the Big Wheel, Noah. It looks great. You ever been on a Big Wheel?"

"Yes," he lied.

"Were you scared?"

"No," he lied again. Some years back he'd watched Dad drag Mum on a big wheel at Crewe Park, and when it eventually stopped at the top he'd swung back and forwards so violently she screamed. Dad laughed and did it all the more, but on the ground below a crowd gathered, some people were concerned, but many more were amused, as the couple rowed furiously. Dean wanted to shrink up and disappear, much the same as he did now as Mickey questioned him. "I'll meet you by the gates at half six," he offered.

"Half six?" She sounded harsh.

"If I can get away…"

"Half six will be great, Deano! I can't wait."

"Mickey, I really will stop going to see her." He wanted to tell her. It was right to tell her. Miss Jones was crazy. The idea of living with her, the two of them in an empty world, in a world without Mickey was more than he could bear to think. "She's going to go crazy with me!"

"Will she?" Mickey was going to say something funny, but stopped when she saw his face. He was deeply troubled. "Dean, I think you should do whatever you want to do. Don't listen to me. If you want to help her out it's okay by me!"

"I don't want to anymore." Something stirred inside him, and he felt angry towards Miss Jones. He was trapped and felt suffocated by her. It would end. He had to be strong enough to say it.

Mickey touched his arm. "I'll see you half six, Noah," she smiled, trying to reassure him.

*

The stink in the cellar caught Dean's throat, and he fancied that he saw a rat in the corner beside a pile of old papers. He didn't know whether to tell Miss Jones, but remembered her fear of spiders and guessed that rats would be even more horrible to her. It was awkward. His skin crawled, and he wanted someone to take responsibility and help him out. He was scared too. After a moment of uncertainty he took a flying kick at the papers and a cloud of thick dust exploded into the dank air of the cellar. Much to his relief there wasn't a rat. His scalp froze and tingled, and he shrugged his shoulders. It was awful. He felt an oppressive sense of responsibility.

A light cut through the dust as Miss Jones pulled open the door above, and walked carefully down rickety steps towards him. She struggled with a walking stick in one hand, and a drink in the other, and despite his feelings he felt a surge of sympathy for her, and a sudden pang of disdain for himself. She'd let him into her life and offered him this – a possible future against a dying world – and yet now he felt nothing but sadness and pity for her and berated himself for his loss of enthusiasm. All he could think about was Mickey, and it hurt him when he wasn't with her. A split cut through his conscience in the same way light had cut through the dark, and he felt Miss Jones would see right into him and discover his betrayal.

"How's it going, Dean?" she asked, holding the drink towards him.

"Great. Bit dusty."

"I can see. You mind it doesn't get on your chest!"

"I might have to go soon," he said nervously. It was too hard to find the right words to say. She looked pathetic.

"Right." Miss Jones felt troubled again. "Are you going out?"

"I might go to thc fair."

"Right," she said again, at a loss, not knowing what to say.

"I think it might be good, you know…everyone else is going from school…"

"Of course, you must. It'll be fun, Dean!" She tried to laugh, but her voice felt squashed in her chest. She wondered what went on between them, and fear grew inside her, and yet she knew she must not announce it. To put him under pressure would be unfair.

"I'll probably come back tomorrow." He peered intently into her face, and tried to see her expression in the darkness of the cellar. His heart beating with anticipation of seeing Mickey made him less concerned, and now he felt Miss Jones had given him permission all he wanted to do was to go as soon as he could.

"You go and have a really good time," she said as cheerfully as she could muster. The word 'probably' cut her to the quick.

And with that, Dean smiled and quickly mounted the stairs and left the house. Miss Jones stayed in the dark for a while, and understood its bleak emptiness.

*

Even though he was early Dean knew Mickey would be waiting for him at the gates. It thrilled him that she was, and when they stood face to face he felt such warmth that everything stopped again – his worry; his guilt; the chime of the clock over the rooftops; the flight of starlings as they looped towards the line of wires straddling the railway track. Everything dissolved into now, the moment, and Mickey's lovely face. They pushed their bikes along the tarmac track, and left them in racks before entering the fair. A dark-haired man stamped the backs of their hands and they tried not to smudge the ink until it dried. Dean wanted to hold Mickey's hand, and it felt like an age until it was dry enough. The closer they got to the wonderful machinery the louder it became – music blaring until their eardrums tingled, and laughter erupted at the powerful and consuming thrill it gave them. They saw other kids from school. Boys frowned and were disdainful, throwing insults at them, while girls giggled and said things behind their hands as they pushed each other and then threw their heads back in raucous laughter. It didn't matter.

The sun began to set behind the tall trees bordering Shrewbridge Road, and threw long shadows across the sweep of grass. A blackbird flapped precariously near to the Big Wheel before dropping into a hedgerow, and more people walked the straight paths from all sides of the park, their faces alive and full of expectation. As Dean watched them he felt a strange warmth, and had an urge to say hello to everyone.

"Come on, Noah," Mickey shouted, "Let's go on the Big Wheel!"

Without a trace of fear Dean followed as she cut across the grass towards the wheel. Lights came on as they approached, and they joined a small queue, faces alive as the wheel slowly turned and stopped, and turned and stopped again as it filled. And then it was their turn, and they were on. The metal arm fell across their laps, the seat moved and swayed, and Dean looked at Mickey's happy face and laughed as they rose above the tops of the caravans and growling engines that blew diesel fumes below them. People looked up as they looked down, and everyone seemed blissfully happy. They were alive, Dean thought. They had this moment. They were above the tops of the trees, and then the rooftops, and the church tower shrank below them until they floated under the increasing shine of stars. If they reached up just a little more they could pluck the moon from the deep and dark blue sky, and roll it between their hands to illuminate their faces, so that the whole of Nantwich would see the thrill of this moment. Dean looked down over the flat map of the town, and traced a finger through the streets, stopping at Cronkinson Oak, moving again to Wellington Road, and circled his finger around Miss Jones' big and cavernous house. Its deep set windows, and huge front door looked like features on a hungry face – eyes wide, mouth wider, as it devoured all and everything.

"Look we're at the top!" Mickey yelled. "We're on top of the world! Dean we're on top of the world!"

Dean turned to her. Her eyes shone and the dark centres pulled him in, moved him towards her until their lips touched in a powerful and intoxicating kiss. The chair moved as a wind muscled gently, and they squealed with delight as they clutched each other in a wonderfully anxious embrace.

"Tomorrow I'm going to tell her it's all over!" Dean announced as he peered intently into her face again. "I'm going to stop helping her. It is mad. It's crazy. Who cares anyway!" he laughed.

"What will she say?" Mickey asked, her face soft in the glow of bright and coloured lights.

"She'll probably go off on one!"

"Will she be okay, do you think?"

"I don't care."

"Be careful. She sounds old."

"She is. Very old."

As the wheel dipped and dropped them down to earth for the last time, Dean felt exhilarated. They clambered off the hard seat, and ran towards the Waltzers, hands held in a tight and frantic grip. Dean felt drunker than any can had made him. He stopped, and pulled Mickey back and in towards him. "I love you," he said, heart beating like a jackhammer under his shirt.

"I love you too, Noah," she replied, and touched his face.

Seventeen /

Dean was already awake, basking in his warm reverie, tasting Mickey on his lips, when he heard the banging on the front door. He sat bolt upright, eyes wide with fear. Who would make such a noise at this time of night? He heard his mum tumble out of bed, and stumble around the room, and despite an overwhelming fear threatening to immobilise him, he too struggled out of bed and fumbled in the dark to find his clothes. He was too scared to put the light on, but a crack of bright light cut like a razor under his door as Patsy ran downstairs. Her words were garbled and confused, but Dean heard the terror in her voice. He managed to open the door, and was shocked to see Mark, bare-chested, on the landing, zipping up his jeans. He held a mobile phone in his hand, but they shook so much he dropped it. An intense blue light from the keypad went out, and he heard a high pitched squeak as the phone died. Mark dashed back into the bedroom, grabbed his shirt and jacket, and paused at the top of the stairs before he crept down.

Downstairs the commotion continued, and now Dean heard a voice in the street, a rough and raucous voice cursing the heavens. It was his dad. Billy was back. Dean held onto the stair-rail, frightened that his shaking legs would give way and he'd fall. He thought he was going to be sick, and held a hand against his stomach and pressed hard, trying to keep it down. Mark ran from the kitchen into the hall, into the lounge, before going back to the kitchen again. He said nothing, absolutely nothing. His words froze in his chest, his mouth was a tight line, lips white, and jaws locked in terror.

Billy Cartwright was back and he'd kill her.

A window rattled and bulged as Billy pressed his face against the glass. His breath steamed obscene patterns around a white faced wrath, and fingers clawed against the flimsy obstacle. No matter what he said or did or promised, his rage was too-well nurtured in a jealous heart, and despite a performance of a life-time to get outside the cell, his drive to get even was more massive, more overwhelming, and so completely nihilistic nothing mattered other than a need to afflict complete destruction and gain revenge. Had he realised Mark Tomlinson, the social worker, lurked inside, he would have torn glass and brick and stone with his teeth to get at him.

"Oh, my god, oh, my god, oh, my god," was all Patsy managed to say, her voice rising with each word. Her eyes were so wide Dean thought her eyeballs would fall out. *"Oh, my god, oh, my god! Mrs Anderson! Mrs Anderson! Call the police! Call the police!"* She thumped and slapped her hand against the wall.

The noise outside exploded as something was thrown against the door, and Dean felt his legs give way. It was Dad. It shouldn't be like this. Not now. Everything was alright. He'd felt good for the first time and now it was going to go away again. He saw Mark again, running around, trying to find a way out, and Dean suddenly felt mad with anger and wanted to get a knife and kill him. He tried to shout, but couldn't get the words out. He pulled himself up, swaying like a drunk, and tried again. This time the words blasted in a high-pitched tirade against the social worker. *"You bastard! Bastard! You bloody bastard! It's your bloody fault! Bastard! Bastard!"* His teeth ground together after each word, gnashed and gritted in his fury. He imagined Dad punching his face until blood spurted out. Dean wanted to be big, monstrous, so that he could grab Mark and kill him, and then turn on his Dad if he had to and stop him too. He saw his mother try to hold Mark, to stop him from going, to beg him to protect her, but Mark shoved her aside, knocked her to the floor. Another loud explosion ruptured glass and wood in the lounge window, and the door thudded several times as Billy kicked it.

"No, Billy! Please, Billy!" she screamed.

Dean saw a blue light and in his confusion thought it was the light on the mobile phone. It filled the room and he heard a shrill siren. It was the police. The banging stopped immediately and before tyres skidded to a halt Billy was off, running through gardens, clambering up walls, kicking out at dogs. In time he would return. In time he would exact an equal measure of pain for every day he'd spent inside.

Dean lay down at the top of the stairs. Patsy fell to her knees, covering her head. The police managed to push the door open, and a policewoman carefully crept in over the glass and splintered doorframe. Her eyes darted nervously from Patsy, up to Dean, and then onto Mark. The social worker started to say something, but stopped. He sat on a kitchen stool and sobbed.

The policewoman tried to lift Patsy, but nearly fell too as the woman lolled like a rag-doll in her arms. "Go see to the kid," she shouted, as another policeman forced his way in, and within a second Dean felt strong hands grab his arms and lift him onto his feet.

"Who was it son? Do you know who it was?"

"No." Dean shook his head.

"We'll get the bastard," the policeman said, trying to reassure him.

"The bastard's downstairs," Dean whispered hoarsely.

"What? What do you mean, son?"

"He's the bastard." Dean pointed to Mark who hugged himself and swayed like an idiot. The social worker's hair stood on end, and his face was as white as the moon. Little whimpering sounds, shrill and annoying, made Dean want to hurt him. He felt bigger and stronger than the man, and hated him for his weakness.

A strange quietness fell upon the house and street. Outside people congregated and arched necks towards Mrs Anderson as she filled ears with earnest and acid whispers. Her face danced delightedly and the people were whipped into gleeful appreciation of her froth and bile. Dean watched them from the corner of the house. Inside, amidst the chaos, too many police officers choreographed their way through broken glass and minds and attempted to string together any semblance of sense. The boy watched and listened and eventually crept out of the back door, pushing his bicycle over the broken fence strewn over the path at the side of the house. Patsy and Mark were so entrapped in the giddiness of shock and narcissistic distress it made them blind. Their tongues looped silently as they tried to manufacture an excuse, a reason, an explanation. Dean's small frame became invisible and despite the fact that he shook from fear and shock, he managed to slip away. All the time his eyes pierced the dark, ever mindful that his dad lurked dangerously, somewhere in the black shadows on the fringe of lights. The claustrophobia of the house was a greater threat. In there he was trapped. Control would be taken away from him and he'd lie whimpering powerlessly in another hostel, another place of safety. Out here he had a modicum of freedom, and even so little seemed so much. Now he craved for one thing only – to see Mickey, to hold her and to let out a cry of pain so loud it would rock the sandstone church to its foundations.

*

Paddy's Field looked to be empty. That's what Dean wanted. Mist hung like a fat duvet over the river and along the allotments to the other edge where the mucky canal lay, white cobwebs, heavy with droplets, sagged in the early morning light. Dean disturbed a heron, and it flapped awkwardly for a moment before becoming graceful as its big, wide wings filled and climbed on the air. Dean had ridden around for hours, watching and waiting for the dawn to streak the black sky with grey, like oil on a dirty puddle, and now as the sun rose under the clouds it became a red ball, making the dark and heavy clouds blush as it looked up their skirts. It was hard to think. An explosion of glass replayed over and over in his head, a silent image of shrapnel bursting in a strange and beautiful way before a terrible cacophony erupted and even now pierced his ears. His heart was a lead weight. He looked at the allotments, empty now;

the season was finishing, and the gardeners prepared for the winter. Behind one of the sheds he found wooden boxes. Time passed as he stared at them not understanding what they meant, until slowly he became conscious of another maggot thought chewing through his daze, which rekindled another dreadful memory and inevitable task. Despite his weariness and misery, he recalled his promise to take them to Miss Jones. He knew then that he needed to take them to her later, as a kind of parting gift, and say what he needed to say. Dean had to finish with it all. He had to tell her straight. What is the point of trying to live? What is the use of holding on? If he was going to die it would be a relief; he'd get away from the mess. He'd take the boxes and say goodbye. It was something to do. He sat down among them, turning a box upside-down and into a makeshift seat. The world was a wreck, like a burned out car he found earlier on a dirt-track in the fields off Kings Lane as he wandered through the dank and cheerless early morning. Joy-riders often dumped cars here, and for once Dean felt a weird kind of respect for them. It would feel good to wreck everything, to have or hold no respect for anyone. What was the point of caring? What was the point of having anything? All those bits and pieces that made it work were a tangle, a mess. The engine smouldered, and when the wind caught the embers under the broken chassis they flickered briefly and eventually died. Wisps of acrid smoke wafted into his eyes and on his face but it made no difference to the already dry and hardened skin. He felt no pain now.

He remembered the fragments of enquiry and comment in the shards of wreckage and glass earlier that night – Mum would have to go to the police station. Mark would have to go with her to explain his fear and shame. Dean imagined them being taken out, heads under a blanket in the hope no-one would see their stupid faces. Dad would be hiding and waiting. The police said he'd come out of prison and got tanked-up in the nearest pub. He was a man on a mission, they said. The policewoman wanted Dean to be taken somewhere, and she said a social worker would come and sort it, but Dean had had a belly full of social workers so he did a runner. What would a *place of safety* be? Dean wondered. Where would it be? There was nowhere safe except for the moment when he lost himself in Mickey's kiss. In the instant he remembered her again he wanted to push the memory away. It would be useless holding onto Mickey. He was a kid. Kids didn't fall in love. If anyone knew they'd try to stop it. They wouldn't understand. They'd do everything they could to stop it, so what would be the point? Mickey wouldn't want to live like this – sitting in an allotment, every muscle aching as nerves stretched at every slight noise. And if Dad knew about them…well, it didn't bear thinking about. It would be best to stop everything with everyone and run away properly. He'd heard about kids doing that. They'd gone to the city and despite mad parents trying to find them, they'd disappeared good and proper. It would be good to do that. It would be good to make everyone worry themselves sick. Serve them right. But the more the thought grew the more he felt a chill run through him. He realised how lonely it would be. It was bad enough now, but to be in a place where he didn't even know the streets, the houses, the sound of the church bells, the faces of the people, filled him with dread. In Nantwich he knew almost every nook and cranny. He knew who was who and he knew where to hide and how to avoid them. In a flash he imagined trying to hide or run from Mickey, to eradicate her from this awful life, and a pain seared through him. It was just too awful trying to push her away. Mickey's face came into his thoughts, and he felt a sudden thrill. Could he really never see her again?

He looked at his bike. The sun shone on the chrome handlebars and they shone like red-hot metal. He wished he could like it again, and recapture the thrill of the first ride, but it was just a lump of metal now. It meant nothing. It was like the mangled wreck of the car, or the inside of his head, all twisted and disgusting, and meaning nothing. He wondered if Mickey would add to the tangle.

She might drop him. She might tell him to get lost. If she knew about his dad, and his mum, and the bloody social worker, she'd run a mile. There was no point. Everything he thought about burnt-out and left him low. He heard a noise in the distance and saw an old man as he wandered down the path holding a tatty shopping bag and a pair of shears. As he came closer Dean hoped he wouldn't notice him hunched on the boxes. His old face looked like the soft-focus photographs in Kendal's Photo Shop, in the dim morning light, and a wisp of breath clouded his face and moved beyond the flat cap which nearly covered his eyes. The boy held onto his own breath so as not to signal his presence, but he watched as the man noticed the bike, and within seconds fixed him with a quick eye and a down-turned mouth.

The man was startled when he saw Dean. The shock rushed through him like an electric pulse, and he reacted immediately. "What are you doing here?" he demanded. "This is private land. You shouldn't be on this land! You…you…" He stopped. It would be better not to provoke the boy. Nowadays no-one was safe. Kids could be dangerous. "What are you doing?" he asked, gentling his tone.

"Nothing."

"Nothing, young fella? What are you doing here?"

Dean peered at his old and wrinkled face and wondered whether to reply at all. Should he sit defiantly and ignore him, or let rip and give him a mouthful? But before any thought took hold he heard himself say wearily, "I'm tired." Deep inside his head he knew he couldn't blank him, or face him out – his energy diminished to the point of extinction, and besides, what would be the point?

"Tired?" the old man repeated. His face softened and he responded quietly, as if coaxing an edgy dog, "No wonder, young man, you should be home in bed at this time. What's up? What's the problem, fella?" He saw the distress in the child's face and sensed he would be okay, not like the usual rabble that destroyed a gardener's efforts in a moment of bloody-minded vandalism. Anyway, that lot would be stinking in their beds at this time of the day, he thought. "You got a problem?" he asked again.

"No. Nothing." Dean didn't have the strength to say or do anything.

"You're not one of those glue-sniffers are you? You don't look well. Have you had drugs or booze, young fella?"

"No. No. I haven't." Dean said, wanting to get angry and defend himself, but feeling so weary he wanted to lie down in the cold grass and sleep.

"Do you want me to get someone for you? Are you ill?"

"No. I'm okay. I'll go. I was a bit wobbly, that's all. I'll go now. I just needed a second…I've got to do my paper-round…" Dean lied and started to push himself up, but then really did feel giddy, and he swayed momentarily. He nearly tumbled as he reached for the bike.

"Be careful, son!" the old man said, moving towards the boy, reaching out to hold him.

Dean flinched, and moved quickly to avoid his touch, and squatted just beyond his reach, the bike forming a barrier between them.

The man moved back anxiously. "You can stay there if you want, fella, just so long as you don't get into any mischief."

"No. It's okay. I'm going in a minute."

"It startled me, see, you being there this early in the morning. I didn't expect to see anyone here at this time. If you've got a paper-round it makes sense you'd be early, son. You can stay longer if you like. I've got a flask. Do you like tea?"

"I've got to go. I've got stuff to do." Dean thought of Mickey. For some reason she came into his mind again, and he thrilled as he thought of her and recalled her warmth and the softness of her lips. He remembered the taste, and a strange sensation ran through him, leaving him breathless. For a moment he bathed in her memory, and craved to see her again. Despite the gloom, the despair, the edge-cold-cut of the early day, he craved for her touch.

The man coughed, breaking Dean's reverie, and smiled. "You can have a cup of tea if you want, fella."

The old man looked okay. He stood off him, and yet communicated his concern well-enough for Dean to feel safe. Dean looked at the boxes, and remembered his need to put an end to Miss Jones' expectations. Something else had to come to an end. "Please can I have some of these boxes?"

"What for?" He was thrilled at the boy's sudden display of manners, and lost any sense of threat now.

"For Miss Jones."

"Who's she then?" the old man asked. "Your Granny?"

"No. She's an old woman I know."

"She want them for sticks?" He *was* a good lad, he thought. The boy was courteous and he obviously cared.

"What?"

"She wants sticks, for firewood?"

"Yes," Dean lied again. He knew if he agreed it would take the pressure off him and he could go.

"You can take them for me. I've no use for them. Just thrown them out last week. If they're any use to you may as well have them."

Dean struggled to his feet and for a moment watched the old man as he rattled his keys and unlocked the big, rusty padlock on his shed before going in, his feet scuffing the damp floorboards. The boy looked at the boxes. He could take four or five. They'd fit on his bike, though he'd have to walk with them. It would be a bit of a struggle and he wondered how to hold them together. The old man watched through the door and offered him some string. Dean agreed, and held his bike while the man helped him to tie them up. They didn't speak, but Dean watched his thick fingers expertly pull loops and ties.

"There you are. Come back if you want some more, fella."

"Thank you." Dean smiled weakly.

"You are a sad young man. What's the matter with you? Do you want me to come with you, take you home? What paper-shop do you work at? Do you want me to tell them you're poorly? What's your name, son?"

The old man's concern made Dean's eyes burn with tears, but he fought to hold them back. Should he give him a false name, like he had with Miss Jones? And what could he say was up? My Dad's an alcoholic who just came out of prison and tried to beat my mother up because she was in bed having *sex* with my *social worker*, but she only did that because my Dad's a bastard, and the end of the world is coming because Miss Jones says it is, and I don't want to believe her no more, but if the end of the world is coming, I'd be really, really sad because I never got to see Mickey.. .

"I'll be late at the shop. I've got to go. Thanks… I've got to go." Dean blurted. The idea of Mickey getting hurt really affected him. He wanted to see her. He wanted to tell her how much he wanted to live. She understood. She knew it was a stupid waste of life worrying about things.

"My name's Dean," he said suddenly.

The old man told him to take care of himself, and he meant it. He watched the boy struggle to hold the boxes, and wanted to go after him, but then thought better of it. Later he'd enquire after the boy in Carrington's Newsagents, see if they knew him. The sun struggled too as it tried to fill the heavy sky with a little heat and light. A hooter blared along Millstone Lane as Harvey's tannery called its men to work. After rooting in the damp shed, the man paused at the door and sighed before plunging a fork into the cold earth. The season was over. It was time to put the allotment to bed. He smiled, and let the thoughts of the child drift away as he stirred the soil.

Eighteen /

This would be the last time and somehow he had to break it to her. He watched as Miss Jones unpacked some tins from a big box.

"Just the job! Must have been a weight?"

Dean shuffled his feet. It had, but he shook his head and smiled. He watched her every move, tensed himself. He felt ashamed, and unkind. It had to be said and done with. Her hunched back angled precariously over the box, and he felt sick, chest tightening, breath hard to draw, as he watched her awkwardness and age. She had grown ugly to him. He had hope now, and in his hope his eyes had seen sunshine and possibility.

"I put them on my bike. Makes it easier," he said feebly, hoping she wouldn't pick-up the anxiety in his voice. She didn't miss a trick, always on the look-out for signs. Always.

"Oh, yes, of course." Her preoccupation with the latest haul kept her attention away from him. It was important work, counting, working out, seeing how much more time they bought.

"Miss Jones…" It had to be now. It had to be said, to jump in and risk drowning. If he left it any longer he wondered if he would ever find the courage.

"Yes?" she said absently, placing some tins under the floorboards.

"I won't be coming again." His voice was a whisper as he watched for a reaction. His guilt hung on him like a tail, just as she said it did. *We carry guilt around like a tail.* How terrible the prospect of letting her down, not wanting to believe anymore.

"You won't what?" she asked. "Sorry, I was counting…"

"I won't be coming again." The words were terrible, stark and real. He felt cold, and his body trembled slightly with the ache of tension that arose in him. It was as if he'd hurled a stone at her, aiming to shock her into reality. This was the way it had to be, and short of doing that there seemed to be no other way in which she would hear him.

She turned quickly, her eyes stabbing into his. He looked down at his feet and cleared his throat, getting ready to defend himself. In his short life he felt emotions that were uncertain, huge and chaotic. It would be better to run, to shove her away and make a dash for freedom so that he could breathe again. He had to tell her, make it clear. End it.

"I don't care about it anymore, Miss Jones," he stammered, wrestling with the words. It was so hard to disentangle from her passionate presence.

"What are you saying?" Her mouth tightened as her eyes shrivelled into two dark, shrill points, and her tongue darted out and over her thin, dry lips. She became a lizard, stub-nosed, wary and winding-up a reaction.

"I don't want this." His heart pounded against his bones, and his ribs felt as if they'd crack under her scrutiny. How awful it was to end it. How awful, and yet he knew he couldn't do other than this. It was time not to believe anymore. It was time to live and to hope and to feel like the world was okay. His feet pathered the dry dust on the floorboards making a nervous dance as he anticipated her rage.

She stood as upright as her crooked back would allow.

"What?" Her face creased in pain. He'd wounded her with the very thought it might be over. It didn't look like him anymore – no longer the sweet-faced kid who crept into her heart and mind.

"I've got to go now, see..." He pointed to the door, his hand showing them both where he wanted to go.

"Go? Go where?"

"I've got to get away."

"What? Get away? What, from me? What have I done? How can you say that? All our plans will be ruined!" A high-pitched note rose as she felt anxiety and disappointment rise in her. She'd never given way to hysteria; her sense of discipline had been an iron rod driven through to the core, rigid and entirely trustworthy, but at this moment the sense of betrayal shook her so violently she envisioned what people meant when they said they were *losing it.* She struggled to regain control, not to fling her arms and fists at him, to slap his small face, and cause the big eyes to drop big tears of repentance. How much she'd come to rely on him. How much! It was against all she'd imagined possible. Such failure! She was a fool!

"Miss Jones, I… I…"

"I trusted you," she said coldly "I let you into my secret and then made provision for you, for your future. And it's that easy is it*? I've had enough Miss Jones, cheerio!* Is it *that easy?* You were my greatest ally. My best friend! You are my boy! *My boy!*" Her voice broke and she let out a huge cry which cut through to his bones.

He shook his head vigorously. "It's me. I've changed… I've…" Her words scared him more now than ever. Her words rang like prison bars, clanged like a steel-shuttered window, and he knew now how dark it had all become, how airless and joyless. *Her boy?* How could he be? How could he be anybody's boy?

She stood upright now, and pushed a hand through her hair, tugged the elastic band holding the bun hard against her scalp, before coughing and shaking her head, letting the thin grey hair fall across her wild and flushing face. The blood boiled and burned. She steeled herself. Her eyes wanted to burst and let out her agony of disappointment, but she would not show it, would not let him know how ferociously this hurt. A beating heart ached inside her and she wondered, feared, if a stroke would stop this, put an end to it all, all this, the planning, the preparation, the cost. What betrayal. It was enough to kill her.

"Anyway, it's your choice! Go! I don't need you. There'll be enough here for *me* now. Go on! Go! I won't keep you; hold you against your will. Go on, you're free!" She busied herself again with the boards, replacing them over the hole in the sitting room floor, her fingers scrabbling in the dust, and she ignored the thin boy who stood awkwardly by the door. It was as if, suddenly, he'd become invisible. *I will survive*, she repeated again and again in her head, feeling the brain boil under the fragile skull, pressuring the blue veins into bulges on her porcelain-white temples. The pressure built as she tried to ignore him.

Dean wanted to go, but his legs were rigid and his breath caught fast in his chest, felt like a cold stone lodged in the airways. He knew he was letting her down, but look, she was old, a pathetic old woman. God! How much he wanted to hate her and make it easier to go – but he had slowly grown towards the light she showed him, encouraged him to see. The light had diminished over the recent past and now he fought with his misguided sense of loyalty to find himself, to hold on to a new sense of things. He moved to the door. He was so near to going, so near to escaping from all this, from her, a withered old lady. She shrank before his eyes, as the illusion had before her. He could see it now. She was the way of all of them, all grown-ups were like this. Sodding stupid! *Stupid bastards*! Admitting to his sense of loss, the loss of dependency, propelled him towards a different possibility, and one where he would take the risk of letting life back in. There was another way to be. He knew he had to become it.

"You'll be sorry when it comes, and you'll be damned! You'll be damned!" she said suddenly, her eyes wide and wild. "Don't you come running back here, young man, when it begins. You will suffer along with them. You are a traitor. A traitor! When the end comes, don't come back here crawling like snake on your belly. You will deserve it!"

He reached for the door handle, cranked his heavy heart and tired legs into such a wild leap as he flew along the path, across the blue-bricks, under the apple tree, under the blue sky a thousand miles high, his lungs filling with a sweetness of air he had long lost the taste for. He could breathe! At last he could breathe again!

Later when he stood at the end of the road, looking back at

the old house, he tried to recall when the world shifted and turned in the way it had. When had his life taken on such a drive, manifested such a dread of dying? This weird creation of fear cultivated anxiety, and anxiety had changed the way in which he'd lived. If life had been awful before it was doubly so now, and this sudden grab for freedom, to take the risk of going, breaking away, was the hardest decision he'd ever had to take, and despite his age he felt as if he'd grown old before his time. At the age of twelve he had witnessed the terrible visions, heard the prophecies of doom, and in the end all it served to do was to push him to take a breath and feel what it means to breathe again.

His eyes opened on the world, and it buzzed before him, in innocence and light. But now, how would it resolve itself? What joy would be there for him?

Dean looked back along Wellington Road towards the big house hunched against the sky, and remembered the beginning, of the end, of the world.

Nineteen /

It was another cheerless day. Paper blew through the Perspex bus shelters which stood by the Civic Hall, and the street-cleaner slowly worked his way through another night's rubbish. The regular sound of his brushing was ignored by a few pigeons who'd escaped the recent purge by the town council to eradicate them, and they flapped from their perches, circled the church and landed with a swirl on the pedestrianised Square. A dog sniffed the benches, wagged its tail at the boy who sat in the middle under the War Memorial, but when he didn't respond it resumed its search for interesting scents. A black van, in Chatwin's Bakery livery, bumped over the ramps and pulled up in front of the confectioner's shop facing Church Walk. The man quickly got out and rushed to the back where he proceeded to noisily unload racks of bread and cakes. He glanced at the boy, thinking he must be waiting to do his paper-round, and felt sufficiently secure that he wouldn't make a grab for the pastries.

Dean looked at the worn slabs. They were dampened with an early morning drench, and with his eyes he traced the pattern of lichen which drew nourishment from the stain. It was cold but if he felt it, it didn't show. His fleece covered his mouth and the hood nestled just over the base of his ears, and he could feel his breath warm as it blew gently back as he exhaled; he caught the smell of his coat, musty like Miss Jones smell had been. His hands were deep in his pockets and they were warm now, and still. Earlier, as he cycled through the empty streets they become stiff with the cold, and the fingertips ached nearly as much as his bones and heart. It was the third night he'd wandered around the town, dashing in the alleys running behind Arnold and Albert Street, avoiding the police car that occasionally nosed slowly around the rows and terraces. In James Hall Street, at three in the morning, a car suddenly appeared from the alley behind Cowap's Shop, but Dean ducked behind the privet hedge bordering the edges of the grassland around the Nantwich Glass workshops, and waited until it disappeared into Beam Street.

His hands were okay now, warm and nimble, and he'd be able to steer the bike and use the brakes if he needed to, but he'd stay here a while longer and then he'd go. Maybe later he'd risk it and come back; the Square offered shelter, being surrounded by tall Victorian buildings, as well as the black-strapped timbers of several old Tudor houses. However, if the walkways were full of people he'd continue to skulk around, keep a low profile, like a criminal on the run. It excited him to think that he could keep it up indefinitely.

On market days he would go and root around the fruit and vegetable stalls to pick up food, and he knew he wasn't averse to nicking something from the cake shop or supermarket if he had to. Nantwich was a small town, and he knew a lot of people. Got to keep moving, he thought. Move from place to place and there would be less of a chance of him being caught. Dean thought he might go and see if the old man was on his allotment, and speculated on a cup of hot tea – but he decided it would be risky. Maybe the less he saw or talked to anyone, the better. The only place of safety was out here on the streets; here, where he had it all under control.

A man he knew as Paddy came and sat with him on the benches around the War Memorial. Paddy was mad, and although he looked at Dean and talked and talked, he didn't say anything other than mad stuff. Paddy would be safe, Dean thought. No-one listened to him, and if they did nothing made sufficient sense anyway. Dean just watched him now, having overcome the initial doubt he felt; watched without moving, without responding, no smiles, no nods, just a blank face, an inscrutable face. It seemed to suit Paddy. The Irishman sucked endlessly on cigarettes and his fingers were nicotine stained, the nails thick and torn like pale plastic plugs stuck under the rough skin, and every so often he'd let out a high-pitched laugh as he pointed a stubby finger towards the figure of Christ strung under the sandstone canopy on the lofty memorial. Paddy scratched the white stubble on his cheek and slowly wandered away, disappearing down Mill Street, as he made his way to his flat on Riverside.

From somewhere deep in the town Dean heard a whistle rise and fall in a cheerful tune, and then boisterous voices. It would be the postmen in the Pepper Street Office, getting loaded-up, pushing big bags on the racks at the front of red and white bikes. They'd be along soon. They'd tried to talk to him a couple of times in the past, but got fed-up and didn't bother now. They let him be. Dean decided it was time to move anyway and slowly wheeled his bike to his side, placed a foot on the pedal and with a push, mounted it and rode away. Two pigeons flapped momentarily before resuming their pecking and poking. Just as Dean disappeared down Castle Street, Paddy came back again and made his way to the benches, his back hunched, shambling along slowly until he sat down and looking dead ahead, talked and talked.

Dean stopped on the River Weaver Bridge and looked down into the water. It was high now, and very deep. He couldn't ever remember a time when it was possible to see into it; it had never been clear. Once on a school trip he marvelled at the clear water in a Welsh river. Mr Smith said the Weaver's water was brown on account of the salt and sandstone. Mr Smith also said grimly that global warming would melt the polar icecaps and the seas would rise and rise and rise, while glaciers melted in the mountains, and so the land would disappear under a huge weight of water and people would fight over the remaining scraps of territory. Nantwich would disappear altogether, he'd said sombrely, on account of it being not much above sea level, and the river would swell, and the end would come, if, if people didn't change their ways. And he knew they couldn't. People can't change.

Billy's face came to mind when a jet high in the sky rumbled on its way as it nosed along and opened up a memory. Some time back, after a particularly physical argument, Billy tried to make it up to Patsy. He was hard-up, it was mid winter, and he needed a drink.

Almost as an afterthought they included Dean in the negotiations as they couldn't decide what to do together. The bedroom door was soundly shut and Billy didn't have imagination beyond it. When they tried to decide what to do as a 'family' and argued to the point where it felt dangerous, Dean blurted that he'd like to go to the airport and see the planes coming in and out. Kids at school spoke of such things, but they'd experienced the flights from the inside when they were holiday bound. The local airport had a viewing lounge, and it would be okay for Dean, it would be enough. He remembered too that his dad had talked about a childhood ambition to be a pilot. Patsy winced, but agreed to the idea. Dean pinned every vestige of hope he had onto the idea. To be a family doing something together and having fun seemed like an outrageous notion and he trembled as he prayed that he wouldn't spoil it. On this day out he would behave impeccably.

It was a cynical need to salvage something for Billy and he poked and prodded Dean, trying to induce an enthusiasm in the boy he couldn't feel himself. It was hard for Dean as his parents had argued before leaving home, spat and cursed in a car hired for the day and nearly had an accident when Billy pushed his foot hard on the accelerator to make a point. The day was a concession, but he still had the power.

"Do you rate it then?" Billy asked.

"Yeah. It's cool!" Dean lied, trying to force reluctant lines to unfold on his brow.

"Look at that short-arsed little bitch!" Billy exclaimed.

Dean thought he meant a propeller driven aeroplane landing awkwardly against the wind, but his dad eyed a small blonde walking through the big lounge.

The glass-domed lounge took Dean's breath away when he first entered it and he screwed up his eyes against a strong light. As he adjusted to the glare he noticed tall windows, and beyond on the outside, a jet with twin-engines swooped onto the strip of grey tarmac, bounced, blasted a shock of blue smoke from its wheels, bounced again and rushed beyond his view. It was the scariest, most beautiful moment of his life. He'd never seen such power and grace, but despite this almost overpowering sensation, there, at the back of his mind, his dad lurked and threatened to disqualify anything remotely positive.

"What do you reckon?" Patsy asked, trying to understand the look on Dean's face.

"It's brilliant." His voice was lost in the busy space. "Where's Dad?" he asked, suddenly realizing Billy had gone.

"Over there." Patsy nodded towards a huge screen hanging above a bar, where Billy elbowed his way to the front with a borrowed tenner in his hand.

For several hours Dean watched the traffic coming and going, enjoyed the colourful insignia painted on the tails of the aircraft, and longed to be inside the big booming creatures which shook the glass and seat where he watched with wide eyes. But eventually the parade grew monotonous and the excitement faded as the day drew on. Patsy flicked disinterestedly through a magazine and read with indifference about the inanely stupid and unreal lives of celebrities. They hadn't got a clue, she thought, as she looked at cruel photographs of dishevelled fashion divas and footballers who'd taken their eye off the ball.

Two elderly couples dressed in light coloured clothes played cards and lifted their spirits. It was winter and they were escaping for a long holiday in the sun. They'd checked in the luggage, received the boarding passes and now made a determined effort to enjoy every minute. Their laughter irritated Patsy, and Dean watched as she kept turning and frowning at them. Dean became irritated too and hated them for their greyness and slack-skinned features. One woman's arms hung in wrinkled sheets of white flesh and despite the darkening sky outside she basked in the thought of a hot sun. Patsy and Dean waited without hope or suitcases.

Later, when Billy came back and slumped beside them, he laughed and hissed, "You look a right miserable pair of bastards."

"You've got to drive back!" Patsy yelled. "Look at the state of you!"

They started to argue with such vehemence two security guards were called for and escorted them away. Dean followed behind, his face fixed, eyes unfocussed on the curious crowd who either giggled or grumbled at such a scene. People don't change. They aren't capable of it.

Dean shivered, looked at the river again and distracted himself with the marvellous fact that at the point of drowning a boy called Kenny Ludford had been pulled out of this river by a passing fireman who not only knew how to extricate the boy from the water but also knew enough about first aid to give him mouth to mouth. Another boy, Tony Dobbin, wasn't so lucky. He didn't come up again. His foot got caught on a submerged supermarket trolley which held onto him until his lungs filled and his heart stopped. Dean wondered who had been the luckier.

Today Dean hoped he'd catch up with Mickey. He'd ridden nearly every road and lane in the town in the hope of seeing her, and sometimes felt mad with his longing to talk with her. She'd understand, and he hoped that she wouldn't judge him for what his parents did. It was acutely painful to think about them. Deep down he still felt responsible for their unhappiness, and their subsequent fury. If he'd never been born maybe they would have been okay and social workers and the police and the like would have kept their noses well and truly out of their business. Dean knew he couldn't go back home now. Maybe if he stayed away they'd get back together and begin to talk things over, and then they'd come looking for him. Just now it was impossible to face his mother's despair or his father's fury and all he craved for was a glimpse of Mickey's face and some reassurance that she still liked him. Maybe when she knew how bad things were she'd help him out in some way. However, Dean was wise enough to keep away from the school gates, or any place where they'd expect a kid to be, so he wandered around and around on the off-chance that they'd run into each other like they did before. He was frustrated he'd never asked her where she lived.

A police car slowed and stopped by the lights, and a young policeman peered through the window, recognised the kid, turned to his partner and said, 'It's Billy Cartwright's kid!' He tried to wind down the window, to stop the child, but Dean had gone, moved away quickly, pretending not to have seen the car. Despite blasting the siren and turning the blue light on, Dean evaded them easily, disappearing in the streets running down towards Wellington Road. But just as he neared the station crossing, he veered away along a footpath running alongside the track towards Shrewbridge Road and another loop of the River Weaver.

Miss Jones' street was somewhere he skilfully avoided whenever he cycled around the town. There were plenty of places to go without passing the house in Wellington Road. He dreamed about her often in his fitful sleep as he hunched under the benches in the cricket pavilion, or by the canal side on the aqueduct running over the end of Welsh Row; saw her face as if through a telescope, and always with that terrible expression, the last one he saw as he ran out of the house, and then the hopeless scrabbling of her fingers in dust. In the dream they managed to work away until they held him and she hugged him so hard his ribs cracked. And then he woke, heavy with sadness, and guilt.

"Hiya!"

Dean didn't hear at first, he was too engrossed in his dark thoughts of Miss Jones.

"Hiya! Dean! Dean! Noah!" The voice was louder, more eager.

He glanced over his shoulder and saw a girl pedalling furiously towards him. He didn't recognise her at first, until she wobbled under the weight of her enthusiasm when she realized it was him, and he saw the transient look of concern and delight on her face.

"Hiya, Noah, what are you doing? Where have you been?" she demanded and stopped just before she crashed into his back wheel. "I've been worried sick about you!"

"Hello, Mickey." Dean suddenly felt light-headed, and his knees buckled.

"I've been looking everywhere for you! Where have you been?"

"There's been trouble…" he started, gripping the bike hard until his knuckles whitened.

"I heard, Dean. I heard some stuff…"

"I…I…I can't go home right now." He wanted to find something to say to her, something nice and good, but as hard as he searched for words all he could find was dark, and heavy, and terribly sad. Despite the hours and hours of thinking about her, craving for her, he didn't know how to start, didn't know what to say. "I've been looking for you too," he blurted.

"We must have kept missing each other." Mickey grabbed him, and let her bike clatter onto the tarmac of the footpath. "I couldn't sleep so I thought I'd come out now, early, before anyone misses me. I thought if I kept looking hard enough I'd see you. I knew deep down I'd find you, Dean."

"Every day I looked for you," he cried. "I thought you wanted to see me. I thought we were an item."

"I looked for you, in school, the next day. I looked round for you and I thought you were avoiding me. I asked loads of kids but they said you'd run away on account of your dad trying to kill… someone…" She was tearful now, her eyes burning as she hugged him.

"Is that what they're saying?"

"The Head at school said if anyone knew where you were they had to tell him at once. He said you must be found because you were at risk, or something... Dean? Dean did your dad try to kill you?"

A rumble shook the surface under their feet as the Shrewsbury train moved along the track. Within a moment the train rushed by them, a short distance away just beyond bent and rusty railings, its power pushing them threateningly towards the children, the noise brutally enveloping their senses. Dean peered into her face, anticipated what she was about to ask, but he wanted to tell her something far more important; he wanted to say how much he loved her. She saw his eyes wide and dark, and she knew. The train whistled, and being so close the sound hit them with such force it felt like an act of violence. Both flinched and hunched under the weight of the noise, and as they did their eyes locked as they gazed at each other. As air settled again, Mickey kissed him.

*

Later on Dean waited outside the door of the supermarket, straddled his bike, one foot against a pedal in anticipation of a quick dash away from this place. Every time the doors opened he got a blast of warm air, but more importantly, he could watch from this vantage point for anyone he knew who would report him. Not that it mattered much anyway. Nothing would make him go back home, or to a place of safety. He wasn't going to be palmed off with people who didn't know him, who couldn't understand. He was going to be alright now he'd found Mickey. It was going to be okay. He got some kind of satisfaction watching the faces of people going in and out laden with bags of shopping, talking, laughing, squabbling, shouting, moaning, doing all sorts of things but always ignorant or in denial of what was coming. Dean didn't fear the end of the world now. He didn't want it, but at least he understood something. After dreading the end for so long, every minute was a beginning – a new moment of wonder. Every waking moment would be filled with his craving for life and as long as Mickey was with him at the very last moment, it would be okay. With her he felt no more pain. In this moment Dean knew the uselessness of life and living, and his inability to change anything, anyone. All things would inevitably be as they were and whatever he yearned for wouldn't happen. He looked back on the days when he wanted to make his mum and dad into a family – but he failed because they couldn't love him, they were incapable of giving him love. So Dean thought his sadness would grow bigger and bigger and bigger until it became depression, and he would wait for his hair to fall out, and the black rings to form under his eyes, like they had with Auntie Jessie because she too couldn't have what she wanted. Uncle Ralph had gone and he wasn't coming back. And then he thought Miss Jones had saved him; that she had given him something to live for – but it was a terrible antidote to life – more awful than dying. But now he had Mickey it was different. It really didn't matter anymore.

He waited patiently for Mickey. When she came out of the supermarket it would be time to move on again. She'd gone in to buy some food and stuff, and they were going to sneak back to her home in Queen's Drive. Her parents would be at work, and they would be safe there until late afternoon. And then they'd plan how to keep him safe – to find him some place to hide. He pressed down hard on the handlebars; the front tyre looked a bit flat. It was okay. He touched the valve, rubbed spit onto its tip to see if there was a leak of air, and as he did he became aware of someone watching him. When he looked up a woman smiled at him, in a funny kind of way. She looked like she was sorry for him or something. He moved to get past her, but she blocked his way and reached out to touch his arm.

"I thought I recognized you," she said, softly.

Dean didn't know her.

"I met you a few weeks ago at the old lady's house. Remember me? I'm Tracey."

She'd got it wrong. She'd mistaken him for someone else.

"I'd just taken your Granny home. She wasn't very well. I took her home in my taxi."

The memory started to seep back into his consciousness. He pictured her standing on the step and he'd wondered who she was, why she was there when Miss Jones didn't let anyone into the house. It was the day after his birthday. He'd gone to show Miss Jones his bike.

"I was so sorry to hear about her," she said. "She seemed a nice lady."

He couldn't make sense of what she said, and the very quiet voice she said it in. She stood staring into his face, her eyebrows creased into a frown, smiling in a sad way. Her hand reached out and touched his face. Her fingers were icy cold and he flinched.

"You must be upset. I'm sorry. I don't mean to upset you. Do you think it will be alright for me to go to the funeral? Just to the service in the church. I'd like to pay my respects. I didn't know her well, but I…."

He couldn't speak. She spoke a few more words, filled with sadness, then touched his face again and went. He watched her climb into a taxi and drive away. Exhaust fumes blew from the back and danced like ghosts before thinning into the cold air and disappearing. His knuckles turned blue as he gripped the handlebars, and had he not had the bike for support he would have fallen. Miss Jones was *dead.*

Mickey saw his face and quickened her pace. She noticed a woman turn and look at him as she walked away, and at first she thought it was Dean's mum. They'd been sussed.

"Dean," she hissed in his ear. "Dean!"

He was frozen to the spot, unable to respond. He saw her face, felt her tug on his arm, but it was as if she stood behind a plate glass window. Her mouth opened, her limbs moved, but she was so far, far away.

"Dean, what's the matter? I've got the stuff, look! Who was

that? Who was it, Dean? Speak to me!"

"I…I…" His head spun. A moment ago he'd felt such ease, such peace. Nothing had mattered, but now he felt a massive sense of guilt. He'd killed Miss Jones. He was certain of it. "Miss Jones is dead," he said, his voice like a razor cutting into his throat. It was too painful to form words, too painful to speak them.

"What?" Mickey asked, her eyes flitting quickly over Dean's crumpling face. "What's the matter, Dean?" her voice tumbled as if falling over a cliff. The words became lost as people surged and shoved around them, like a sea sucking them towards a dangerous undertow. She'd lose him. They'd take him away. "Dean, please tell me what it is? Quick, we've got to go!"

"Miss Jones is dead! Dead! I killed her!" He turned towards her, his face an agony of guilt and shame. Walking away from the old woman had taken away her life, and he'd done that. He was responsible. A tiny thought, like a maggot, chewed somewhere at the back of his brain, and as it tore the fragile cells, spilling more shame, more guilt, he looked at Mickey and wanted to wail like a banshee.

"You've done what?" Mickey was scared now.

"I killed the old lady," he said, almost imperceptibly.

But Mickey heard him, and a sudden, dreadful thought reared through her mind. She hardly knew him. She fancied him and stuff, but she didn't really know him. A plastic bottle crashed between her feet and split, and she felt cold liquid against her legs as the Coke fizzed and spurted and the bottle began to spin. She heard another crash, and someone cursed and told her to be careful as she spilled the contents of her carrier bag.

"What do you mean, you killed her?" she insisted, her face pale and drawn. "You killed the old lady? The *crazy* lady? What do you mean you killed her?" Mickey wanted to slap him, but as she looked into his eyes, and saw the black points unfocused and hopeless, she shrank back. She really didn't know who he was. She'd kissed him – that's all. All she'd done was kiss him. No more than that.

Dean didn't know what to do as she let her hand slip from under his arm. She shrank further and further away until she became a blur, another smudge in a sea of accusatory faces. He wanted to say something, but the pain in his throat had grown so great he thought he'd choke. Gasping for air he pushed against the pedal on his bike and moved against the flow of this dreadful tide. He didn't know where to go. Maybe he'd jump from the Weaver Bridge. Maybe he'd jump into the canal at Basin End, it was deep and black enough so that he'd sink in the mud and never be found. Maybe he'd go home. He'd be certain to drown there.

Twenty /

"Where are you going?" she asked.

Dean looked at his mother. Her face was white, and lank hair fell across her cheeks and edged into the corners of her mouth. Nicotine stained fingers rubbed the dark rings under her eyes. The stink of cigarettes hung over everything. The door frame had been repaired and he looked at the mess of bolts and padlocks she'd had screwed haphazardly to secure the door.

"Where are you going?" she asked again, but more frantically.

He didn't answer. He hoped she'd flick a channel and be absorbed into another soap where people screamed at each other, slept with each other, cheated on each other, so that she could find an escape from the world.

"What do you want to eat?" she asked, without turning to look at him. "Will you get me some chips?"

Dean couldn't remember the last time he'd eaten. It didn't matter. He'd had enough cans and cigarettes to quell his appetite, but the gnawing sense of guilt and shame couldn't be assuaged by food or alcohol. His bike lay at an awkward angle against the wall, and he noticed a long scratch along the frame. It didn't matter either. It could rust away for all he cared. Everything came to an end. Everything went. Nothing could be kept. There was no point. It would be better to let it go. It would be letter to let go.

"Get me some chips? Where are you going?"

A chain rattled as he slipped the bolt, and after shoving the door hard he blinked against the light. He came up for air for the first time in days. The sky was wrapped in a dirty grey sheet which wrinkled miserably all the way from his bed, up over the church where a bell rang incessantly, slowly, and spread forever and forever to blot out the sun. Eyes shrivelled into cinder-black points, two small dots shrinking to keep the day at bay.

"Get me some chips will you, Sweetie?"

She heard the door scrape and bang behind him.

*

All day long he wandered around the town looking for memories to give him a sense that he belonged there, and whenever he saw someone looking at him he turned and went in the opposite direction. There was nothing substantial to hold on to. It was late afternoon when he noticed the heaviness in his legs. Several times he'd sat on the damp benches in the Town Square, and watched the day as it shifted along, sometimes busy, often quiet and occasionally deserted. This was Nantwich. This was his home town. If the end of the world came it would get hell of a battering, he thought. And if the end of the world came it would deserve it. The day darkened as did his eyes, and he felt too tired to wander any longer. There was only one place left he felt compelled to see.

Over the red-bricked walls and into the garden he heaved his heavy heart and legs, not wanting to be there, but unable to resist it. The house stood empty and dark and foreboding and he felt his heart beat in a manic rhythm of palpitations. It was here where it all began and it seemed like an age ago, in another life. Surely another boy must have experienced this? Dean couldn't fathom the strange sensations coursing through him making him feel distant, like an outsider looking in. As he moved pictures flooded his imagination and he saw a scruffy kid stealing apples while an awkward old lady stumped her way down the blue brick path to shout and berate him and then accept him. His face looked pale, but not as pale as the face that stared out at him from the mirror in the bathroom back at home.

A slight breeze ruffled his hair and he shivered. It served to ground him and he quickly opened up to his present reality. Dean Cartwright stood in the garden of Miss Jones, the woman who wanted to save his life and for her reward he had killed her. He knew the moment of rejection had been too much for her and he felt his heart slow as if beating through treacle and all energy left him. Unsure now of why he'd returned to her house he wondered what to do, but an idea came to mind and nagged him until he went with it. For some reason he wanted, needed, to get into the house. What would it mean to him to stand among the dreams and desires they'd shared and know that she'd gone despite planning for her weird immortality? All the world's terrible possibilities hadn't touched her at all. But he had. Dean Cartwright.

It was easy enough to shove hard on the quarter light in the kitchen window frame and push it open. Most of her windows were rotten and she'd steadfastly refused to spend money for replacements despite the obvious, and now qualified risk they presented. He reached through and just managed to get a fingertip on the lever holding the large pane in place. The finger crept along until two fingers touched the rusty metal, and then a third. That was enough of a hold, and Dean pulled and felt it slide open with ease. Clambering over the kitchen sink and draining board he scuffed the dull metal and felt momentarily guilty until the full force of her absence hit him again. It didn't matter now. The absolute silence of the house, its uncanny stillness, bore down on him like a huge rock and he fought to get his breath. If ever a place was haunted this would be, now after the physical presence of Miss Jones departed to be filled with her angry and demented ghost – a guardian of everything she prized so dearly. Dean's mouth was dry and his fingers tingled. He felt an urgent need to pee but didn't want to go into the dark closet she'd used for a toilet. It didn't have a light and once the door shut, he remembered, it was pitch black. He recalled fumbling in the dark several times in the past. Now it would be the spookiest place imaginable. Outside a police car sounded its siren as it hurtled down Wellington Road and Dean was sure someone had seen him enter. He crouched on the dusty floor beside an untidy sack of rags, probably something she'd deemed as useful, and he held his breath until he heard the pulse in his ears, like water pumping through a tight pipe. The siren faded and he allowed himself to slowly release breath and tension, and draw a lung full of dank air.

How powerfully scents and odours grab the mind and wring from it the most arcane of memories. In one breath he realized newspaper cuttings, tongue sandwiches, cardboard and the smell of black plastic bin liners. The kitchen released a tinge of gas and something boiled, and when Dean pushed through into the scullery he was met with a smell and an image of the old woman herself, hunched in the gloom, reeking of that odd odour of ageing. She was everywhere. As each room was entered she followed him, stood alongside him, and tried to touch his face, or hug him, and even now he was just as repelled by her. The odour clung to him and sat on his skin and in his hair and he frantically tried to recall the warm loveliness of Mickey's skin, a fragrance now so elusive, and the more he tried to imagine her, the smell, the feel, the face, nothing would come. He feared Miss Jones would enshroud him and hold him forever.

Dean wondered whether he ought to burn the house down. Perhaps if he took away the opportunity for her stuff to be plundered by God-knows-who she would leave him alone, but he knew he would never be able to cauterise the final image he had of her face – disturbed, disillusioned and dreadful. It would forever look at him and demand to know why he had cheated her and dumped her. Her boy had been capable of such betrayal and had taken away everything she'd planned and schemed for. He had to get out. It was crazy coming in here like this and it just made things worse. He didn't know what to do. Every time he tried to make a move nothing happened and he started to cry at the futile attempts he made to move his feet. Closing his eyes he prayed Miss Jones was safe in Heaven and the world could end now and kill everybody if it had to be so.

"Please God let me move. Please God kill me now if you

have to. I'm so sorry!" He would die. He wouldn't stay in the house and live on the rations of betrayal. Movement came back, and he cautiously shuffled his feet, and wondered if God really had answered his prayer. In the hallway he avoided the boxes and the bags and glimpsed into her living area, so small now under the huge weight of boxes and crates. On a rickety coffee table he saw a pile of papers and despite not wanting to look he instantly recognised his name written on an envelope. It was for him. A letter. She must have known he'd come back. She'd left it for him. Time stopped for the boy. What would she say; what could she possibly want to tell him? He picked it up and held it between his fingers and cranked himself up as best he could to open it. The flap opened with ease. Inside he saw a piece of folded paper. Her handwriting was difficult to read and as he carefully unfolded the sheet he found it hard to make sense of her scribble. He knelt on the dry floorboards and scuffed his knees. In the gloom he read –

Dear Dean,

Everything I have is yours. Do what you want with it. I killed my brother and now my reward is that you will kill me. I failed to see his danger and couldn't stop him, and now your betrayal is apt and I deserve it. You are so much like him. I wish I could hold you for a moment. You didn't like it, did you, to be touched by me? When you came into my life you awakened him and I thought my love, our sharing, would be my redemption. I think I should die and I do not say that with any self pity. There is nothing to stay alive for. You have made me face him. The walls are dismantled. Everything I have is yours. I hope it will not be a burden. You are my boy.

My love,
Miss Jones.

Dean understood it.

He folded the letter and put it back in the envelope. There

was no point in keeping it. Outside he'd throw it away in a litter bin, tear it into a thousand pieces and shove it alongside the stink of takeaways and empty cola cans. The legacy was too much to contemplate. His dad's face flickered in his mind like a thug in an old movie, eyes wide, brow creased into a sinister expression, a mouth leering with contempt and avarice.

*

Paddy, the mad Irishman, sat next to Dean and spat several times while he drew on a fat cigarette rolled from dog-ends he'd picked from the street. The smell caught the back of Dean's throat and he pulled his head back to escape a trail of smoke drifting his way. It was very early in the morning and breath was already leaving its momentary trace on the air. In his pocket the letter crumpled and rustled slightly when he moved.

"You got a light, Paddy?" he asked casually.

"What?" the man said aggressively.

"You got a light?"

"What? A light?"

"Yeah. Can I have a light?"

"You ain't a smoker! You ain't old enough!" With a look of deep abhorrence Paddy lurched to his feet and briskly walked away babbling incoherently before he stopped in front of a newsagent, turned and doubled back. "You want a light?"

"It doesn't matter."

"What?"

"It doesn't matter. I don't smoke."

"What?"

Dean moved on again and in front of the library in Beam Street he peered into a bin, angled by some drunk's kick the night before. Pulling the letter from his pocket he tore it until the thickness of layers became too much and then let the pieces fall like snow into the bin's gaping mouth. The job was almost done.

*

The undertaker from the Co-op funeral services watched the kid across the road while he arranged the two small wreaths on top of the coffin and closed the hatch at the back of the limousine. He'd been there for quite a while, and other than neighbours, Mr Bryant and his wife, there was no-one else present. Sad, the undertaker reflected, that a life had passed and there were few here to see the passing and say goodbye. He wondered whether she'd been a difficult lady, or whether a generation of family and friends had gone before her. Whatever, he'd sing at the top of his voice even if the church pews were nearly empty. He always did. In the town he was something of a celebrity because he'd appeared in Coronation Street, doing exactly what he did now – being smart, dark and grey, and singing at the top of his voice. He nodded to his colleagues and the hearse coughed into life. Respectfully, they nodded back towards his tall and stately frame, and joined him in the big, black limousinc, and when the doors shut, he cracked a few jokes and they stifled laughter in the heavy chests of their winter coats.

As they drove slowly down Wellington Road and towards the town he glanced in the wing mirror on his side and saw the boy following behind on his bike. The boy stood on his pedals as he tried to keep up with the hearse, and the one other car, containing Mr and Mrs Bryant, which followed.

"Slow down, Derek," he said. "There's a kid behind trying to keep up."

"What?"

"A kid on a bike. Maybe he knew the old bird. Don't lose him. I'll have a word with him if I get the chance."

The car slowed. As it turned into Church Lane a few people stopped and watched and an elderly man took off his hat and bowed.

He wore a trilby with a wide black band. Miss Jones would have liked that. He turned to a woman who slowly approached the wide gates to the church.

"Do you know who it is?" she enquired, looking full of it, waiting to announce everything she knew.

"No. Who is it?" he enquired.

"It's Miss Jones who lived in the big house in Wellington Road. Her father was a big-wig in the town. Don't you remember, they came here twenty or thirty years ago from Derby or Nottingham or somewhere down there. She kept herself pretty much to herself. She never really fitted into Nantwich."

The old man nodded and looked straight ahead as the coffin passed with its small cortege. He didn't want to hear anymore, but the woman persisted.

"They think she had a fall. Whether it was on account of the drink I don't know."

"Let her rest in peace," he said, bluntly.

She paused for a moment but then turned to another woman. "Of course, it might have been a stroke. I'm not sure. I think she'd gone a bit strange, you know, did odd things." She raised her eyebrows and nodded towards the retreating coffin as it disappeared through the high church door.

The small group of people broke away, the elderly man putting his hat back on, while the woman continued expounding the details she knew or fabricated.

"They reckon the house is full from top to bottom with groceries and things. They say it's like a warehouse. They think she'd gone a bit loopy. Tens of thousands of cans and tins and bottles apparently! You hear about these things, don't you? You never know what goes on in people's minds. Anyway, I must get on. There's a good deal on tinned salmon in the new shop down Mill Street. Maybe I should call at the old dear's house and see what's on offer there." She laughed, turned quickly and walked away towards the

Square, not noticing the young boy standing behind the railings in Churchyardside.

Dean waited for a long time. He didn't know how long a funeral lasted. They wouldn't let him go to Uncle Ralph's. It was easy enough to hide away today. On Market day the town was heaving, and he crept between the tweedy farmers' wives, and big, robust men who strung the pavements as they sauntered between the public houses. Dean decided to stand just inside the porch of the Information Office across from the church, so that he could see, but he regretted it when Paddy grabbed his arm and peered into his face. The Irishman poked a gnarled and stained finger under his nose and told him it was time to shave. Someone laughed, but Dean shrugged off the big hand, and pushed away from Paddy's nonsense, across the path until he stood on the church steps that fell into a recess and along the front of the church.

Within minutes the doors opened again, and the coffin was wheeled back out into the chilly day. Tracey, the taxi driver waited discreetly at the back before slipping out through the side door, and Mr and Mrs Bryant walked as soberly as they could given that they hardly knew Miss Jones. They'd agreed it was a decent thing to do. The undertaker from the Co-op blinked in the light, and cleared his throat. He'd sung well, and enjoyed the two hymns, and after all, he'd chosen them in the absence of family and no written instructions from the deceased. He noticed that the boy still hung around, and he tried to attract his attention before climbing back into the hearse and as they made their way to the cemetery in Whitehouse Lane he spotted him again. It was a long ride for the kid, so he repeated his instruction for Derek to take his time. The vicar sat behind him, tapping his Bible and Order of Service, his long nails slightly curled and well manicured. He played guitar in a Charismatic Group, though his finger-picking wasn't up to much.

"So you didn't know her?" the undertaker asked, as if they'd been deep in conversation.

"No. I saw her around the town sometimes, but not often. Bit of a loner. I don't know much about her at all to be honest."

"She didn't have any family by the looks of it either. Parents long since dead, and there's talk she had a brother who died a long time ago, too."

"Who's going to sort out her things?"

"Supersaver probably," the undertaker said dryly, making Derek laugh.

"Oh, no, she was definitely a Marks and Spencer woman," the vicar said sardonically.

"No, definitely Supersaver," the undertaker insisted. "She really had an eye for a bargain," he said without any hint of humour. "Haven't you heard?"

"Heard what?"

"She was a... how do you put this? She was a well-provisioned woman."

"Well proportioned, surely?"

"Well provisioned," he repeated, turning slightly to catch the vicar's expression.

*

Dean got near enough to hear the vicar reading from his book. He leaned his bike against a small brick building where a big wheelie bin full of dead flowers stood, and tried not to scratch the frame on a tap which stuck out of the side of the wall. He felt self-conscious and didn't want anyone to see him as he crept between the graves. The man in a long black overcoat had stared at him all morning and Dean tried to manoeuvre to his blind side. But the man moved, turned his head, and with a discreet twist of his hand beckoned the boy to come nearer. Dean didn't. He stopped and watched and listened.

"Dust to dust, ashes to ashes..."

It was all he caught of the vicar's words, and he was too smart to be caught as they filed away from the graveside. Later on he would visit her, put something on the grave.

*

Afterwards Dean rode slowly down to Paddy's Field. The short cold days ensured that no-one went there much, except for the few youths who went to break windows and steal stuff from the sheds. He did that once in what now seemed a million years ago, and for no reason, it was just something kids did. The old man wasn't there, so he wouldn't have to make conversation with him. The light was failing and a bright full-moon rose just above the buildings beyond the river. It would freeze tonight for sure but it wasn't right to go home just yet. Patsy watched endless soaps, capitulating to the tyranny of the mundane, and smoked until she coughed up her guts and her wrath. Billy was nowhere to be seen, and yet he heard endless speculation as Mrs Anderson cursed and gossiped in a voice always loud enough to be heard and understood. Mark, the social worker, had disappeared too, though Dean felt just as indifferent now to him as he did to everyone. He'd heard Mrs Anderson say he'd been sacked, and that his balls were being used by the women in the local golf-club.

Dean took a cigarette from a crumpled packet and pulled a can from inside his jacket. He'd started smoking again and after an initial bout of nausea when he pulled hard and sucked the smoke into his lungs, he persevered and got the hang of it again. Now it made him slightly light-headed and he liked the feeling. When he could he liked to smoke and drink because the sensation was exquisite and for a short time made him feel okay. The can fizzed and bubbled when he forced back the ring and he sucked the froth from off the ice-cold rim. The strong Special Brew would make the picture of Mickey fade from his mind, and even though he wanted to think about her and remember the warmth of her kisses, he couldn't get beyond the despair which now ran through him, making his blood cold and his bones ache. And beyond all this, the alcohol obliterated the awful image of Miss Jones' face as he re-ran the scene again and again and again, the time of his betrayal, the time of his going, the time of her death. Now, he was left at exactly the same place from where he started. Dean Cartwright was unlovable and it was his own fault. He took a long swig of the thick and bitter beer and waited for it to work its magic.

*

At the same moment Mickey stood in front of the dreadlocked youth worker in the Methodist Church Hall and wanted to say more but wasn't sure how much to trust this relatively new woman. She clutched the Nantwich Chronicle to her small breasts while Lorraine peered intently into her eyes. Lorraine liked Mickey a lot, and made time for her when she noticed how down in the dumps she looked.

"Why do you kids always have a friend who's in trouble? Mickey, come on! Is it something you've done?"

"I don't know…"

"You don't know what? Look Mickey I can keep this confidential as long as you're not using, selling, or dealing in any way with drugs or selling your body." Lorraine smiled as if it was a joke, but Mickey understood.

"It really is about my friend…well, he was sort of my boyfriend."

"I see. Pregnant are you, Mickey?"

"No!" Mickey protested. "We never did that. We were just getting it together when he told me he killed an old woman."

"Mickey, are you serious?"

"Yes."

"Who is he? Do I know him?"

"No. He didn't ever come to stuff like this. He was a bit of a loner. At school he always kept on the edge of things. I've been trying to find him but we were always missing each other. Something must have happened to him. His dad kicked off not long ago and the headmaster said we were to watch out for him because he was at risk."

"What is his name, Mickey?" Lorraine was firmer now, and crouched slightly to look right into Mickey's eyes. "This is serious stuff, Mickey. If he's hurt somebody…"

"But he didn't!" Mickey insisted. "Look!" She showed Lorraine the newspaper. Mickey had read it many times and wondered if Dean knew about this stuff. Kids at school said the old woman was a loon, a crazy old bird, but no-one offered an explanation why; being old, being alone, were apparently enough to raise such inane and spurious speculations.

"What am I looking at, Mickey?"

"This. Here, look, this stuff about the old lady."

There was a short article describing the life of Miss Jones, and in summary it suggested there were no suspicious circumstances. She'd been found in her home in Wellington Road holding an old theatre ticket for a performance of The Tempest. It is thought she'd died peacefully in her sleep. There was no mention of anything else.

"Tell me all," Lorraine insisted after reading the newspaper text.

Mickey said how bad she felt. She'd judged him and let him down. Of course he'd spooked her with his talk but now she was sure he'd got it wrong and wanted to help him get it straight.

"What would you like me to do?" Lorraine asked, in a non-committal voice. It was getting late and she wanted to go home.

"I don't know…I don't know what to say." Mickey felt disappointed, let down by the woman. "I suppose I'll just have to keep looking for him and tell him…"

"I'd do that, Mickey. That seems a good way forward." Lorraine smiled as warmly as she could, but Mickey saw through it.

*

Dean heard someone laughing from down at the end of the allotments, laughing and cheering. He'd better go. They'd be the wreckers. Other voices joined in now, raucous and high on something. Dean pulled behind the old man's shed, picking the bike up so the wheels and gears wouldn't move and whir and give him away. Gently he put it down in the grass which had started to get a coating of frost like icing on a cake. It sparkled in the moonlight and looked lovely, soft and still.

The voices came nearer. They were coming along the path.

"You should see the bloody stuff! Masses and masses of it!"

"I've got enough to last for a month!" a voice announced breathlessly, excited and strained.

"Are you going back for more?"

"Course I bloody well am! Keep going till the cops get wind! I'm going to dump this at home and get some sacks so I can fit more in. Better get cracking. News travels quick round Nantwich. You'd be a dozy bugger to miss this opportunity! Someone had been in there before and probably bagged the best stuff."

"It doesn't belong to no-one now though does it?" Someone asked trying to justify whatever it was they did. "She had no-one I heard. So it isn't nicking really, is it?"

"Nah, is it hell! Mad old bugger! Bet she's turning in her grave!"

Dean listened as their voices shrank into the dark night. The thought was slow to come, struggling from under the seeping and insidious weight of drink, and for a while he stood in a weird kind of trance as if their words were meant especially for him. They were implanting an idea, but it was hard to understand it at all, to make sense, to pull it out of the dull head and acknowledge what it meant. But then it dawned on Dean that they were talking about Miss Jones.

Grabbing his bike he steamed over the sodden path and scrambled over shale humps spread by the gardeners. He shot across the Town Square and a kid from the flats nearly strayed into his path, and shouted when the stuff he carried cascaded from his over-full arms onto the pavement. He passed several people laden with bags and boxes, their arms full, and their faces flashing with big grins, laughing, or whispering in conspiratorial voices. Within minutes Dean was at the end of Wellington Road, crashing his wheels across the railway tracks as he jumped the crossing. A man scuttled with his fat wife along the pavement, carrying bags stuffed with tins and bottles. He clenched a cigarette in the corner of his mouth and laughed at Dean. "I could do with that bike, kid. Here, I'll give you a quid if you help me carry this stuff!"

Dean leapt off his bike and nearly smashed him in the face, and the man's fat wife squawked when he grabbed her arm and tried to wrench a bin liner from her tight grip.

"You little bastard! Sod off! Go and get your own stuff! There's enough of it for everyone between here and bloody Crewe!"

"You're thieves!" he yelled, the pitch of his voice high, and his throat so constricted with fury it felt like he'd swallowed glass. He grabbed his bike and held onto the handlebars as he mounted but he pushed too hard and his foot slipped and he toppled over, crashing against a privet hedge. The bike clattered behind him, and the man made a grab for it.

Dean couldn't care less now. As he moved onto his elbows and knees, pulling himself away from the hedge, he saw the crowd ahead. Shouting and squabbling, grabbing and mauling, they pushed their way through Miss Jones' front door, which by now had shattered. Feet crunched on the fragments of glass, and kicked the wooden panel whenever it swung across their way. Boxes spilled their contents over the small lawn, and onto the street, and small kids fought to grab a can, a bottle, a packet. Everywhere the contents of the house, Miss Jones' insurance, was erupting and exploding as the people became mad with greed.

Dean picked himself up, and didn't notice the man loading his bags onto the handle-bars of his bike, and then quickly push his way home, his fat wife whooping behind him. Dean stood in deep shock, mouth wide, eyes bewildered. His heart ached. His head swam, and he felt a surge of nausea explode into vomit over the pavement. He spewed deep from the pit of his being. Dean Cartwright had set this madness in motion. Dean Cartwright was responsible for this.

He walked slowly, unsteadily towards the house, where the windows blinked against the rising moon, and beyond them he saw people pouring through the rooms, faces glowing, eyes wide, mouths agape as they plundered her home. A window broke somewhere. He saw a woman hold up the newspaper cuttings, the magazine articles, shake her head and then throw them up into the air above the heads of the crowd. Feet clapped across the landing upstairs, and floorboards creaked and groaned as men heaved and strained to prise them open and rob the stash underneath. Dean remembered Miss Jones holding up the cigarette packet. He remembered the apple tree, and the cinema that had fallen under the work of ants. Something made him turn around, and across the street, under the light of the streetlamp, he saw several faces. Mickey stood - mouth open, aghast at what she witnessed, and when she saw Dean, she screamed so loudly there was a momentary hush in the house. The riot stopped as people caught the awful shrill note. Mickey ran away into the night.

Dean stood, motionless and weary.

A fight broke out. Voices were raised, and several people ran from the house, fearing the brawl. Dean looked through the doorway, and was shoved, trampled and barged as they passed.

In the middle of the riot was his dad, fists flying, boots weighing in with a frightening power. He ploughed through them, spitting in his drink-fuelled rage, overflowing with venom. Snake face. Tongue inflicting its dreadful bile on the world.

Dean blinked and looked up at the sky. The moon hung lower than he'd ever seen, and was the colour of steel. He wanted to lie down and rest, to sleep. He wanted to curl-up and give way to his exhaustion. It was pointless. He fell slowly to his knees. Through his weariness he heard a brutal and persistent voice calling his name. It was his dad, face bashed and bloodied who stood over him now, grabbed his collar, and yanked him to his feet.

"Where the friggin' hell have you been?" he hollered in Dean's face, speckling the boy's face with his blood and snot. "Too friggin' good for me now are you?"

"No," Dean croaked.

"I've been looking for you! Where've you been?"

"Nowhere," Dean replied, breathlessly, "Nowhere…"

"No-one can be friggin' nowhere. Everyone has got to be friggin' somewhere!"

Dean felt something deep within him. His hatred, his loathing for his father simmered and surged slowly upwards, burning his heart and then his head. *"I'm here, Dad. I'm bloody well here!"* His voice rose as his heart hardened in rage. He grabbed his dad's thick wrists and despite feeling powerless, he hung on.

"Get in here and give me a hand," his father demanded, shrugging away Dean's thin fingers. "You can come and bloody well help me now you useless little shit!"

"No!" Dean shouted, spittle spraying his father's face.

"What? What did you friggin' say?"

"No! I said, no! This is all my stuff and you can't have it!"

"What? You get your arse in here and you friggin' well…"

"No!"

Dean didn't flinch when he felt the fist, not on the first dull thud, nor on the last. He sank to his knees, and eventually, through a deep and painless fog he watched several policemen wrestle his father to the ground. Just beyond them, partly hidden by a door which swung dangerously on broken hinges, he saw Mickey's face. She'd come back. Her lips parted as she watched him fall, and he remembered the sweetness of her kisses, and the gentle heat of her body.

There was no feeling now. No sadness. No tears. Dean lay down his head, closed his eyes, and someone held him, cradled him. His fingers slowly scrabbled in the dust. Voices dimmed into silence, and stillness descended. He opened his bloodied eyes for a moment and saw Mickey again as she leant over him; another face in a circle of faces. And beyond them he saw the moon as it fell towards the earth, and he smiled weakly as the world darkened and softly came to an end.

Supplement Publications
2007